THE TESTAMENT OF LOKI

THE
TESTAMENT
OF LOKI

JOANNE M. HARRIS

GOLLANCZ

LONDON

First published in Great Britain in 2018 by Gollancz
an imprint of the Orion Publishing Group Ltd
Carmelite House, 50 Victoria Embankment
London EC4Y 0DZ

An Hachette UK Company

1 3 5 7 9 10 8 6 4 2

A CIP catalogue record for this book is
available from the British Library.

ISBN (Cased) 978 1 473 20239 9
ISBN (Export Trade Paperback) 978 1 473 20240 5

Typeset by Input Data Services Ltd, Somerset

Printed and bound in Great Britain
by Clays Ltd, St Ives plc

www.joanne-harris.co.uk
www.gollancz.co.uk

CHARACTERS

Loki – Your Humble Narrator. Not-quite demon, not-quite god. Handsome, charismatic and brilliant hero of this troubled tale. World traveller, lover of jam tarts and sometime survivor of Ragnarók. Rumours of my death are not entirely inaccurate, still pending, facing enquiry.

Jumps – seventeen-year-old human. Not entirely impossible. Has an inexplicable love of things with pictures of animals on them.

Evan – pizza lover and games freak. RPG player extraordinaire.

Stella – gossip; mean girl; lover of shiny, spangly things. Strangely irresistible to humans of the opposite sex.

Twinkle – fluffy white dog.

Odin – Allfather. Onetime leader of the gods, blood-brother to Yours Truly.

Thor – son of Odin; the Thunderer. All bark, no bite.

Freyja – Warrior Princess. Apparently.

Sleipnir – horse. Kinda.

Jormungand – giant snake.

Smá-rákki – goblin.

Nancy Wickerman – girl of the Folk.

Jonathan Gift – academic with delusions of grandeur.

Gullveig-Heid – the Golden One; the Sorceress. Nasty, vengeful, venal, vain. All my favourite qualities in one irresistible package.

The Oracle – Mimir's Head. Harbinger of Last Times. Prophet of the New Age. Keeper of Runes. Whisperer of Secrets. As slick as a sackful of weasels, and about as trustworthy.

Darkness

*Last night I dreamed I was in Asgard
again.*
Well, I guess that's gin for you.

Lokabrenna, 5:16

1

*A SGARD WAS FALLING. The plain below was cratered with fires
and laddered with smoke. Ragnarók, the End of the Worlds, lay upon
us like a pall. Odin had fallen; and Thor; and Týr. Gullveig-Heid,
the Sorceress, stood at the helm of the Fleet of the Dead. Dark Lord
Surt, on dragon's wings, approached from out of Chaos, and where his
shadow fell, the dark was absolute, and terrible. Bif-rost was broken,
and as I fell, clutching at the last of my glam, I saw the great bridge
come apart at last in a fractal of brightness, spilling its millions of
cantrips and runes into the wild and shattered air, so that, for a
moment, everything was rainbow . . .*

OK, stop. Stop. Wind back. That's the authorized version; the
tourist's guide to Ragnarók. Bit much to take in all at once, I
know; and yet you'll need to understand some of what happened in order to grasp the magnitude of our rise and fall.
Luckily – or maybe not – there's an official record. Delivered
first as a prophecy, it's now all that passes for history among
what's left of our followers. The Prophecy of the Oracle: a poem
of thirty-six stanzas, outlining the rise and fall of the Worlds,
and retold over the centuries by every bard who wielded a lute,
or hack with a penchant for drama.

That was the first Age, Ymir's time.
There was no land or sea.
Just void between two darknesses,
No stars by which to see.

From the birth of the Worlds in fire and ice to their end in frozen darkness, the Oracle predicted it all. The rise of the gods of Asgard, their Golden Age, their eventual fall, was laid out in those thirty-six stanzas. The struggle out of Chaos; the quest for the runes of the Elder Script; the many adventures and exploits of Odin, leader of the clan; of Thor, his mighty though somewhat intellectually challenged son; of one-handed Týr; of Freyja of the Falcon Cloak, and Hawkeye Heimdall, and Balder the Fair; and, of course, Loki, the Trickster (that's me): recruited from Chaos by Odin himself, though not given credit in the text for any of his virtues, his role in the narrative reduced to the series of tragic events which marred the latter part of his career, much as the *Titanic* has unfairly become a byword for disaster, rather than a celebration of its many sterling qualities. Still, water under the bridge, now. But the fact remains: there was more to me than trickery and betrayal. Not much more; nevertheless, my point stands. Never trust an Oracle.

The Aesir came. On Ida's plain
The new gods built their kingdom.
Here they raised their citadel, their courts,
Their seats of wisdom.

The Oracle predicted that, too: the building of the Sky Citadel; its rainbow bridge; its gleaming halls, the beauty and the splendour. Then came the creeping of unrest; the breaking of our brotherhood; the final betrayal of the gods by one whom Odin had himself betrayed. Our end was inescapable: our fate was woven into the tale like a double skein of mortality. That

4

knowledge tainted everything. Even at the pinnacle of our achievements, the prophecy of the Oracle cast its shadow over us. And worst of all, *it was a lie* – a lie designed to bring about the very doom we sought to escape. The Aesir fell. Game over. Boo hoo.

So. To recap. The story so far: god (that's Odin) meets demon (that's me). God recruits demon from Chaos, with a view to exploiting his talents. God's friends and fellow-deities take a somewhat dim view of this, as, through a combination of hubris, predestination and increasingly bad life choices, demon goes a bit off the rails; falls into bad company; wreaks havoc; causes the odd death and eventually finds himself chained to a couple of rocks in Netherworld; is rescued by the Sorceress just in time to play his part in the engineering of Ragnarók, including the fall of his erstwhile friends, before realizing that the house always wins, whichever colour card you play—

I could have swung the outcome, you know. Even then, if Odin had acknowledged his mistake, I like to think they could have been saved. After all, it wouldn't have been the first time my quick thinking saved the gods from the brink of disaster. If he'd believed in me from the start, things might have been different. But Odin believed in the Oracle. That thrice-damned bauble had his ear, and somehow it managed to steer us towards the rocks we'd been trying to avoid. And Odin was a stiff-necked fool, and the rest of the gods always hated me. And so we lost Asgard, and they fell – Thor, Týr, even the Old Man himself.

> *I see your fate, o sons of earth.*
> *I hear the battle calling.*
> *Odin's folk prepare to ride*
> *Against the shadows falling.*

As for Yours Truly, I plunged to my fate in the arms of my

nemesis, Heimdall, having just thrown the Oracle – Mimir's severed and calcified Head – from the ruins of Asgard into the icy waste below. And in those last moments of freefall, with the giant shadow of Chaos looming above me, oblivion seemed the most promising of my few remaining options. The Prophecy put it quite well:

> Once more the wolf at Hel's gate greets
> Asgard's heroes, one by one.
> Battle rages, Worlds collide.
> Stars fall. Once more, Death has won.

Actually, in my case, Death wasn't really the problem. The Ruler of Hel owed me a favour, and as I fell into the dark, I was already working out a scheme to talk her into redeeming it. No, the problem was Chaos: the element into which I'd been born, and into which I would be reclaimed as soon as I left my corporeal form – and knowing the Lord of Chaos, I guessed my welcome wouldn't involve tea and little fairy cakes.

There's a special place reserved for renegades of Chaos. It has no bars, it has no doors, and yet it constrains more efficiently than any dungeon of the known Worlds. The Black Fortress of Netherworld: a prison more secure than Death, because Death at least is escapable – in theory, at any rate – and no one I knew of had ever escaped a cell in the Black Fortress. I'd seen some bad things in my time – and done a few, if truth be told. I'd laughed in the face of Death more times than Thor could shake a hammer at, but right now, things were not looking good for Your Humble Narrator.

Don't think I didn't have a plan. I *always* have a plan. But as a traitor, both to the gods and to their enemies in Chaos, I was currently *persona non grata* all across the Nine Worlds. If I survived my fall from the sky (which currently didn't seem likely), and if I escaped Surt's shadow (which seemed even less so), there would be nowhere for me to hide. Wherever I went, whatever I did, Death was the only escape for me. And so I fell, and hit the ground, which turned out to be every bit as hard as it had looked from the top of Bif-rost.

Ouch.

Stop there for a moment. Take a second to contemplate the tragedy of my demise. The tragedy and the irony; because, as I slipped into darkness, believing the Worlds had ended, still hoping to enter Hel's kingdom, or perhaps simply to disperse into a glorious trail of fire, I was cruelly snatched away at the moment of my dissolution, and thrown into the most terrible place imagined by god or demon, the Black Fortress of Nether-world, where the fun was just beginning.

You see, that *wasn't* the end of the Worlds. Turns out it was only the end of *our* world; the end of our supremacy. So many gods fall into the trap of assuming that the Worlds will end when their little kingdoms collapse. In fact, the Worlds are like the tide, expanding and contracting, while gods – and men, and demons – roll like sand under the waves. We were no excep-tion. The Aesir of Asgard, overthrown and humbled into the dust. So shoot me – I don't grieve for them, who never would have grieved for me.

And so I was damned – but dry your tears. There isn't a dun-geon I can't escape, given time and incentive. My time in the Black Fortress gave me both, in more than ample quantities. This is the story of how I escaped the most secure dungeon in all of the Nine Worlds, and some of what happened afterwards, and some of the lessons I learnt on the way. I can't pretend it made me a wiser, humbler person, but I did pick up a few things – things about stories, and friendships, and dreams, and what it's like to be human.

Yes, human. Didn't I tell you once that *god* and *dog* are only a revolution apart? In spite of all the splendour and pomp and exhortations to *be more god*; of holy wars and heresies; of mir-acles and martyrdoms; everything turns, and turns, and turns.

Order; Chaos; darkness; light. Rinse and repeat. Reboot and replay.

So, once more with feeling: Let—
                                                    there—
                                                    be—
                                                        light.

2

THEY TOLD THE WORLDS THAT I was dead. Trust me, Death is better by far than the punishment dealt to me. Death has a kind of dignity. Even Hel, that empire of dust, would have been a blessed relief. Quite apart from the fact that its ruler was a relative, and therefore open to bribery, it remains the one place in the Worlds where Chaos has no sway, and where, by and large, the deceased can stay put.

But there is a special place reserved for those who dared to shape the Worlds; who held the seats of office; whose crowning arrogance was to assume that godhood was eternal. The Oracle describes it thus:

> *I see a hall on the shores of Death*
> *A-crawl with snakes and serpents.*
> *Netherworld, in which the damned*
> *Await the time of judgement.*

Except that the time of judgement was past. The verdict: perpetual twilight, along with the gods of yesteryear; gods from Worlds we never knew and empires that were already dust when Asgard's walls were rising. A painfully slow dissolution, with, in the case of Yours Truly, an added dose of suffering, delivered by none other than my monstrous son – Jormungand, Devourer of Gods, the good old World Serpent in poison. Both of us chained to the same rock, much in the same way that Odin himself had once left me bound not so long ago, with nothing to do but struggle and scream and watch the seconds and minutes float past like flotsam on the river.

I know what you're thinking. Yes, my *son*. That's what you get when demon blood grows hot and irresponsible. And yes, I *had* a wife in Asgard, and yes, she was better than I deserved, but Angrboda of Ironwood was more than just alluring. She gave me three children: Fenris, Hel, and the Serpent Jormungand – frankly, the thickest of the bunch, and by far the least appealing. His conversation in Netherworld – such as it was – was limited to angry hissing, slightly angrier hissing and furious hissing, all of which drizzled venom down my bound and helpless body, as well as producing a terrible stench. All in all, not what you'd call the best kind of father–son bonding. Which is why, in despair, I turned to Dream, even though that glimmer of hope hurt far more than submission.

You see, no faith can truly die until the last of the faithful are gone: and sometimes the faithful are stubbornly, cruelly persistent. Even when their fallen gods plead to be forgotten, yearning for the silence of death and the peace of dissolution, there's always a zealot who just won't quit, or a temple for tourists to gawk at, or an inscription on a stone, or a statue in the sand – anything to make Men dream—

Or, of course, a story.

Stories are the worst of all for keeping those torches burning. Stories told by firelight; whispered in the darkness; kept in carefully handwritten tomes; passed down through generations; written down in secret codes or scratched on pieces of bark and stone. Stories are how gods are born. They remain as a form of worship. And stories are what kept us alive – albeit in a twilight state; stripped of all our powers; tormented by our memories; feeling ourselves slip away, but still present in stories and dreams.

Humans are avid dreamers, of course. Their appetite for stories is vast; and every night they create new dreams; new, ephemeral Worlds to explore. Some of those Worlds are tiny, no larger than a soap-bubble. Some are as tall as glaciers; implacable as Destiny. Some last for less than a second or two; others may last up to a minute. Just long enough, in theory, for *someone* – let's say, a renegade god – to enter the dream and, from there, to follow the silver thread that leads into the dreamer's sleeping mind—

It can be done, in theory. But it isn't easy. To take control of a dreamer; to inhabit his consciousness – that takes a special kind of skill. Frankly, not all humans *want* to be possessed by a god. And their dreams are mostly volatile things; too weak for us to grasp at. It would take thousands – *millions* – of people *sharing the exact same dream* to give it any kind of strength, or provide even a chance of escape.

But Hope is a cruel torturer, worst of all the demons. While there was hope, we could not turn away from what was happening. Through reflections in Dream, we watched everything we knew disappear. We watched as our runes were forgotten, replaced by the new Roman alphabet. We saw the rise of a new god, enforcing his message of love and peace with a series of wars and purges. We watched the dark days of the Folk, when stories (and even dreams) were banned, and just to speak our names was a crime. We lost ourselves in darkness, and the pain was unimaginable.

And yet somehow, even through those times, our stories remained alive in the Worlds. A layer of darkness was lifted. We watched: on occasion we would see reflections of ourselves in Dream. Sometimes there were paintings, or perhaps a piece of music; some shared experience of the Folk that seemed to offer a kind of hope. And then there were *books*; there was *reading*; a thing we'd scarcely bothered with, back in the day, when stories were something that flew from mouth to mouth, and runes were something you carved in stone. And then there was the final part of the Oracle's prophecy, the verse that seemed to offer us a hope of something better:

> *I see a new world rising. Green*
> *And lovely from the ocean.*
> *Mountains rise, bright torrents flow,*
> *Eagles hunt for salmon.*

Of course, that could have been another of the Oracle's tricks: a misdirection to keep us in hope, and therefore prolong our torment. With the passing of time, that World seemed increasingly out of reach. Watching through Dream became almost too painful for us to bear. Everything seemed to indicate that the new World was not for us. Its mountains and its rivers were for other gods to rule and enjoy. One by one, we succumbed to despair; we closed our eyes to the green world.

But demons are tougher in some ways than gods. And though I missed corporeal form (especially the food, sleep and sex), my primal state *was* discorporate. Boredom was as much my foe as torment in that darkness: and with nothing left to hope for, what else was there to do but watch?

And so I watched as a new World was built. I watched as a man set foot on the Moon. I watched the rise of the paperback; the movies; computers; video games. Order reigned: an Order that owed little to our influence. It seemed as if the gods of old had been put aside for ever.

But Order, it seems, cannot exist without a certain amount of Chaos. My element is fire; and fire never goes out of fashion. In homes and around campfires; in lightning and in wildfire; in dreams and stories I was revered. I was almost worshipped. Order, for all its rules, loved to dream. And there, after years of searching, I found, hidden among the dreams of the Folk, some corner of a foreign field that was forever Asgard.

You see, just like the Worlds themselves, the Folk and their dreams were expanding. Television, computer games, e-books, apps: all these concepts I'd glimpsed in the dark had come together to make a world in which dreams could not just be shared, but *manipulated*. And the river Dream runs through that too, that world they call the *internet* – a fitting term for a medium able to catch the gods themselves—

And finally I began to see the possibility of escape.

3

LIKE HIS HALF-SIBLING, ODIN'S HORSE, Jormungand could pass between Worlds. In a previous Aspect, the Serpent had happily circled the One Sea, and, tail in its mouth, had spanned the Worlds from Dream to Pandaemonium. If I could persuade it to break out of Netherworld and into Dream, then I could use its momentum to crash my way into that world in which bright Asgard still endured, and thence into the corporeal World, perhaps even into physical form—

I know. It was a gamble. But then, I've always been lucky. Besides, what did I have to lose? My cell in Netherworld? My chains?

The first problem I encountered was trying to sell my plan to the snake. Jormungand wasn't the brightest spark, and he'd never been fond of me. But he was a prisoner too, and I guessed that even such as he might be open to the concept of escape. I started with the Prophecy, and its promise of brave new Worlds. But Jormungand hated poetry almost as much as I did, and all I got in lieu of response was a faceful of his venom.

I set my sights lower.

'I know a way,' I told him with exaggerated care. 'I can see a way out of this place. A way I could be persuaded to share – for the right kind of cooperation.'

Jormungand belched; it smelt vile, but I could tell he was interested.

'I can lead you there,' I said. 'But you'd have to release me.'

Well, *there* was a challenge, to start with. Jorgmungand wasn't built for dexterity. All he had was his teeth – not exactly precise when it came to the kind of task I had in mind. He hissed at me suspiciously, releasing a miasma of stench that made the whole of my body convulse. Of course, it wasn't *my* body at all; but the Black Fortress is built on sensations, all of them very unpleasant. I screwed my eyes shut against the venomous mist from the serpent's jaws, and tried again.

'All you need to do,' I said with more confidence than I felt, 'is to release me *with your mind*. These chains aren't real; they're like everything else in this place, built from dreams and ephemera. All you need to release me is to really *want* me to be free.'

A bit New Age for the snake, I know. I realized that a little too late. Jormungand gave another hiss, exposing his giant fangs and sending out a double jet of venom into my face.

'Dammit, Jorgi, that *hurts*!'

Jormungand made a guttural noise that sounded suspiciously like a purr.

'You enjoy it, don't you?' I said. 'You love making me suffer.'

The snake gave an undulating shrug, as if to say: *So shoot me, it's my nature.*

'But don't you see what you're doing?' I said. 'Your hatred for me is keeping you here. Without it, we could both be free. Can't you at least give it a try?'

The snake gave another hiss, but I thought I sensed a slight relaxing of its slimy coils. I pushed my advantage a little more.

'Freedom,' I said. 'Remember that? Remember being in the ocean? Remember the shoals of herring, the way they used to slip so sweetly down your throat? Remember the seals, and the cuttlefish? Remember how good they tasted?'

15

Of course, I'd never tasted them, but I was going for dramatic effect. Jormungand made the purring sound again.

'Remember how quiet it was in the sea?' I went on, gaining momentum. 'Remember how quiet and restful it was—'

The Serpent gave a dangerous hiss. Apparently, Jormungand wasn't a fan of rest and relaxation. Correcting myself, I changed tack.

'Remember the ocean storms?' I said. 'Remember how the wind lashed the waves? Remember how you loved to smash the merchant-ships with the tip of your tail? Remember how good it made you feel?'

The snake gave a thoughtful little belch.

'That's right,' I went on, soothingly. 'And remember how much *better* it felt than simply tormenting Yours Truly. In fact,' I went on hastily, 'think how much better tormenting me would feel if I was back in the flesh? Imagine what you could do to me then? Wouldn't that be *wonderful*?'

Jorgi said nothing, but I could smell his eagerness.

'All you have to do,' I said, 'is let me take you into Dream. I know a place, a wonderful place, where you and I can run amok and cause Chaos to our hearts' content. Trust me. I know where it is. All you have to do is let me go, and, I promise you, we can both be free—'

For a moment, I let him take in the idea. I knew he wasn't quick off the mark, but the fact that he wasn't actually spitting venom into my face was already a positive sign.

Then Jormungand purred, and I felt the chains around me slacken. Similarly, the rock on which I had spent the centuries began to lose substance, taking on the ephemeral form of Dream at its most deadly. I reached for the snake; felt its bristling scales like teeth embedded in the sheath of slime. I hauled myself onto its back, trying to ignore the stench, and held on with every particle of strength as the creature began to move, slowly, very slowly at first, and then with increasing momentum, smashing through walls like a thresher through grain, taking down ceilings and corridors; punching through torments and oubliettes; eating its ravenous path through anything that stood in its way; heading relentlessly upwards through countless levels of Netherworld towards the mouth of the Fortress.

For a moment I saw the gates, and the river Dream beyond them, a shining expanse of ephemera, dotted with islands and skerries and rocks, which might have looked almost beautiful to anyone as yet unaware of its deadly potency – and then the Serpent crashed through the gate, with Yours Truly still clinging to its spines, and we were both immersed in Dream: the choking, toxic wellspring of Dream, charged with the deepest fears of the Folk, roiling with lethal ephemera.

I know. It wouldn't have been my first choice of escape route, either. But it was the only choice I had; and with the added momentum offered by the Serpent, I'd hoped to spend as little time in the maelstrom as I possibly could. Not that Time has much meaning in Dream. A second blossoms into days; a minute into a lifetime. But I knew where I needed to be. I'd seen it too often to be in doubt. A dream shared by many; towering tall; held together by fragments of code, like millions of runemarks. A dream like a net, designed to catch the very gods in its gleaming mesh – although to be fair, my current goals were rather less ambitious. I searched for it now, and desperately, among the flotsam and jetsam of Dream, and, seeing it, I rode the snake into that dream of Asgard. Asgard. Oh my. Even in Dream, it was a world of marvels. There was the Sky Citadel, standing tall with Bif-rost arching towards it. There was Valhalla, and Odin's high seat with Hugin and Munin, his ravens, soaring above it. There was the world of the Folk, down below, and Ida's plain all flowered and green beneath a sky of the shade of blue that only exists in memories. And far away, on the horizon, there was a distant shimmer of something more: something that shone as bright as the sun, all swimming with colours and runelight.

For a moment the Serpent and I were poised on Asgard's

parapet. I knew it was a dream, and yet it felt so pure, so *powerful* – surely beyond the power of any single human to build. And I was *corporeal*: I could smell the ocean, the ozone in the atmosphere, the flowers from Idun's garden. I inspected my current Aspect. Not *quite* my own, but close enough – though the headgear was unfamiliar. But I was, if not myself, then at least as close as any dream could get. Who was responsible for this? Who could have dreamed this place into being? Once more, I looked at that glow in the sky. Tangled with runelight, it beckoned and shone like a luminous, living thing. Could one of the other gods have survived? Had Gullveig-Heid escaped Ragnarók? Could this even be a *new* god, bringing a new World out of Dream?

Then I looked up, and it hit me. This was no ordinary dream. Printed across the sky in letters that must have been a thousand feet high, letters that, like the Bif-rost of old, were made up of millions of tiny runes, coded together to create a web of something vast and unbreakable, I read:

NOW CHOOSE YOUR CHARACTER.

We were in a computer game.

4

ITS NAME WAS *Asgard!*™ – with an exclamation mark, like a 50s musical, and that little rune alongside, as if somehow to prove ownership. The premise, to hold the Sky Citadel against an assault from our enemies – Ice Folk, Rock Folk, renegade demons and so forth. There were a number of possible ways to play, according to character. You could play a Warrior (Thor); a General (Odin); or a Warrior Princess (Freyja) depicted as a generic female in impossibly scanty armour.

I know. You'd have thought that in a World as advanced as this one, such gross misrepresentation would have been in-conceivable. I mean, seriously, *Freyja*? If I'd created a game in which Elder Age gods came back to life, I certainly wouldn't have chosen *her*. Not that she couldn't fight when she had to, but Freyja was always too touchy for words, besides not being a fan of mine. All in all, there were plenty of things about this game that I wouldn't have planned, least of all the fact that I was clearly one of the bad guys. Talk about stereotyping. Of *course* the guy from Chaos would be representing the black hats.

Still, minor inaccuracies aside, it seemed like a pretty cool game. In fact, there was a whole world to be discovered in there – battles with giants; problems to solve; goblin minions to destroy; unlikely treasures to be found; a quest to reawaken a group of sleeping comrades buried under a layer of ice – its primary objective being the eventual defeat of the boss monster (me) and the reclaiming of Asgard.

I'll admit, it gave me the chills. So familiar, and yet so strange. So like the bubble-worlds of Dream, and yet so much more durable. But for me, the important thing was that during the course of this game the player seemed to enter a state of intense suggestibility, *becoming* his character; speaking his lines, maybe even sharing his thoughts. And that's where the gulf between the Worlds narrowed to the point at which you could *almost* cross—

Oh yes. I was familiar with the principle involved. I'd watched the process many times from my cell in Netherworld. Not that I meant to participate, but I understood how it worked. And now at last I had reached the point at which it might possibly work for me.

The snake was looking suspicious. As well it might; unlike myself, it had entered this place without prior knowledge, and it was beginning to understand that this might not be a conventional dream. In Aspect it was much as before, minus the stench and the sheath of slime, which frankly was an improvement, and yet I could sense its growing unease. The change of Aspect. Corporeal form. The strangely familiar landscape.

I looked into the blameless sky.

Below me, the Serpent followed my gaze.

YOU HAVE CHOSEN THOR!

announced the giant letters in the sky. Martial music began to play. I looked around, only to see all the goblin minions rushing to take cover as *something* appeared on the horizon. Something fast. Something big. Something that made the ground shake.

The Serpent gave a low hiss. Quietly, I slid off its back to stand on the open parapet.

Ah.

The basic premise of this game seemed to be adversarial in nature. YOU HAVE CHOSEN THOR, it said. And sure enough, coming over Bif-rost was the Thunderer, in Aspect, wielding his great hammer, his face twisted into a pretzel of rage—

The serpent gave a mighty hiss. I couldn't really blame it. The last time they'd met hadn't ended well for my monstrous progeny. The Oracle describes it thus:

> *Now the snake that binds the world*
> *Strikes in rage at wrathful Thor.*
> *Thunderer wins the battle, but falls*
> *To the monster's raging maw.*

Which made for a certain awkwardness now as the Thunderer strode into view. Of course, this wasn't *really* Thor. The real Thor was somewhere in Netherworld, still trapped in his own personal hell; but *this* Aspect of Thor had the red beard, the hammer and the attitude. He also had a kind of corset made from shining metal, which I thought looked rather silly, and a helmet with horns on, which made him look like a giant cow.

Still, my plan had never been to engage in combat. For a start, I don't enjoy pain, and if my assessment was correct, this game would involve quite a lot of it.

I ducked beneath the parapet just at the moment at which Meta-Thor's hammer smashed into the massive wall only inches from my head – accompanied by a brief fanfare from an invisible orchestra – while at the same time I heard his voice roaring like a hurricane:

Flee, thou creature of Chaos, before the might of Thor, the Thunderer!

Yeah. I had to laugh at that. Even Bragi the Bard, who had written some cheesy lines in his time, would have balked at that one.

I shall rend thee limb from limb. Tonight, I shall feast in Valhalla, and pick my teeth with thy sharpened bones!

The language was ridiculous. But I had to admit, the *sentiment* was Thor. The last time I'd seen him, at Ragnarók, he'd promised to tear me limb from limb. Luckily, I'd brought along a distraction; and one that was more than ready to fight.

I flinched as once again the hammer crashed into the parapet, sending a massive plume of black smoke and pulverized rock into the air. But the Serpent was between us, lunging at the Thunderer. Thor struck at it with his hammer; the blow was enough to send the Serpent flying through the gleaming air – until it struck an invisible wall, and bounced off it with an air of almost comic astonishment. Well, yes. I should have said. That's the thing about this World: easy enough for us to get in; not so easy to get out. The Serpent gave an enormous hiss and went for the barrier again. When it bounced off for the second time, its violent rage was enough to make the parapet on which I was standing shake.

I grabbed at the nearest minion. It was a goblin of some kind, about the size of a large dog, its furry face half hidden beneath an oversized round helmet.

'Whose dream is this?' I demanded.

The minion goggled at me from eyes of a luminous, wedding-ring gold. For a moment I wondered if it could speak. Then it squeaked: 'Let me go, Captain, let me *go*! I didn't do nuffink! It wasn't me!'

I held it fast by the scruff of the neck. 'You know me?'

The goblin looked surprised. 'Everyone knows you, Captain,' it said, as if I'd said something ludicrous. 'Quick, you gotta get ready! It's Thor!'

Well, that was certainly true enough. Thor – or whatever Aspect of Thor happened to be a prisoner here – though briefly distracted by Jormungand, was heading straight towards me.

'What weapons do I have? What glam?'

The goblin goggled at me idiotically.

'Don't tell me I have nothing,' I said, considering for a moment the possibility of holding the creature over my head and using it as some kind of shield. 'This game, this battle – this

22

World – has rules. What chance do I have if I'm unarmed?'

The goblin gave a whole-body shrug. 'Well, you *are* the Trickster,' it said. 'You've got a bunch of tricks you can use.'

'What kind of tricks?' I said.

'I dunno,' said the goblin. 'You're the god, remember? I'm just a minion of evil.'

I sketched a runeshape in the air, without any great expectation. Somewhat to my surprise, there was a fanfare – and a shining disc of silvery light sprang into being in mid-air a foot or so from my face.

A runeshield. And just in time, too: the Thunderer struck at me again. I felt the impact against the shield: a bone-crunching blow that in any other circumstance would have meant the end of Yours Truly. As it was, I guessed the shield wouldn't last more than another couple of strikes – not that I meant to be around for long enough to find out.

I made a leap for higher ground, still holding the runeshield between us. There was a ledge above the parapet, ending in a blank stone wall. Nowhere to run; nowhere to hide; nothing but the sickening drop to Ida's plain below me. But I wasn't planning to hang about for Meta-Thor to finish me. All I needed was the chance to connect with whoever was playing the game. One dreamer was all I needed: one mind. One player to choose my perspective, rather than that of the Thunderer. And I could sense *hundreds* of minds at work here; hundreds of silver strands interlinked. *One* of them had to be suitable. They couldn't *all* be rooting for Thor. Surely one of them, at least, would be sympathetic to an alternative point of view?

Meta-Thor started to climb. Now I could practically hear the hundreds of interlinked voices, urging him to crush my skull, to peel me like an orange—

I tried a delaying tactic. 'Er, can we talk about this?' I said.

Meta-Thor looked a little confused.

I tried a different idiom. '*I prithee, o brother, o Mighty One.* Er – look, could we possibly do this some other time?'

I started to edge away from him, keeping an eye out for Jor-mungand. The World Serpent had finally stopped its mindless pounding of the outer wall, and was currently circling Asgard's walls with a look of angry bafflement. But Meta-Thor was moving again, and I had to pursue my argument.

'I mean, quite apart from the fact that this *isn't* Asgard, you're not *actually* Thor, and I could use some *help* here—' I addressed this final plea to the universe in general as that damned fanfare came again, and Meta-Thor, with a howl of triumph, hurtled towards me, hammer in hand, ready to smash me against the wall.

I attempted to use the shield again, but instead of a fanfare, it simply produced a sad little twanging sound, as if I'd stepped on Bragi's lute. I raised both my arms, thought of Asgard, and—

The World Serpent, having finally identified the real enemy, hurtled into Meta-Thor, striking him in the small of the back. Thor stumbled forwards, hitting the wall and pulverizing the rocky ledge on which I had been standing. I fell, arms flailing through the air, to be caught by Meta-Thor, who seized me by the hair as I fell and drew me into a crushing embrace—

Ouch. So, I could feel actual *pain* in this odd little bubble-world. Interesting in principle, but not something I was eager to pursue in practice.

'Please,' I said. 'I can help you escape. Just let me go. I swear I will. I swear, I'll find a way to free *all* of the gods if you let me go . . .'

Meta-Thor growled. His hands found my throat. His eyes were bloodshot and desperate; the eyes of a man who has long since ceased to hope, or to believe in anything. I might even have felt sorry for him, if I hadn't been otherwise engaged. Behind him, on the parapet, the World Serpent shook its hoary head free of the rubble and debris of Asgard. It opened its jaws. The stench was immense. Its fangs were the size of ice-picks. I'd counted on it attacking Thor in preference to me, and to be fair, barring one detail, my plan was going swimmingly.

The thing was, I'd rather counted on not being in the vicinity when Jormungand made his move. I addressed a blasphemous prayer – to the game, to the players, to the universe in general:

Please. Just give me a break, OK? Have you any idea what it's like, being me?

At which point, the Serpent struck with the bludgeoning force of a battering-ram, and, thrown free of Thor's embrace, I was flung over the parapet, and, screaming and cursing and pinwheeling, I fell once again towards Ida's plain, while all around me the fanfare played, and the letters in the sky above proclaimed in a tumult of Northlights:

GAME OVER!

And I was reborn into flesh.

5

GODS, WHAT A FEELING. What a trip. I swear there's nothing like it. Emerging like a newborn from Dream into a living body; feeling that rush of sensations – heat; cold; hunger; lust; exhilaration; appetite – seeing colours; hearing sounds – no, there's nothing like it. Which is why it didn't occur to me until a little later that there was something very slightly odd about the whole experience.

When Odin first called me from Chaos, I determined my own Aspect: that of a young man with red hair and a certain louche charm. When rescued from bondage by Gullveig-Heid, restored to the height of my powers, I naturally resumed my corporeal form. In the game of *Asgard!*™ I had assumed the Aspect of the character created in my image: not quite an accurate portrait, but close enough to identify. But this time, it was different. This time, I *had* no corporeal form; no glam to create one. Yet here I was, in the physical world, in a physical body.

The initial shock was tremendous. I wondered if I'd lost my mind. So many sensations all at once, crammed into this jacket of flesh. I couldn't breathe. My vision swam. I fell to my knees on a hard wooden floor that smelt of dust and beeswax. The sounds of battle rang in my ears; the brassy taste of blood filled my mouth and once more I was falling from Asgard's broken parapet . . .

I lay on the dusty floor for a while and listened to my deafening heart. Slowly, the panic receded; the nausea became bearable; I opened my eyes and saw a room that was dimly lit by a glowing box. Discarded clothes lay on the ground. There were pictures on the walls of a man who I thought looked vaguely familiar. The bed was unmade; the curtains were drawn. I realized that it must be night.

I held up my arms. They were skinny, but functional. For a moment I thought I saw the silvery gleam of the runemark *Kaen*, although unlike my own rune, this one seemed to be reversed –

– but no, on further investigation, it was only a pale scar that happened to *look* like a runemark. There were other scars there, too, braceleting half the length of my arm. I knew they were not accidental, although I didn't know how I knew. And suddenly, there was something else; something that had me scrambling to my feet and heading full-tilt towards what I knew to be the bathroom. There was a mirror over the sink (no time for me to marvel yet at *how* I knew these things), and I turned on the overhead light to scrutinize my features.

I know. It's a cliché. So shoot me – but I was a little afraid of what I might see in the mirror. *What if I was ugly?* I thought. Call me shallow, if you like, but I've always been irresistible. The thought that my current Aspect might not be as alluring as the one I'd always inhabited filled me with a nameless dread.

Oh.

Well, I wasn't ugly. That was a relief, for a start. In fact, as the impact of seeing myself for the first time began to wear off, I was even inclined to approve. Eyes, grey; hair, nondescript (but *that* could be changed); a mouth that looked more serious than the one I had become used to (still, I sensed that a healthy dose of laughter might work wonders). The skin was reassuringly good; the cheekbones, average; the general appearance somewhat gauche as well as rather skinny, but with a little effort, I felt that maybe I could work with it. And yet, I couldn't help thinking that there was something important that I'd missed.

And then it struck me. Yes, of course. I should have seen it straight away, except that I'd been a prisoner in Netherworld for centuries, and my mind had been on other things. But now I saw it clearly. The hair; the shape of the jaw-line; the absence of something significant in the trouser region –

I stared at my reflection again. No doubt about it.

I was a girl.

6

*W*ELL, *IT COULD BE WORSE*, I thought. In previous Aspects
I had already been a horse, a bridesmaid, a gadfly, a hawk, a
snake and an old woman. I'd even given birth – not an experience I was keen to repeat, but at least I wasn't entirely new to
the concept of gender fluidity. And scrutinizing my reflection,
I was inclined to believe I'd been lucky. I was young, I looked
healthy; I was even passably attractive, although the short hair
seemed a little severe compared to what I was used to.

I was wearing some kind of shapeless black hooded garment
over a pair of leggings (*Jeans*, whispered a distant voice in my
mind), and boots of sturdy leather. On my left arm (the one
with the ladder of rune-shaped scars), I wore a stack of bracelets
made of some braided material in a number of bright colours.
My ears were pierced in several places, as was my left eyebrow,
and small diamond studs inserted. My breasts were disappoint-
ingly small, although, as the offspring of a fire demon and a
combustible, I'd never found mammaries particularly fascinat-
ing. I was just starting to investigate my rather more promising
nether regions when the whispering voice that had spoken to
me identifying the jean-things spoke up rather more sharply.

What the hell are you doing? it said.

That must be my host, I thought. I'll admit, I'd been so busy exploring my current Aspect that I'd hardly given any thought to its original occupant. Frankly, I'd expected them to vacate the premises. Apparently, they hadn't.

'Oh. Sorry,' I said aloud.

If anything, my host seemed more upset than ever. *Who are you? What are you doing?*

'I don't want you to panic,' I said. 'But – remember that computer game? The one you were playing a moment ago? The one with the silver-tongued, handsome dude, and the big, hairy psychopath?'

Now I'm hearing voices, said my host. *Marvellous. That's all I need.*

'No, really,' I said helpfully. 'That was me. I'm Loki.'

Oh, God. I really am going crazy. That, or Evan spiked my drink. That's right. He must have done. Come to think of it, it's precisely the kind of thing he would think was funny. I'm going to kill him. Where's my phone? I'm going to kill him for real this time.

I made a mental note to myself to remember this Evan person. He sounded cool.

I tried again. 'You know, *crazy* is such a negative word. I prefer *disordered*. Order's so dull. Chaos is where the party is.'

My host put her fingers in her ears, and, taking control of the voice, began to shout: 'I'm not listening. Bla, bla, bla. I'm not listening. Bla, bla, bla – there's nobody there!'

I waited till she was out of breath. Then I took control again, and said:

'OK. Is it my turn again?'

For a moment, there was no coherent response; just a kind of mental squall. I let it run its course, much as the parent of a small child might ignore a tantrum. (Of course, unlike *my* children, she wasn't likely to try and destroy the Nine Worlds, or to devour the Sun and Moon, or put an end to Humanity.) Then, the clamour seemed to recede, and I took the opportunity to say:

'I know this must feel very strange. Trust me, I know how

you feel. But here we are, and before you say something *really* hurtful, let me just tell you that no, you're not dreaming, yes, this is real, and however hard you try to escape, I'll still be here. I'm persistent. It's one of my many qualities.'

There was a long, long silence.

You're saying I'm not crazy? That I'm not tripping out at all?

'For all I know, you're mad as a fish. But everything that can be dreamed is real, at least on some level. *You* dreamed *me*. And here I am. Simple as *Fé, Úr, Thúris.*'

What?

'I'm sorry. Simple as A, B, C. It's going to take me a while to adapt to your local idiom. Plus, there's the genitalia, which, frankly, may also take some getting used to.'

Stop it! Let me get this clear. You're saying you're Loki? As in Loki, the Trickster of Asgard? Son of Laufey, Father of Lies, sire of the Serpent, blood of the Wolf, yadda yadda yadda?

'Absolutely, in person,' I said. 'Well, actually, *not* in person. Or at least, not in the person I'm *accustomed* to being in, which doesn't mean to imply that I'm not *very* grateful for your hospitality.'

Yeah, said the voice, sounding calmer now. *I'm totally not buying this. This is all a crazy hallucination. That, or a trick. Or maybe I'm just zoning out, the way I sometimes do in class. Or it's a virus, I dunno, something like sleeping sickness. Doesn't that affect the brain? Or is that just the zombie plague? Is there even a zombie plague? Or did I make that up, as well?*

I tried to explain about Dream, and the gods, and our long incarceration in the dungeons of Netherworld. I dwelt upon the paradox of what we call Reality; its infinite possibilities; the Aspects of ourselves we leave scattered across the Nine Worlds. I explained how even Death is subject to the rules of Order and Chaos; how nothing ever really dies, but our volatile essence can be distilled into Aspects of ourselves like perfume into a bottle; all of them separate, but equally real, equally true to the formula.

There was a long, long silence.

Then the voice said, very calmly: *When I see Evan, I'm going to kill him. And then I'm going to kill him again, just to make sure.*

For a moment I wondered whether Thor had managed to follow me into my host. The sentiment – even the words themselves – seemed eerily familiar. Then I thought that maybe my host had simply played too many games of *Asgard!™*, and had thus acquired some of the Thunderer's less appealing mannerisms.

She must have caught my train of thought. *But Asgard's just a game*, she said, *made up of light and pixels. It isn't real. How could it be?*

I shrugged. 'You say *pixel*, I say *ephemera*. Dream's made up of them, sweetheart: millions of tiny particles. You pulled me out of Dream, and as such I'm as real as anything else that can be imagined. More so than some, in fact,' I went on, thinking of the stranger types of ephemera I'd encountered on my travels through Chaos. '*You* may not be aware of this, but there's actually a theory that those particles make up *everything*, and that Dream itself is only a part of an even greater reality.'

I waited for my new host to process this information. I could feel her struggling – against me, Reality, you name it, the whole Nine Worlds.

This is total bullshit, she said. *This is all a figment of my over-developed imagination. I mean, why would a god choose me? And why Loki? Loki's the bad guy!*

'I was misunderstood,' I said. 'Someday I'll tell you the story. But I was falling. You saved me. Some part of you must have reached out. You must have felt a connection—'

But why you, rather than—

'Rather than who?'

Nothing. No one, said my host. *God, now I'm arguing with myself. That's what comes of reading too much instead of being on the netball team. Just close your eyes. He'll go away as soon as he sees you're on to him. He's just a part of you, you know. A fragment of*

*your subconscious. There's nothing he can do to you that you haven't
already done to yourself. Just close your eyes and count to ten. One.
Two. Three —*

I waited. I had plenty of time. Slowly, I felt her resistance collapse; her disbelief and panic recede. Then the inner voice said:

Are you still there?

''Fraid so.'

When will you be leaving?

That was inhospitable, even rather hurtful, I thought. 'You
know,' I said, '*some* people might feel privileged, being host to
a god of Asgard.'

The inner presence seemed to shrug. *No offence*, it said. *But
I have enough identity problems as it is without having a Norse god
living in my mind. And besides, how do I know you're Loki? I mean,
you don't sound like Loki to me.*

I was offended. 'What do you mean?'

*Well, Loki was in the olden days. Shouldn't you be saying things
like 'Come with me unto Valhalla, brother, wherein we shall feast with
our ancestors?'*

I briefly rested my head in my hands. 'Where did you get *that*
rubbish from?'

Everywhere. Films, books, games —

'Oh, please.' I could see that I was going to have my work cut
out with this one. 'How old are you, nine?'

A blast of resentment from my host. *Don't be ridiculous.
Seventeen.*

'You can't be serious,' I said.

*At least I'm not a has-been from a bunch of stupid old legends. And
if I'd known you were a dick, I wouldn't have bothered reading them
in the first place.*

I sighed. 'Oh, gods. You *are* seventeen. I'm sorry – er – what
was your name?'

My host gave a sniff. *They call me Jumps.*

'OK. OK, I'm sorry, Jumps. We started off on the wrong foot.
Could we maybe start again? It isn't easy, dying, then being

tortured for centuries, then finding myself in the body of some-one who doesn't want me around. I mean. Just give me a break, OK? Think of me as—' I searched for a concept that she might understand. 'Think of me as a refugee. A refugee from a war zone. Would you really turn me away? Knowing all I'd been through?'

A sullen silence. Then: *OK. I'll give it a try. You know, I loved those stories.*

'Well, I guess that's a start. I have to admit, the legends are cool, although they don't exactly show me in the most flattering light. I'll have to put the record straight. Remind me to do that sometime. Still, if I was your favourite, they must have got *some* of it right. Right?'

I never said you were my favourite, said my host, with a pinch of amusement.

'What?'

I thought you were OK, but you were never my favourite.

'Oh.'

Well, *that* really *did* hurt my feelings. I'd kind of assumed that the reason I'd ended up in this body was because its original owner and I had an intimate connection. And now she was trying to tell me that I wasn't even her first choice?

Instinctively, I searched her mind. It felt a little like searching through a complex storage system. There were many galleries, archives and directories filled with all kinds of information: memories, facts, vocabularies, fantasies, feelings. I sensed that some of these would be hard to access – locked doors, leading to unlit places – but there was enough in the well-lit, open sec-tion for me to find what I was looking for. I came upon a gallery devoted to the gods of Asgard – comics, books, posters, games, you name it. Oh, she was a fan, all right, even if her version of us was almost absurdly far from the truth. And now I suddenly realized why those pictures on the wall had seemed vaguely familiar.

I sat down in astonishment.

'*Thor?* You're telling me *Thor* was your favourite?'

My host gave a kind of mental shrug. *Well, you know—*

'That animal? The guy who used to pick me up by the hair? The man whose favourite party trick was necking fourteen barrels of mead and then killing all the guests? A man so tragically incompetent that he once actually mistook the World Serpent for a *cat*?'

You may be inside my mind, said Jumps, *but you're not going to tell me what to think.*

'OK. OK. You're the boss.'

There followed a lengthy silence, during which my stomach growled lustily. 'I think that's a call to breakfast,' I said. 'I take it we agree on *that.*'

Jumps just gave that shrug again. *I'm not hungry.*

'Are you insane? I'm *starving!*'

A shiver of denial; the sense of something buried deep in one of those directories. It was odd, and rather disturbing; my previous incarnation had never once resisted any kind of pleasure. Besides, it had been centuries since I'd experienced as much as a dry crust, let alone a jam tart or a cup of wine.

'Come with me unto Valhalla, Jumps, wherein we shall feast with our ancestors,' I said.

No, we can't— began my host.

'Come on, live a little,' I said.

And then, with the same instinct that had driven me to rifle through my host's mind, I stepped forward and took control of the body.

7

IT FELT A LITTLE LIKE TAKING the reins of a speeding chariot. For a moment I sensed protest, but I simply pushed harder at the host mind until the resistance failed. Then I just followed my instincts and hers – *bedroom, passageway, kitchen* – until I found myself in front of a large white box, which, when opened, revealed an exhilarating quantity of all manner of victuals.

Fridge, said Jumps' voice in my mind. She sounded very far away. To be honest, I didn't really care: there was a plump roast fowl, and cheese, bread, milk, various unidentified (but nevertheless delicious) sweetmeats and, best of all, something like beer, in strange cold metal cylinders which I took some time to prise open, but, with the help of my internal handbook, eventually discovered the little cantrip (*Ring-pull*, whispered Jumps) that sealed its foaming contents.

Full disclosure: I might have gone a bit overboard. From time to time, I heard Jumps' voice, saying things like *Calories*, and *Saturated fats*, and *But I never drink beer*, but to be fair, I wasn't really paying attention. I moved from the fridge to the pantry, then on to a series of boxes and tins, containing something flat, brown and unexpectedly delicious.

Chocolate, oh no, moaned the voice of Jumps in my head – then suddenly she was back again, struggling hard to regain control.

'Ouch!' The door of the pantry slammed shut, rather hard, against my hand. The pain – that very *corporeal* pain, so unlike the existential kind that tortured us in Netherworld – was like plunging into a bucket of ice. 'What the hell was *that* for?' I said. It wasn't as if she couldn't feel it, just because I was in her. In fact, I could sense her pain and distress, though much of the latter seemed mixed up with the fact that I'd eaten the chocolate, which, from a quick search through the mental directory marked FOOD, seemed to be some kind of poison that would instantly change my appearance into that of a bloated troll.

I glanced at my reflection in the kitchen window. I couldn't see any difference. I'd survived the chocolate easily – the harder challenge, it seemed, was surviving Jumps.

You were completely out of control! I heard her scolding in my mind. *I had to stop you somehow. My God, when my parents see what you've done—*

I pointed out the supreme bad taste of invoking one god whilst serving as host to another. 'Besides, I was hungry. You were, too.'

She laughed. *I'm always hungry. So what? That doesn't mean I'm going to just stuff my face with doughnuts and cheese whenever I happen to feel like it.*

'Why not?' I was genuinely curious.

Because— she began. *Oh, what's the use? You're a guy. What do you know?* I sensed her struggling to explain, so I opened an archive marked HUNGER and reached for a series of images. A blonde not unlike Freyja, standing on a sunset beach; another woman wearing nothing much but a pair of very unconvincing wings; a kind of box with numbers on it and a memory, not so far away, of children, chanting:

Land whale, land whale, Josephine the land whale.

'Who's Josephine?' I said.

I am, said Jumps.

'Weird name,' I said. 'What's a land whale?'

Stop it! said Jumps. *That's private!*

'What, this stuff about junior school? I just assumed it was public domain—'

Well, it's not, said Jumps, annoyed. *Just stop poking around, all right? And step away from the chocolate.*

I did. To be honest, I was feeling a little sick. Centuries without corporeal food had slightly tipped me over the edge, and besides, I was never a creature of moderation.

And you'll have to tidy that up, said Jumps, indicating the mess on the floor. Well, I'd dropped a couple of things, including some chicken bones, a lot of packaging and some slimy stuff (*Yoghurt,* said Jumps) that had looked more promising than it had tasted.

I took a moment to envision a world in which I was supposed to clean the floor.

'You don't have servants to do that?' I said. It occurred to me with an unpleasant start that perhaps my host *was* a servant, but her laughter at my question was enough to quell my doubts.

Servants? You must be joking, she said. *We just clear up after we eat. I mean, what are you, an animal?*

'Not currently,' I told her. 'But not being entirely used to this, I'm on a bit of a learning curve.'

She gave a dismissive kind of shrug. *Let's just get this done,* she said. *It's really late. I need to sleep. And then, when I wake up—*

'Oh no, you don't.' I didn't need to be a genius to catch the thought she was trying to hide. She was thinking that if she went to sleep, I'd be gone when she awoke. 'I'm not planning to move out just yet. You let me in, and I'm staying here. So pull up an extra chair, Jumps. I'm going to be around a while.'

I could tell she didn't believe me. No matter; I wasn't leaving. I finished cleaning the floor, which was made from some kind of smooth brown tile, and tipped the rubbish into a bag. Then I went to the bedroom and started to take off my clothes.

'Why do you have your eyes shut?' I said, as I dropped the shapeless black over-garment onto the cluttered bedroom floor.

I don't want you watching me, said Jumps.

I had to laugh. 'I'm *in* you. I know what you know. I feel what you feel. You think that closing your eyes will change that?'

That shrug again. *Whatever.*

'OK.' I waited until she was dressed again, this time in a shapeless pink garment – *nightie* – printed with pictures of penguins. I opened my eyes. The light was still on. Jumps picked up an object – *phone* – with a little screen, adorned with a picture of a cat. For a moment she blinked at the screen. I watched her fingers move quickly over the pads that she thought of as *keys* – an apt term, I thought, for a thing designed to unlock secrets. I quickly understood that these keys were made to open windows – windows marked with mysterious names like SNAPCHAT, E-MAIL and INSTAGRAM. I lingered at one marked FACEBOOK, but Jumps passed over it quickly. Instead she opened a window marked MUSIC. I sensed her impatience; her desire to keep me from the Book of Faces. I understood that there was some kind of equivalent of this book in her mind, which, if I were to open it, would give me access to family, friends – everyone in Jumps' life. But Jumps was not ready to share it with me.

Now, fixing something over my ears – *Headphones* – I heard music: not the kind I was used to, but something soft and melancholy. I could hear words: a kind of lament, although much of the idiom was strange; and the instruments were new to me. At least there were no lutes, I thought. That had to be a bonus.

'Trying to lull me to sleep?' I said, fully intending to stay awake – I had no idea how my reborn self would function in this Aspect, or how much control I would lose if I gave myself to Dream.

Jumps just gave that shrug again – a combination of shoulder-shrug and adolescent head-waggle – and closed her eyes without a word. I suppose I could have opened them, but the bed was warm and soft, and the pleasure of once more being in the flesh was enough to dim my fears. Sleep would be so good, I thought. Sleep would be so very good. But would I awaken in the flesh, or back in the dungeon of fallen gods? Still fighting, I slipped into the dark, and awoke to the sound of Jumps saying:

Fuck!

I'd survived my first night.

8

'F UCK!' REPEATED JUMPS, OUT LOUD. 'Why did this have to happen *today*?'

I stretched, enjoying the sunlight. The phone sitting by the side of the bed showed me some blinking numbers. I could feel Jumps wanting to hurry; but I was still half-dazed with sleep, and saw no reason to move as yet, or take control of the body. Had I dreamed? I thought I had. Something half-remembered seemed to linger in my consciousness. The memory of a hill, some runes, and then an object that shone like the sun—

At the back of my mind – *our* mind – Jumps was repeating: *You can't be here! You were supposed to be gone by now. I can't have you here with me. Not today.*

I took a deep breath. The dream was gone. Twelve more waking hours lay ahead, all gleaming with potential. Twelve more hours of freedom, I thought. Twelve more hours of precious life. I stretched again. I was hungry. But though Jumps shared my appetite, it wasn't a priority.

What's happening today? I said. *I was thinking breakfast, then maybe a nice long bath, then maybe some clothes that don't look like they've been designed for a cave-troll—*

'I have to get to school!' she said.

School? I looked up the reference in Jumps' inner lexicon. The

41

section marked SCHOOL in our shared space was hidden in the shadows. Many conflicting emotions seemed to coexist in this area. I wondered why she wanted to go when clearly she didn't enjoy it.

It looks terrible. Let's go with Plan A.

'There is no Plan A. I have to go.'

But I could feel her ambivalence as I searched her mind more thoroughly. On the one hand, there was the fear of authority – never much of an influence where I was concerned, of course. On the other, there was the growing fear that I might somehow reveal myself in front of people who mattered, people who would judge her because of what I did. Her peers seemed to matter enormously; especially a person named *Stella,* whose name seemed at the same time to conjure both admiration and venom. Most of all, there was something called EXAMS, which seemed to matter even more than the Stella person.

'What's an EXAM?' I said.

She growled and tipped the phone onto the floor. 'Why are you still *here*?' she said. 'Why can't you just be a dream?' She dived into the mess at the foot of her bed in an attempt to re-trieve the phone. I noticed that much of the floor space seemed occupied by objects of a similar sort, the nature of which was strange to me, but all of which seemed to run on cantrips of one sort or another. The phone, however, seemed to have great importance to my host; it housed the Book of Faces; a link to all her acquaintances; games; pictures of funny cats – even, some-how, I sensed, the time.

'Cool gadget,' I told her, slipping into her idiom. (This was easy, given our proximity and my access to that internal lexi-con.) 'Order or Chaos?'

The question was moot. Her insistence on cleaning the kitchen suggested the former, but honestly, the state of her bedroom floor was hardly Idun's boudoir. Not to mention the pictures – *posters* – on the bedroom wall, most of which seemed to feature some kind of bastardized Aspect of Thor. Of course, the Thor I knew was a lot less well-groomed and would never have been seen dead in that golden armour, but at least the hammer was recognizable enough. Call me vain if you like, but I couldn't help wondering what *I* looked like in this fantasy version of Asgard.

'Order or Chaos, *what*?' said Jumps, trying to struggle into her clothes without opening her eyes.

'What's the source of your power?' I said. 'Because if it's Order, this place needs a clean, and if it's Chaos, then I'm toast.'

I felt her struggling to understand. 'Power? I don't have any *power*,' she said. 'I'm a seventeen-year-old girl. I go to school. I hang out with my friends. Most days I barely get to control the TV remote. What are you talking about, power?'

She couldn't lie to me, of course. I was in her consciousness. She really believed what she was saying, and yet, I could sense it in her, the glam: what we in the old days called the Fire. But the Fire that drives the Folk is a different element. They burn so bright, and yet they are so completely unaware of the power within their control. Their dreams created the River that runs through all of the known Worlds, and at the same time they seem completely ignorant of their inner resources – a power that dragged me out of Dream and here, into this stolen skin.

She must have caught a part of my thought. In any case, I sensed mistrust. I could tell she still didn't quite believe in my existence: still thought I might be nothing but a casual visitor in her mind.

Opening her eyes again, she picked up the phone from its place on the floor. 'I'm texting Evan,' she said aloud. 'If he's behind this, I'll kill him.'

It was a forlorn hope, at best. I could tell even she wasn't convinced. But this Evan sounded OK, and besides, the sooner she could be persuaded I was real, the sooner I could work on my own plan, which consisted of exploring this world and enjoying whatever it offered.

I looked around the bedroom. Thor's face – or at least this

World's version of him – continued to stare out at me from half a dozen clippings, drawings and posters.

Why couldn't you have been him? said Jumps. *Why did it have to be you?*

I sighed. Joined as intimately as we were, tact was not an option.

'I get it,' I said. 'You don't like me. Join the club.'

It isn't that. It's just—

'I know when you're lying, Jumps,' I said.

'I'm texting Evan,' she said. 'Do you mind? We'll talk about this later.'

I watched as Jumps summoned cantrips on her phone. The letters were not quite familiar, being based on the new Roman alphabet, but given that I knew what she knew, it wasn't hard for me to translate.

Meet me at your place. NEED TO TALK. J x

'So what about EXAMS?' I said.

'I don't have to be in until later,' she said. 'I've got English Lit. in the afternoon.'

She pulled on a pair of ankle-socks with little cats printed on them. What with the penguin nightdress, I guessed she must really like animals.

'So, I'm free until then,' she went on, 'and we're going to talk to Evan. And then, whoever the hell you are, you're getting the fuck out of my mind.'

9

THE WAY TO EVAN'S PLACE LED us through a series of streets and alleyways that Jumps simply thought of as *The Village*. Its name was *Malbry*, I understood – pronounced to rhyme with *strawberry* – and Jumps had lived here all her life. I'd spent less than twenty-four hours in her mind, but I could feel my awareness of all things Jumps growing at a startling rate: her idiom was no longer strange; her body no longer unfamiliar. And now, as we crossed the Village, there were memories at every turn, on every piece of stonework; in the park, with its ancient climbing-frame and the swing on which she used to sit while her father pushed her and they laughed—

Stop that!

'What? What did I do?'

Poking around in my memories again. Those things are private. Leave them alone.

I gave an inward shrug. 'OK. If that's the way you want to be—' I sent her a mental picture of myself, sitting bolt upright on a sofa, the cushions of which were covered in transparent plastic sheeting. A woman with hair that seemed to be carved from a single piece of blonde driftwood glared as she handed me a glass filled with some kind of beverage. *Stay there, sit still and don't spill your juice,* the woman said. *And don't you be touching anything.*

'That's my Auntie Cora,' said Jumps. 'How did you even know about her? She moved to Australia when I was six. I haven't thought about her for years.'

I pointed out that her memory was now largely a shared resource. 'I can't sit still and not touch anything. I may be a visitor in your mind, but I know what's in the cupboards. So, you'd better get used to it, Jumps. I won't put my feet on the furniture, but I'm damned if I'm going to ask you every time I need a glass of water.'

I let that register for a moment. When she finally replied, it was in a subdued tone. 'I don't want you in here,' she said. 'Can't you just go somewhere else?'

I had to laugh. In her mouth, the laughter sounded strange and a little mad. 'I wish I could,' I told her. 'But I'd need somewhere else to go. Preferably somewhere that *isn't* designed to keep my disembodied self in a state of perpetual torment. And that, dear Jumps, is the rub. Until I find more suitable accommodation, I'm afraid you're stuck with me.'

She didn't believe me. I could tell. There was still something hidden in there, some kind of a plan that she wasn't ready to reveal. Evan was a part of it: I sensed that much, although his face was obscured by clouds. Funny, that: I could see Aunt Cora in detail, and yet her best friend was a mystery.

'I can't see into *your* mind,' said Jumps. 'Why should you see into mine?'

'Trust me, you don't want to,' I said. 'Thirty seconds in there and you'd probably go crazy.'

That was true. I knew *that* much. My mind was a whole lot bigger than hers, with entire rooms full of directories given up to torment, rage, wickedness, pain and various kinds of insanity – well, that's Chaos for you, of course – as well as some somewhat complicated personal issues, involving sex, guilt and feelings. I wasn't about to let one of the Folk loose among my demons, especially as *her* mind, such as it was, seemed to consist mostly of funny cat videos, penguin socks and vague nostalgia for childhood; plus Facebook, existential angst, mean girls from school and acute public embarrassment, with long and unnecessary compendia given over to images of physical perfection, along with a whole lot of needless guilt regarding the consumption of food. Which reminded me . . .

'Breakfast.'

'I never have breakfast.'

'Well, I *do*.'

We passed a woman walking a dog, who looked at us in a peculiar way. The dog didn't look too impressed, either. From Jumps' reaction, I gathered that people talking to themselves wasn't generally approved of in Malbry.

Must you? said Jumps, reverting to our initial, less public form of communication.

'Must I what?'

Be so bloody talkative!

I shrugged her shoulders. It felt good. I shrugged them again, for the fun of it. 'I haven't had much to talk about over the past few hundred years. I'm rather enjoying the novelty.' I sent her a mental picture of one of the less traumatic antechambers of the Black Fortress – not a very clear picture, and only for a moment. But I sensed her horror and disbelief, along with something else I might use, and I grinned in secret to myself.

'See, Jumps,' I told her. 'You *can* see into my mind. If I want you to, that is.'

I don't want to, said Jumps. *Not ever again.*

'We'll see about that, shall we?' I said.

We walked in silence the rest of the way.

10

E VAN'S PLACE WAS A DUN-COLOURED box made of something called *concrete*. It was very high, and we entered through
a portal (*lift*), powered by arcane and complex mechanisms that
Jumps barely even noticed.

I have to say, I was a little surprised at her casual attitude.
Her world was filled with energies, glamours and cantrips, and
yet her mind – such as it was – still dwelt mostly on clothing,
school and objects shaped like animals. It made no sense. In fact,
I was starting to believe that she had no right to the body we
shared, and that I would be far better off as its only occupant.

I could probably take it by force too, if it came to a mental
fight – and yet I *needed* my annoying host, at least until I learnt
to manage in this world without her. My history of fitting into
social groups was patchy at best, and if others learnt of my
illegal occupancy, it was likely that Jumps and I would find
ourselves imprisoned in what the inner compendium referred
to as *The Nuthatch*, which, on investigation, seemed considerably less pastoral than the name suggested.

I filed the plan for another day. Jumps could feel my thoughts,
to a point, and I didn't want to make her even more suspicious
than she already was. Instead I tried to stay quiet, even though
I was filled with questions, not least about the individual we

were on our way to consult. The image Jumps had given me of her friend Evan was of a character not unlike me: her respect for him was beyond doubt, though he also seemed prone to practical jokes – I felt we could be soulmates. Which made it all the more of a shock, when we finally reached the door to Evan's flat (*flat* – an odd name, for something that towered above the rest of the place like Bif-rost), to find, not a sage or a warrior, but a young man in a metal chair, who did not stand up when we entered, but fixed us with a cockeyed grin and said:

'So, what's with the drama?'

I looked around the flat. Compared to Jumps' house, it was sparse. Most of the walls were covered in books – more books than I had ever seen. A desk – also piled with books. A computer by the window. A kitchen area, open plan, with a kind of island for serving food, and, to my delight, a fridge. I understood that the boy lived with his mother, who, according to Jumps, worked at the local hospital. I could see an animal of some kind – maybe a dog – sleeping in a basket. While Jumps was otherwise engaged, I sneaked a look inside her mind. A series of mental images behind a door marked EVAN served as an introduction: some younger versions of the boy, some with the metal chair, some not; a lot of game, computer and RPG references that I glossed over as tedious; a great deal of affection; some awe; an inexplicable sadness; some practical jokes (including one rather good one involving a duck, some pastry and a school fire hose, which I filed away for later), plus an assorted variety of snippets and scenes from Jumps' past, many featuring that mysterious chant of *Land whale, land whale* – which seemed to affect her so profoundly.

Nothing much to interest me there. I turned to my environment. In spite of Jumps' reluctance, breakfast had been much on my mind, and I was sure that Evan would have something suitable tucked away. I made for the fridge, sidestepping his chair. And then, looking out of the window, I saw something that raised the hairs on the back of my neck (I was already starting to think of Jumps' physical Aspect as my own) and sent little flashes of energy racing all over my body.

It was just a hill, that was all. A hill with, at its summit, a square stone tower of some kind, flanked with green slopes, behind which lay a mountain range, with seven peaks, wreathed in mist, on the horizon. All of it perfectly ordinary. But it gave me a shock somehow: a galvanic kick of recognition that went right down to my boots. I'd seen these things before, I knew. Perhaps in a dream. I was sure of it.

'What's that?'

Jumps said: *Please. Will you just shut up? Anyone would think you hadn't ever seen a hill before.*

Evan wheeled his metal chair over to the window. 'What's what?'

'Nothing,' said Jumps quickly. 'I just—'

'How about breakfast?' I went on, taking over the sentence before Jumps could move in to stop me. 'I'm starving.'

Evan raised his eyebrows. 'OK? Well, there's toast—'

'Yes, toast,' I said firmly, while Jumps protested vainly in my mind. 'Toast and – cheese, and chocolate. But you can leave out the yoghurt. That stuff makes me want to puke.'

Evan laughed. 'Now you're being weird. But what the hell?' He wheeled his chair over to the fridge. 'Be my guest.' I noticed then that there was something about his eyes. They seemed slightly out of alignment, as if looking in different directions.

Stop it, said Jumps. *He's got a glass eye. No big deal. Stop staring. And don't mention the wheelchair, all right? He must be having one of his bad days.*

Bad days. I sensed a reference to something in their shared past. If it was relevant to my needs, I guessed she'd fill me in soon enough. I shrugged and began to go through the fridge's contents. I recognized some items and sampled a few unfamiliar ones. Evan watched me from his chair, quizzical but smiling.

'Why don't you stand up?' I said, through a mouthful of cold apple pie.

Jumps had a quiet tantrum in her corner of our shared space. Whether this was at my question or the eating of the pie I was as yet uncertain.

Evan grinned. 'OK, who the hell are you,' he said. 'And what have you done with the real Jumps?'

11

THANK THE GODS. HE UNDERSTANDS. It seemed almost too much to hope for the human to have grasped the situation so clearly. But Jumps had a lot of respect for him, a sentiment that bordered on worship. I understood that Evan was smart, possibly almost as smart as me.

I looked at him. He was grinning.

'I am Loki, the Trickster,' I said. 'Son of Farbauti and Laufey. You may know me from legends, tales or such games as *Asgard!*™.'

Evan kept on grinning. 'Go on.'

'I have entered the corporeal presence of the one you call Jumps, through a tributary of Dream. As a result, she and I now share the same physical Aspect, although our minds coexist independently. Also, you should probably know that I have sworn to liberate my companions from their current torment, after which we shall, verily, feast with my brothers in Valhalla. Forsooth.' (I added that last part to add *gravitas* to my little speech, and because Jumps appeared to think that was how a real god of Asgard was supposed to talk.)

Evan laughed. 'Sounds like a great idea for a game,' he said. 'So what's the punch-line?'

'The what?' I said.

He doesn't believe you, dummy, said Jumps. *And what's with the verily, forsooth?*

'I thought that was what you wanted,' I said.

What, are you crazy? said Jumps.

'You mean he doesn't believe me?'

Of course he doesn't believe you, Jumps said. *You're telling him his best friend has been taken over by a Norse god, and you're expecting him to say, 'Forsooth, let's unto the realms of Death, thereby to liberate my kinsmen?'*

Well, that *had* kind of been the plan. I'll admit I was a little disappointed.

Evan was still watching me with an expectant look on his face. 'Good game,' he said. 'Shall I be Thor?'

'I'd *so* much rather you didn't,' I said.

'Oh for God's sake, let me explain,' said Jumps, taking control of the voice part once more, while I turned my attention back to the fridge. The physical demands of this body were many, and given that Jumps didn't seem to care, I felt it was up to me to address the current breakfast deficiency. There was something cold that Jumps called *pizza*, which I sensed was forbidden. I therefore made a grab for it, and found it delicious.

The dog, which had been faking sleep, started to take an interest, and ambled over to see if there was anything going begging. It was the most stupid-looking dog I'd ever seen: white and fluffy, with the longest tongue outside of Netherworld. I dropped the dog a piece of crust and it cavorted joyfully.

'So,' Jumps was saying, 'either I'm nuts and my life is over, or maybe you, like, spiked my drink with acid, or something, in which case, I won't get mad, but please, *please* tell me now, because *this isn't funny at all!*'

Oh, great. Now she was crying. Plus she was talking so fast that I could barely swallow my pizza. I said:

'Do you mind? I'm eating.'

'Fuck *off!*' said Jumps, and spat out my mouthful of pizza onto the kitchen floor. The dog obligingly cleaned it up.

There was a moment's silence. Then Evan said: 'OK. Sit down. Stop shouting. Step away from the fucking pizza.'

He sounded calm enough, so I did. Besides, it was hard to enjoy a meal with Jumps running riot in my space. She trusted Evan, in spite of the fact that she knew he wasn't trustworthy. *Underneath*, she trusted him. I could see it in her thoughts. It occurred to me that I'd once had a relationship very like this. Brothers in blood: peas in a pod; him and me against the Worlds. It didn't end well, of course (none of them did), but people are like that. Ridiculous.

'OK,' said Evan, when Jumps and I were both sitting down beside him. His metal chair made little ticking sounds as he rocked it gently to and fro as Jumps retold her story. 'Let's start from the beginning, shall we?'

'I was playing *Asgard!*™,' said Jumps in a shaky little voice.

Evan gave her a look.

'I know. You were going to show me how. But I was bored, and you weren't answering your messages. I thought I'd just try a level or two. I didn't think it could do any harm. And then, suddenly, *he* was there, inside my head. Talking to me. Eating for two. Going through my memories.' She looked at Evan, who was sitting forward in his metal chair, apparently fascinated. 'Just please tell me you did something,' she said. 'I won't mind. I'll understand. I just don't want this to be real.'

Wait, I said. *Did he actually warn you that this kind of thing might happen?*

No, well, not exactly, said Jumps. *But—*

Evan leaned forward. 'Did he speak? Did he say something just then?'

'Yes. He talks to me *all the time*,' said Jumps, taking a cushion from the couch and hugging it tightly to her chest. 'I've tried to just ignore him. But you don't know what it's like. It's like—'

I spoke aloud. 'Oh, please. Don't play the victim card. Remember, *I'm* the victim here. In fact, the Oracle's Prophecy deals with that most poignantly.' I quoted:

54

I see one bound beneath the court,
Under the Cauldron of Rivers.
The wretch looks like Loki.

I spread my hands. 'Now *that*,' I said, 'is tragedy.'

Evan smiled. 'You're good,' he said. His glass eye watched me unblinkingly. The living one burned with blue fire.

Jumps began to cry again. 'It's not a prank. I swear it's not.' I caught the glimpse of a memory – something from school, something childish, dwarfed by her current horror and fear. Evan was prone to playing pranks. I took it that he and Jumps had been involved in some kind of incident. She had been angry enough at the time to want to pay him back in some way.

But Evan was looking curious. 'Is he there all the time?' he said. 'What does it feel like? Did it happen all at once, or gradually?'

Jumps gave a watery sniff. 'At first I thought it was kind of cool. But that's because I didn't quite believe it was real. It was like a game. But now it's real. Now it's real, and *I want it to stop—*'

'Hang on, please.' I was starting to feel really quite uncomfortable. Not to mention hurt – as if it wasn't bad enough to be condemned to Netherworld, the moment I managed to find my way into a suitable host, I was treated like an intruder.

But you are *an intruder!* wailed Jumps in my mind. *And it isn't your mind, it's mine!*

I had to admit she had a point. But even so, her reaction seemed unnecessarily violent. 'It's always been like this,' I said. 'No one ever gave me a chance. Not in Asgard, not in Dream, nor anywhere in the Middle Worlds. What harm have I done you? None at all. I could have driven you out of your mind, and taken over your Aspect. But I didn't. That would have been wrong.'

'You *thought* about it,' said Jumps.

'So shoot me. Thinking isn't a crime.'

I turned to Evan, who was still watching us both with a look of fascination. The fluffy white dog gave a hopeful whine, in the expectation of pizza. 'You look like a reasonable man,' I said. 'Tell me, what other choice did I have? I saw a line. I grabbed it. And honestly, if I'd had the choice, I wouldn't have chosen to enter the body of a teenage girl with a fucking eating disorder.'

I realized that I'd grabbed those words from Jumps' inner lexicon. Their meaning followed soon after, in a burst of feelings and memories: images of childhood; pictures of fashion magazines, her mother drinking herbal tea, some numbers on a bathroom scale, the Stella person again, and then that chant that seemed to resurface every time she was feeling low: *Land whale, land whale —*

'I'm sorry,' I said. (Where in the Worlds had *that* come from?) 'I didn't mean to say that.'

Now you're apologizing? said Jumps. *How about you just leave?*

I sighed. 'You see? Whatever I do, it always comes down to this in the end. *Get Loki. He doesn't belong. He isn't one of us. He's a freak. Don't trust the freak. Someone dies? Blame the freak. Lock the freak in a dungeon and hang a giant snake in his face.*'

'There were reasons for that,' Evan said.

Well, yes. There were reasons. So shoot me. I wasn't prepared to discuss that now. Whatever he knew had probably come from Odin's side of the argument.

'Whatever,' I told him. 'It's in the past. Can't we move on?'

Evan started to laugh. There was something familiar about that laugh, but I couldn't figure out what it was. Something from a long time ago. Something from another life.

I flicked through the Book of Faces. *Evan. Best friend since childhood. Genius RPG player. Favourite colour: arterial red. Favourite movie:* Tampopo. *Favourite novel:* Les Misérables. *Favourite meal: chilli pizza, with pineapple, and extra jalapeños.*

Not much there, I told myself, although the pizza sounded good. I moved a little closer, trying to see him clearly. He looked pretty ordinary to me, except for that metal chair of his.

Brown hair, no beard, a clever, open, humorous face. Nothing there to recognize, except for the fire in his one living eye. And yet I felt that I knew him, somehow. That somehow, I'd *always* known him.

'You'd better not be who I think you are,' I said.

He grinned. 'I'm disappointed. After all we've been through together, I thought you'd have known me, *Captain.*'

I sat down, rather hard, on one of the vinyl kitchen chairs. I should have known, I told myself. I should have known him by his smile, rare in those days of Asgard, and by his laughter, rarer still, and so often the sign of trouble. Or by his one blue eye, so sharp that it seemed to pierce right through me. And he had called me *Captain.* No one ever called me that. No one since the End of the Worlds. And that's how I knew, beyond a doubt—

Odin was in Evan.

Light

*An absolute only serves to affirm the
reality of its opposite. The moment
your God said: 'Let there be light,'
He created the darkness.*

Lokabrenna, 9:18

1

I HAD TO LAUGH. That Odin of the Aesir, Founder of Worlds, Master of Runes, Chronicler of the Elder Age, should be reduced to taking possession of a young man of the Folk, who, by all appearances, *couldn't even walk*—

'Actually, I *can* walk,' he said. 'But only on my good days.' He went on to explain in unnecessary detail the physical condition of his host, his good and bad days, his medication and his more or less constant joint pain, while I mined Jumps' memories for anything that might give me an edge.

But Jumps had retreated into a space at the back of her tiny mind, where she was curled up, repeating things like *This isn't real*, and *Fuck this shit*, none of which were helpful to me in my current predicament.

'How long have you been in this world?' I said.

'Long enough,' said Odin.

'And how did you get here?'

Odin shrugged. 'Much as you did, I believe. Via the river Dream, which runs through every World there is, or was, or might one day be possible.' He gave me a smile that might almost have been that of a brother or a friend. 'The greatest minds of this World see Reality as a many-branched tree, in which every possible outcome of every possible act is laid out. Sound like anything we know?'

'Yggdrasil,' I said at once. The World Tree, in whose branches – according to lore – the Nine Worlds were suspended.

The General smiled. 'You're quick. This World may seem very different to the one we left, and yet we have much in common. So many branches of science that sound suspiciously like our runelore. So many things that intersect. So many common elements.' He gestured around him. 'Take this town of Malbry. According to this many-worlds theory, there should be a version of this place – and even its inhabitants – in any number of alternate Worlds. Perhaps even in the one we left.'

'Hmm.' Well, it sounded at least as plausible as the theory I'd been taught, which (without going into unnecessary detail) had involved the whole of Creation coming from a giant cow.

'There's lots more,' Odin went on, absently stroking the fluffy white dog that was still cavorting around his feet. 'Something called "quantum theory", and something about a cat in a box, which, like the gods, is both dead and alive. Evan has knowledge of all these things; knowledge that he has shared with me.'

'You don't say,' I remarked. 'Because this is the biggest info dump I've heard since Mimir the Wise came back from Vanaheim minus his body.'

Odin smiled. The Silent One, we used to call him, back in the day. This was the chattiest I'd seen him since he lured me from Chaos. Still, I thought, after Netherworld, perhaps he'd rediscovered the appeal of conversation.

'All we need to know,' he said, 'is that the Worlds have *expanded*. There are possibilities now that we never envisaged.'

'Such as?'

'Going back to our World. Reclaiming our godhood. Finding our friends.'

I had to laugh at that. 'Our *friends*? Wait a minute, would they be the guys who slaughtered my sons, then hunted me down, imprisoned me—'

'Bygones,' said Odin. 'You swore an oath.'

I thought about that for a moment. 'But if, by definition, every possibility exists on some branch or other of the Tree, then maybe *this* reality is the one in which I *break* my oath, and go on to live a rich and happy life on a tropical island somewhere?'

Odin shook his head. 'No.'

'How can you tell?'

'Because,' he said, 'I have a plan.'

Of course. When did the General *not* have a plan?

'And presumably, this plan of yours involves us living happily in our current Aspects, without going out of our way to encounter – shall we say – giant snakes, or the Lords of Chaos, or anything equally likely to upset our equilibrium?'

'Not as such,' said Odin.

'Oh? So what happens?'

'We die,' he said. 'Or maybe not.'

I said: 'Well *that's* a weight off my mind.'

He grinned. Even in this unfamiliar Aspect I would have known that grin anywhere. It was the one that the General always wore when the chips were down: the smile of a gambler about to play the last coin in his pocket.

'Think of this world, this body,' he said, 'as the box in which that cat lingers, neither wholly dead nor alive. If this works, the cat walks free. We get the chance to start again.'

'And what if the cat's already dead?' I said. To be honest, all this stuff about cats was starting to get my goat.

Odin – or was it Evan? – shrugged. 'If it's dead, it's dead,' he said. 'In either case, the cat can't stay in the box for ever. You and I were never meant to live in such a small space as this.'

I thought about that. He did have a point. Living free of torment was a novelty that would fade. Soon, I guessed I'd start to miss the things that made me Loki – my Aspect, my powers, my runes, my glam. Besides, how much longer would Jumps live? Fifty years? Maybe even seventy? And after that, where would I go? Back to Netherworld, or Hel, where I could spend eternity? No, I needed more than that. I needed something more permanent.

'You think we could go home,' I said. 'Is that even possible?'

He shrugged. 'I believe it is. I believe that we can return to the place where our version of Asgard fell. Back to the source of our power.' He let that sink in for a moment, like a lure into the sea. I could see the fish-hooks sticking out at every point, and yet the lure was so shiny that even I was tempted.

To reset the world like a game board, with all its pieces back in place. To rebuild Asgard; to free the gods; to start again, the past erased, to play out another scenario.

'So, are you with me, Captain?' said Odin at last.

I shrugged. 'I guess.'

'So how's your wrist?'

'My wrist?' I said. 'Why?'

'Because we're going to play *Asgard!*™.' said Odin, with a brilliant smile. 'And this time, we're not going to stop until my son is here in the flesh.'

2

M Y SON. BY WHICH HE MEANT Thor, of course. I sensed a stirring of interest in the mind I shared with my host. Of course, I knew that Jumps would spare no effort to help Wonder Boy. In fact, I wondered how she had managed to end up with me at all.

'But the Thor in the game isn't *really* Thor,' I said. 'He's just a construct of pixels and ephemera.'

Odin shook his head. 'Not quite. Just sit down and try to concentrate. I promise it will all become clear.'

I shrugged and did as he asked, looking at the darkened screen of the thing Jumps thought of as a *console*. Evan handed me a black object – *Gamepad*, said Jumps – inscribed with unfamiliar runes.

The dog hung hopefully around, making with the tongue again.

'So, how do I play?' I said.

'You don't. *We* do,' said Evan. And there was something in his face – a presence, and maybe an absence, too, that told me I was speaking to the body's original host, and not its rascally passenger. He turned to Jumps. 'This is going to be hard,' he said. 'But you're going to have to trust me. Will you trust me?'

Jumps shook her head. But I could read her thoughts, and among all the confusion, suspicion and rage I could still feel her essential *belief* in Evan, just as I had believed in the Old Man, even as the bastard had planned to betray me to my enemies.

Evan's voice grew urgent. 'Jumps. Would I do anything to hurt you?'

Once more she shook her head.

'I swear this is going to help,' he said. 'No tricks, no bullshit. I promise.'

Oh, if I'd had a gold ring for every time he'd told me that, by now I would have enough golden rings to rival Draupnir, the Dropper. Jumps may have believed his words, but under that youthful exterior Odin was still as two-faced and duplicitous as he'd ever been in the old days. Fool me once, shame on you. Fool me twice, and watch me rip out your spine with my bare hands and use it as a skipping-rope.

I said: 'Excuse me, but what exactly is my role in all this?'

Evan – or Odin – looked at me. 'You managed to get into *Asgard!*™. I'm very curious as to how.'

'A temporary alliance,' I said.

'With whom?'

I briefly explained how Jormungand had broken me out of my prison cell, omitting to reveal that the snake was currently loose in *Asgard!*™.

Odin – or Evan – listened, with an air of fascination. The fluffy white dog sat at his feet, tongue lolling expectantly. 'Jumps drew you from the game,' he said, 'because you somehow linked with her mind. And now you're going back to create the same link with the Thunderer.'

'A link with Thor?' I protested. 'You seem to forget that old Hammerhead and I parted on somewhat acrimonious terms. And now we're supposed to be *roomies*? It's bad enough sharing this space with its original occupant; I'm not about to share it with the guy who promised to rip off my head and use it as a doorstop.'

'Don't worry.' That was Odin again. I could tell from the gleam in his eyes. A wholly unreliable gleam, promising all kinds of things, with Death at the end of all of them. 'I told you, Captain, I have a plan.'

I pulled a face. It wasn't so much the existence of a plan that filled me with doubt, as the amount of personal discomfort the plan would lead to. I knew from past experience that Thor was a dreadful housemate. Untidy, flatulent, and prone to violence, especially where Yours Truly was concerned. Besides, I was happy in the flesh: the thought of forsaking it, even for an hour, to enter the world of *Asgard!*™ didn't exactly appeal to me.

'What if I get stuck in there? What if I get killed?' I said.

'I trust you to find a way,' Odin said. 'Now – are you ready?'

'What do *you* think?'

'I think you're going to tell me that there's as much chance of getting you to go back into *Asgard!*™ as there is of Jormungand donning top hat and tails and learning to dance the fandango.'

'How well you know me, brother,' I said.

He smiled. 'And yet, it's the only way. My plan requires the Thunderer.'

'So *you* go in and get him,' I said. 'I'll have pizza ready for when you get back.'

Odin shook his head. 'I'm afraid that's not how it works,' he said. 'My host is not strong. The presence of not one, but two alien visitors in his mind might prove fatal to Evan. It *has* to be Jumps. But I promise you,' Odin went on, as Jumps began to protest again, 'this is a necessary step towards getting us out of this borrowed flesh, and back into our true Aspects.'

Damn him. *Our true Aspects*. Baited with fish-hooks, there was the lure the Old Man knew I couldn't resist. I swore in the language of Chaos. Odin waited patiently.

'There really is a way?' I said at last.

He nodded. 'I swear it.'

I sighed. 'All right. Let's get this done.' And, putting my hands on the console, I let Jumps take over the body again, while I attempted to achieve the dreaming, trance-like state of mind that would enable me to enter the bubble-world of *Asgard!*™.

For a moment I thought it wouldn't work. The flat screen flickered into life in front of me. I started to tell Odin no dice, but then I caught sight of Asgard's sky, and Bif-rost, and Ida's plain below, and I felt a sudden dizziness, almost as if I were falling again – and then I was out of the flesh, and standing in front of Asgard's gates in an Aspect I almost recognized.

A blare of martial music, and the words:

NOW CHOOSE YOUR CHARACTER.

And then, as Asgard unfurled once more like an impossible banner of dreams, came the martial music again, and the ominous words:

YOU HAVE CHOSEN THOR.

Well, that's a new definition, I thought. Given a choice of gods to revive, I certainly wouldn't have chosen Thor. But it had to be done if I were to regain my immortal Aspect. Besides, I had a plan of my own. How could Odin have believed otherwise?

And so I took my position and waited for the big guy. He didn't take long. In a rumble of thunder and a wail of guitars, along came my old friend Meta-Thor, fuming and in Aspect; red-bearded, piggy-eyed, small-brained, and homicidal as ever.

I have to say I don't see the point of games like *Asgard!*™. Seems to me there's enough violence in the corporeal world without going off to seek it elsewhere. And though real in so many ways, this world didn't follow normal rules. For one thing, my powers were all wrong – according to Jumps, in this Aspect I could throw runes, summon shields, cross great distances in a single leap, but eating, sleeping and sex were all entirely out of the question, and even such a basic thing as scratching my nose was impossible.

I looked around for the goblin minion I'd seen when I last entered the game. He wasn't there. Or if he was, he was lying low. The World Serpent, too, was lying low; although I guessed it was nearby, ready to show itself at the least opportune moment.

I jumped onto Asgard's parapet, using one of those giant leaps. I guessed a higher vantage point would give me a better chance to attack. Still, I wasn't planning to *kill* Thor. I don't think that was an option, anyway – the rules of the game seemed to allow this Aspect of Thor to die any number of times, and come back to life with no ill effects.

I was less sure of my own survival. As far as I understood the game, my pixellated Aspect could die and be reborn just as he could, but the essential Loki – the part which had lately found refuge in Jumps – was subject to no such assurances. I could just as easily find myself out in the cold if things didn't go the way I had planned. And so it was with no small degree of trepidation that I faced Meta-Thor on the battlements, and wondered just how I was supposed to connect with the mind of the Thunderer.

Then there was no time to wonder much about anything, because Meta-Thor had seen me, and was pounding towards me, hammer raised. The world shook under his mighty tread.

Flee, thou creature of Chaos, before—

'Ah. Hang on a minute,' I said. 'I thought we'd moved past this? Plus whoever wrote this dialogue has *no* idea of how Thor used to speak. I mean, even when his mouth *wasn't* full, it was hardly what you'd call clearly intelligible. So quit with the *verily*, *forsooth*, and let's have a conversation that doesn't sound as if it was written by someone in pantaloons.'

Thor gave an inarticulate bellow of rage and took a leap towards me. It was a pretty giant leap, which brought him from the horizon almost to kissing distance.

I flung up a runeshield just in time and addressed the Thunderer once again. 'It's Loki. Remember me?' I said, dodging to avoid his attack. 'Remember, we had a moment? When I was here with you yesterday?'

Meta-Thor gave a strangled yowl, like a bull trying to swallow a housecat.

I sidestepped an oncoming hammer-blow. 'Give me a break. I'm here to help. Odin sent me to help you.'

He probably doesn't remember, said Jumps' voice dimly at the back of my mind. *He's played a thousand games since then.*

'That many? Wow,' I said.

Well, it's a very popular game.

And then the hammer came down again some six inches from my head, and I had to cast a mindbolt, or be reduced to a smear on the parapet.

A thousand games. A thousand deaths. No wonder Thor was bewildered. I mean, he'd never been what you'd call a giant intellect, and confusion had always tended to make him more aggressive. I jumped to a higher level, somewhere – if this had been Asgard – from which I might have found a vantage point. Jumps' knowledge of the game told me there were weapons there; things I might be able to use.

Thor gave a growl and followed me. For a big guy, he could climb.

'I've come to help,' I said again, as Thor started to tear down the parapet on which I was standing, stone by stone, casting them onto the plain below. 'I swear it. The General sent me.'

Meta-Thor made that noise again, and the parapet started to collapse. Martial music blared from the sky, which I found off-putting.

Come on, said Jumps at the back of my mind. *I thought you were meant to be clever.*

'I thought you were meant to be keeping him from killing me,' I said.

No, said Jumps. *That's your job. Me, I'm just fine either way.*

Wow. That hurt. It really did. After everything I'd done for her, too. I searched the *Asgard!*™ part of her mind for something that I could use against Thor, and found a cantrip that gave me wings. Not the ones I was used to – these were big and unwieldy; more like a dragon's than a bird's – but they carried me out of harm's way, and onto the game version of Bif-rost, which was heartbreakingly like the real thing, and at the same time heartbreakingly not.

Spikes of rainbow-coloured light shot up all around me; I sensed my pixellated self gathering momentum. And in spite of the danger, it felt pretty good to be back on the field of battle. You might think that, being more a creature of intellect than of mere physical action, I wouldn't enjoy waging war. But I do. I always did. That's how the Sorceress, Gullveig-Heid, had managed to lure me to her side in the prelude to Ragnarók.

For a moment, I felt almost nostalgic. Beautiful, ruthless and corrupt, Heidi was the embodiment of everything I most admired. If only she hadn't betrayed me, what might we have achieved, she and I?

> *'Now comes a fire-ship from the east,*
> *With Loki standing at the helm.*
> *The dead arise; the damned are unleashed;*
> *Fear and Chaos ride with them.'*

I realized I'd spoken the verse aloud. The Prophecy of the Oracle rang out over the battlements. I'd forgotten how powerful words had been, in the days of our fellowship. How powerful; how mysterious; how laden with doom and foreboding.

I looked down at Meta-Thor, now approaching the foot of the bridge. For a moment he seemed to halt mid-stride. *Interesting,* I told myself. *It's almost as if he remembers.*

'Remember that?' I asked him. 'Remember the death-ships sailing in? Remember the smell of the campfire smoke, and the sound of the demon wolves howling?'

Meta-Thor looked up at me. His eyes were filled with burning

71

sparks. And then, rather slowly, he started to climb towards me.

I tried another verse of the Oracle's prophecy:

'Flames from the south. Ice from the north.
The sun falls screaming from the sky.
The road to Hel is open wide.
Mountains gape and witches fly.'

Below me, Meta-Thor gave a growl and started to climb faster. And now that he was getting close, I thought I saw something else in his eyes, something more than animal rage. Something like— *Intelligence?*

Of course, with Thor, it was hard to tell. Even in his primary Aspect, he'd never been what you'd call a majestic thinker. But there was purpose to him now; a kind of calculation which had not been there a moment before.

'Is that really you?' I said. 'Do I have your attention now?'

Thor continued to climb, his face a picture of concentration. Now within reach of my perch, he gleamed in purple, red and gold. I could hear his breathing, like a saw through timber.

'Come on,' I said. 'The old Thor never used to be this slow.'

Thor made a sound that managed to combine rage with satisfaction. 'It *is* you,' he said in a low voice. 'I thought I was still dreaming.'

Then he gave a mighty leap and landed right in front of me. *That* wasn't very authentic, I thought. In the old days, Thor had been banned from using Bif-rost after a certain incident involving his goat chariot, some beer and half a roast ox, and besides, even when sober, the big guy was never that nimble.

Still, that wasn't important now. The important part was already done. Thor stood on the Rainbow Bridge, the Thunderer in Aspect: awakened, aware and alert, with murder in his eyes.

Do you have him? said Jumps in my mind. She sounded urgent; excited. And now I found myself going back to my first

72

experience with *Asgard!*™ – the lights, the fanfare, the words in the sky:

YOU HAVE CHOSEN THOR.

I mean, how much clearer could it have been? Rescuing Thor had always been the Old Man's main objective. How disappointed he must have been to find me there in place of his son. How well he had managed to hide his surprise. How cleverly he had handled me.

Trust me. I have a plan, he'd said. And yes, I had believed him. But *trust* him? Who did he think I was? Ten to one his plan involved sacrificing me for Thor: sending me back to Netherworld while the Thunderer was reborn into flesh. I'd known it almost from the start; from the moment he called me *Captain*. Oh, I'd feigned reluctance to make him believe I was on his side, but honestly – it was insulting. Suspicion is my middle name. Of course I'd expected betrayal, and of course I had planned accordingly.

The martial music was at it again. Thor was close enough to touch—

Now! said Jumps. *Now! Take his hand!*

Now was the time for me to bring the Thunderer into the World; to have him take my place in Jumps, and be left once more at the mercy of Dream. But instead of taking his hand, I assumed my most commanding voice and called for my monstrous offspring.

'Hey! Jorgi! Over here!'

I knew the Serpent would respond, wherever it had gone to ground. The link between us was too strong for it to ignore the summons. And, however suspicious it was, I hoped it would not be able to pass up this chance to re-engage with the foe.

What are you doing? demanded Jumps.

I ignored her. *'Over here!'* I called, keeping Thor at arm's length. *'Over here, mudfeeder!'*

There came a rumbling from below; the sound of something stirring.

Please, said Jumps' voice in my mind. *Loki, please, don't do this!*

Trust me, I said. *I've got a plan. And it's better than the General's.*

Then, taking a deep breath, I shouted at the top of my voice: *'HEY, JORGI! COME AND GET ME!'*

The Serpent must have been coiled around the lower part of Asgard's wall. Now it reared into the air, approaching at the speed of Dream towards me and the Thunderer.

Please, no, said Jumps.

I smiled. 'Tell Odin he'll have to trust me,' I said, and then the World Serpent opened its jaws, and several things happened almost at once.

Thor looked down at the Serpent with an air of slowly dawning surprise. The Serpent gave a giant hiss, and I grasped Thor in a full-body embrace and *pushed* him off the Rainbow Bridge, so that both of us dropped onto Jormungand's back, just where the bristling head met the neck. Jormungand hissed and convulsed, but I held on tightly to his mane, urging him once more into flight. We rode, as I had ridden through Dream, the Serpent thrashing and coiling and the Thunderer clinging on to me, towards the letters in the sky which marked the threshold of the game—

'What is this treachery?' said Thor, wrapping a forearm around my throat. My air was cut off. Red flowers began to bloom across my vision. I had seconds to live, no more, I knew; but seconds were all I needed. Summoning every ounce of my will, ignoring the Thunderer's crushing grasp, I urged the World Serpent frantically towards the gleaming threshold of Dream, and up over Asgard, towards a sky that now announced:

GAME OVER!

I heard Jumps' wailing protest, and the echo of Evan's voice in my ears, and then I was back in the flesh once more, and the little white dog was barking like mad and nipping at my ankles.

'What did you do?' Odin said in a voice as soft as it was dangerous. 'Where's my son?'

I feigned surprise. 'You mean, your plan *didn't* involve my return into my human host, whilst simultaneously firing Thor into the only available host not currently occupied by a god?'

He looked down at the fluffy white dog.

'*Twinkle?*' he said, in Evan's voice.

The fluffy white dog rolled over and barked.

I smiled. I'd fulfilled my mission (if not quite according to Odin's plan). And now there was nothing the bastard could do but grit his teeth and live with it.

As for the little white dog, I could see that it was trying to process things. I'd like to say I sympathized. But it's a god-eat-god world out there, and if our positions had been reversed, I doubt he'd have spared any pity for me. So instead I made for the fridge, and, trying not to laugh, I said:

'Hungry work, this, isn't it? Anyone for pizza?'

3

AFTER THAT, I ASSUMED THE Old Man would probably be on the warpath. But Odin was always subtle, and though I had foiled his treacherous plan, he showed no sign of resentment. Instead, he gave his inscrutable smile, fed a biscuit to the dog and said:

'You see, I was right about you. It's good we're on the same side.'

Well, *that* was rich, coming from the man who'd sworn a blood oath to me, then betrayed me to his friends when things got too tough to handle. 'Whatever,' I said. 'My work here is done. Now to enjoy the good life.'

Slowly, Odin shook his head. 'I don't think you understand,' he said. 'You and I can't stay in this world. For a start, that isn't your body. You can't just occupy it indefinitely. And besides—' His living eye darkened. 'Our place here is precarious. Remember the box with the cat inside?'

'Oh, not the bloody cat again,' I said.

He blinked, and Evan resurfaced. The change was so subtle that anyone else might not have seen the difference. But Evan's voice was more hesitant, like that of a boy who'd once stammered; and he sounded almost apologetic as he said: 'I know I'm a massive geek, OK? But I've been ill since I was a kid. I've had a lot of time to read. Science and magic can sometimes sound very close to each other. In fact, all through the Renaissance, science and magic overlapped. In those days scientists believed in alchemy, and the Philosopher's Stone that could turn base metals into gold and give you the secret to eternal life—'

'Just tell me about the cat,' I said with a touch of impatience. It seemed Odin's host was as talkative as he himself had turned out to be. I shot a glance at the little white dog that used to be the Thunderer. Like so many very small dogs, it seemed to believe that it was a wolf, and was trying to eat my shoe.

Evan went on patiently. 'This cat,' he said, 'is like the gods. Neither in this world, nor out of it. And much as the box may seem the safest place to be right now, no cat – or god – can live in a box and expect to survive for long.'

Well, put like that, it made sense, I thought. Whatever else he might be, Odin's host wasn't entirely without insight.

I said: 'What's the alternative? Without the power of the runes, how can we hope to get back to our World and do all those things you were talking about?'

The General smiled. It was odd to see that smile on the face of a boy of the Folk, but it was the General's smile, all right, and I didn't trust it one bit.

'We have one more friend to meet,' he said, 'before I tell you that. Another has taken Aspect from the game of *Asgard!*™. Another has been born into flesh. I'm afraid that your host may not approve.'

'Why not?' Jumps and I both spoke simultaneously.

'Because of the individual of whose current Aspect they have recently declared occupancy.'

I felt Jumps rebel. *Oh, no,* she said.

'I'm sorry,' said Odin. 'I had no choice. She was by far the closest match.'

'Not Stella,' said Jumps aloud. 'Please tell me you didn't ask Stella.'

Odin shrugged. 'I'm sorry,' he said. 'But trust me, Stella can help us. I chose her for a reason, as I chose you for a reason. And with her help, we'll have enough glam between us to do what needs to be done – that is, finding a way out of this World and back into the one we left.'

I pointed out that dying wasn't exactly my idea of a plan.

'No, not Death,' said Odin. 'There are many other Worlds. Worlds in which the old gods may still have a chance of survival. Worlds in which runes are still powerful; Worlds in which we can find our place, and maybe reshape our destiny. My plan is to find a way into one of those other Worlds, and start again with whatever glam we can salvage between us.'

I have to say I was doubtful. Easy to talk about crossing between Worlds, but even in the old days, these things weren't that straightforward. It had taken an army of gods at the peak of the Golden Age, plus a million cantrips and runes, to build the Rainbow Bridge that had linked Asgard to the Middle Worlds. What could the pair of us do now, with not even a runemark between us?

'Trust me,' said the Old Man. 'I've been here somewhat longer than you.'

'How long exactly?'

'Long enough.'

Well, *that* was intriguing. I have to say I'd assumed that I had been the first one to escape. But now, I started to wonder. How long *had* Odin been in this World, quietly weaving his plans for the gods? A week? A year? A lifetime? He certainly seemed on better terms with his host than I was. Were he and Evan a better match? Or had he entered the mind of the boy at such an impressionable age that he and Evan were brothers in blood, united in thought and action?

If so, I thought, gods help the boy. Odin's record of loyalty wasn't exactly flawless. He and I were blood-brothers too, and look how he rewarded *me*.

In the inner space we shared, my host's agitation was growing. 'Why Stella?' she said again. 'Of all the people you could have chosen, why did it have to be Stella?'

I let her ask the question. In fact, I was curious myself. I accessed the Book of Faces. *Stella. Age: seventeen. Favourite colour: pink. Favourite film: Scream. Favourite food: Haribo. Likes: sleepovers; netball; talking about boys.* There was much more everyday stuff in this vein, but from what I could read of Jumps' mind, Stella was nothing but trouble: an erstwhile friend, turned enemy; as confident as Jumps was not; empty-headed, volatile, venal, selfish and vain. And there was something else, as well. Jealousy? Anger? Something more?

Odin shrugged. 'You might as well ask the same question of all of us. Why was it easier for Odin to enter *this* mind, and not another? Why was Jumps' mind more receptive to the Trickster, rather than Thor, whom she preferred? Each of us has some quality that makes us inherently suitable. As for Stella—' Odin smiled. 'Who knows what qualities she may reveal?'

'Which brings me to the question,' I said. 'Who among our colleagues has had the good fortune to merge with this paragon?'

'I'm glad you asked me that,' Odin said.

I thought back to the game of *Asgard!*™: its principal protagonists. We already had the General (Odin) and the Warrior (Thor). The only remaining character was the Warrior Princess, I thought (unless the goblin minions and the sleeping gods under the ice could be said to count as characters).

I looked at the General. 'Freyja?' I said. The Old Man always did have a bit of a soft spot for Freyja.

Odin said nothing, but I thought his host looked a little awkward.

'Freyja? Really? What's the point? All she ever does is preen, complain, and try to seduce people.'

'Perhaps,' said Odin. 'But currently, we need her. More specifically, we need Stella. Or rather, something that Stella has.'

Now Evan was looking more awkward than ever. Between that and the sudden surge of jealousy I sensed in my host, I deduced that Evan might have a soft spot for Stella, too.

'Why?' I said. 'What does she have?'

The General gave his narrow smile. 'Stella has a runemark.'

4

FOR A MOMENT I JUST stared at him. 'In this World? How is that possible?'

First brought into Asgard by Gullveig-Heid; then bartered for by Odin; used by him to build his power and finally handed out to the gods as symbols of their allegiance: runes and rune-marks have always played a crucial part in our sovereignty.

In the old days there were sixteen runes, each with its own set of attributes, from opening doors between the Worlds to building bridges out of thin air. But now our runes were broken and scattered around the Nine Worlds; and I for one had seen no sign of them anywhere in Jumps' world – except of course for that scar on her wrist – *Kaen*, reversed – which coinciden-tally mirrored my own – but which, as far as I could tell, carried no special power.

I wondered if Evan had one, too – a scar, a birthmark, a tattoo – anything that could channel the form and substance of a runemark. But there was nothing visible, not even a spark of the primal Fire. And as for the ridiculous dog that currently served as a host for Thor, there was nothing to suggest that it was unusual in any way, except perhaps for the length of its tongue, apparently designed to make up for the shortness of its legs. It saw me watching it and growled.

'*No*, Twinkle. *Bad dog*,' Evan said.

I made a frankly heroic attempt to suppress my laughter. '*Twinkle?*'

'Yeah. Long story,' Evan said. 'Not my choice of name, obviously.'

Twinkle. Canine. Suspected Poodle-Pomeranian cross. Likes: barking, long walks, splashing in puddles, chasing things, eating leftover human food. Currently serving as host for Thor, who shares most of his interests.

I summoned my composure. 'You were talking about Stella,' I said.

Oh, good, let's talk about Stella, echoed Jumps sarcastically. *Let's talk about how special she is. Let's talk about her runemark. I mean, forget about my exams, or the fact that I'm going crazy—*

'What is it with you and Stella?' I said.

Jumps said: *Whatever. Just do it, OK?*

And so, as I listened and Jumps kept up a counterpoint of internal complaints, Odin explained how, in this world, the runes we had known were corrupted. Runes, the ancient code, from which all the Worlds had once been built, the language of the primal Fire, had somehow in this World been reduced to a simple game of chance. Gone were the words of power: the words that once had adorned the hammer of Thor made meaningless, just pretty shapes for carving onto trinkets.

I had to laugh at that. But it was the laughter of Chaos: bleak and without humour. I knew our runes had been broken the moment Surt's shadow fell over us, but even so, the thought of the gods reduced to little squeaking toys, when once we had ruled with such arrogance—

'Yes, I know. What a joke,' Odin said, although he wasn't laughing. 'Chaos didn't just defeat us at Ragnarók; they broke us into tiny pieces, and scattered the pieces throughout the Worlds. Whatever power we had is gone. But maybe we can find it again. Maybe, in another place, there's the chance to start anew.'

'How are you so sure?' I said.

'The Oracle predicted as much.'

'The *Oracle*! Don't you ever learn?'

Odin gave a twisted smile. 'An Oracle never lies,' he said. 'It may tell the truth perversely, or with malice, but what it reveals is still the truth. There *will* be a new Asgard.' Then he quoted from the text that had already cost us so much: our fellowship; our godhood; our lives:

> '*On what was once the battlefield*
> *A New Age dawns. Its children*
> *Find the golden gaming-boards*
> *Of bright Asgard, the fallen.*'

'*Asgard!*™' I said tartly. '*There's* your golden gaming-board. There's your New Age of the gods. In this World, the Folk play with gods as if they were *Skáktafl* pieces.'

Odin shook his head. 'I'll admit, that's what I thought at first. But whatever can be dreamed can be made reality. The Prophecy promised us new runes, new gods, a new beginning. And I mean to find those new runes with whatever resources this World can provide.'

'But *why*?' I said. 'We're *alive*, in the *flesh*.'

Odin gave me a patient look. '*You* may be enjoying this,' he said, 'but the thought of living this short life, in a body not my own, and in more or less constant pain, doesn't seem to cut it, somehow.'

Well, I guess I could understand that. Odin's host was hardly the most comfortable of Aspects. There was a section of Jumps' mind filled with pictures of Evan as a child – some of him wearing an eyepatch, some of him in the metal chair, some of him walking with some kind of metal frame around his leg, some of him looking healthy. Phrases like *Chronic Fatigue Syndrome* and *nerve avulsion* and *joint hypermobility* swam ominously around these images, although it seemed to me that even Jumps was unsure of their significance. Instead I sensed a mixture of guilt, affection and a low, buzzing anxiety, as if she felt somehow responsible.

Dammit, will you stop that!

'Sorry. My bad.'

I don't feel responsible for him, OK? He's a friend. We go back a long way.

'And what about Stella?'

Jumps sniffed. *Stella doesn't have friends. Stella only has worshippers.*

That certainly sounded like Freyja, I thought, turning my attention once more to Evan's passenger. 'So, if there are no working runes in this World, how can Stella have one?'

'Excellent question,' Odin said. 'One possibility is that Freyja survived Ragnarók with her runemark intact.'

'One *possibility*?' I said. 'Hasn't Freyja told you herself?'

'Freyja,' said Odin, 'has always been – shall we say, somewhat *capricious*? So far I haven't managed to get the full story out of her. Or indeed *any* story.'

That, too, sounded like Freyja. Fickle, flirtatious, shallow and vain, she and Odin had history from which Odin had never recovered. Given what lay between them, I guessed that he had handled things badly. Freyja had always enjoyed wielding power, and Odin's visible neediness had probably brought out the worst in her.

'So how could she have survived?' I said.

Odin looked thoughtful. 'At Ragnarók, the Aesir fell beneath Surt's fiery shadow. Some were dragged into Netherworld; others crossed into the kingdom of Death. Until now I had assumed that the Vanir, too, had suffered this fate. But recently I have come to believe that the Vanir may have remained in the World. And I think they may still be there, suspended in some kind of frozen sleep, awaiting resurrection.'

'You mean, like in the game?' I said. 'You've been playing too much *Asgard!*™.'

Odin smiled. 'That may be true. And yet, even a game may contain elements of reality. Imagine if that part were true. Imagine if we could find them again. Imagine if the runes had survived – maybe even the Oracle—'

'The Oracle?' I said. 'What *for*? Hasn't it already done enough?'

But Odin's one eye was shining. He said: 'The runes, Captain. The New Runes—'

'Oh, please,' I said. 'That's ridiculous. Even if you *could* find the Oracle, do you think it would cooperate? You sent the Oracle to his death at the hands of the enemy. Then, you took his knowledge, his lore, and kept his freaking head alive, just in case it wanted to spout the occasional bit of cryptic verse—'

'It's complicated,' Odin said.

'Isn't it always?'

He grinned at that. 'You need to meet Stella for yourself. Come on. Let's go. If anyone asks why you came in late, you can say I missed the bus and you had to help me.'

'Go where?' I said.

'School, of course. Bring the dog. You push.'

And so we made our way to school, with Thor trotting at our heels, and Jumps still protesting in my mind, in search of – you guessed it – trouble.

5

I HAVE TO SAY I WASN'T thrilled at the prospect of seeing Freyja again. What would she be like in this World? Given my recent experiences with Odin, Thor and myself, I wasn't holding out for anything too impressive. The game had described her as a Warrior Princess.

I *hoped* that was an overstatement. Jumps was no warrior, but I was pretty confident that she could survive a catfight.

The place Jumps referred to as 'school' was maybe a mile and a half from Evan's home. A big, sprawling camp, built from the same kind of concrete; trees to the west; grass beyond; a stretch of black tarmac to the east. On the tarmac I could see a crowd of young people, talking, walking, running. Most were younger than Evan or Jumps. Some were carrying schoolbags. I felt a sudden sadness, all the more unexpected because I had no idea from where it came.

I've got an English Lit. exam, said Jumps. *I mean, when you've finished gawking.*

But Odin didn't seem keen to join the young people walking to class. Instead, he said: 'I see her,' and put out a hand to slow me down.

Inside, Jumps moaned: *We're going to be late. Can't we just go in now?* And then suddenly, I saw her, and everything shrank to a point of light and the heartbeat of the Nine Worlds stopped as if a switch had been thrown.

To be fair, I didn't see Stella at first. Instead I saw the cluster of boys standing all around her, their faces all the more bovine for being at the age of peak testosterone. To me, they looked like a herd of young stags around the one available doe. But even to my human eyes, there was something special about her. In this Aspect I couldn't see her colours, but I sensed that if I'd been able to, they would have almost blinded me.

Oh, for Christ's sake, muttered Jumps.

Odin and I moved closer. The dog Twinkle, whom I'd almost forgotten in the heat of the moment, barked, and then the crowd parted to let us through.

Pff, said Jumps.

I had to stare. Freyja's host was stunning. Eyes the colour of the sea and hair like a miser's fantasy; wearing a pair of shorts apparently designed to show as much buttock as possible and a halter top emblazoned with a picture of a sparkly pink kitten (what was it with the Folk of this World, that made them want to have animals on every item of clothing they possessed?). She looked cool and poised and beautiful – that is, until she opened her mouth, extruded a wad of bubblegum and popped it with the tip of her tongue.

I said: 'Wanna dance?'

The Goddess of Desire gave me a look that suggested nothing but contempt. 'Dogstar. You're a girl again. Can't say it suits you, but I suppose that's the only way you'll ever get to see a woman naked.'

I grinned. That sounded like Freyja, all right.

Jumps muttered something vaguely obscene.

The dog Twinkle started to bark again, sharply and insistently.

Odin looked absurdly pleased. 'See?' he said, addressing me. 'Isn't she just *perfect*?'

Oh, just perfect, growled Jumps. *Why are boys so stupid? Why is everyone so stupid?*

The Goddess shrugged. 'I've known worse. I can work with it. I mean, the hair's a disaster, and the wardrobe looks as if someone brought it in on a goat chariot from some downmarket World's End store—'

Odin gave her a quelling look. 'Perhaps we should talk in private, eh?' he said, with a glance at Stella's entourage, who had been following every word with puppyish adoration.

'Oh, *them*,' said Stella, and snapped her fingers in a gesture of casual dismissal. 'Laters, 'kay?' At once the little group was dispelled as neatly as with a cantrip, and I started to understand why Odin was so pleased. Stella had glamour, and lots of it. Even in this skin I could sense it. It sparkled like cheap jewellery; surrounded her like cheap perfume. But could it be used for our purpose? That remained to be seen, I thought, skimming through Jumps' memory for any information that might lead to a better understanding of the fact that, out of the four of us, Stella was the only one who seemed to have a spark of the primal Fire.

I found very little. Stella was, as I'd suspected, a pretty girl of average intelligence, whose popularity at school was mostly due to good hair, prowess in sports, and a large collection of short skirts, hoop earrings and sparkly animal-print tops. I also gathered that she had once been a close friend of my host's – until, at least, an incident that Jumps kept closely guarded behind one of those unlit doors. I sensed a painful memory, cocooned in conflicting emotions, before Jumps registered my interest and slammed the mental door in my face. A spike of pain flashed through my head.

'*Ow!* What was that for?'

I told you not to do that!

'You have some *major* trust issues,' I said, pressing a hand to my temple. It must have hurt her, too, of course, but she didn't seem to care. The door marked STELLA was firmly shut – which made me all the more curious to know what was behind it. But Jumps was clearly unwilling to tell, and so I went to the horse's mouth and addressed the Goddess directly.

'I hear you've got a runemark,' I said.

Freyja gave me a scornful look. 'Jumps was supposed to bring *Thor*,' she said, addressing Odin. 'What happened? Did you lose him?'

Odin shrugged. 'It didn't work out. For some reason Loki was the best match for this host. But we *do* have Thor. In a way.' He looked down at the fluffy white dog, which was now cavorting around her ankles, still barking excitedly. Thor at least seemed happy enough in his current Aspect: I imagine he and his canine host had more than a few things in common. An optimistic outlook; excellent teeth; a boundless appetite for snacks – in fact, as far as Thor was concerned, he'd probably found his perfect match. I patted his head. He growled at me and bared his little puppy-teeth.

'Cute,' I said. 'Does he do tricks?'

'Sorry,' said Evan. 'He's still confused.'

I shrugged. 'Thor was always confused. But now that we're all together, I'd like to know what's happening. What about this runemark? Where did it come from? What is it?'

Odin looked at Stella. 'Show him. It'll be easier.'

Freyja raised her halter top to reveal her bare midriff. There, just above the band of her shorts, there was a mark – a familiar design, most certainly a runemark. It looked to me like an inked tattoo, but the execution was better than any tattoo I'd ever seen, the colours sharp and bright and clear. And at the heart of the inked design was *Fé*, the rune of wealth and success, Freyja's since the Golden Age; *Fé* unbroken, unreversed and shining with its own inner light.

'Nice,' I said. 'Can I have one?'

Freyja laughed. 'Why, are you having performance issues?'

Odin made a clicking noise, sounding a lot like his ravens. 'The old runes were broken at Ragnarók,' he said. 'The new runes are as yet unknown. Why did yours survive? And how?'

Freya shrugged. 'Don't look at me. I told you before. *I* don't remember anything after Bif-rost fell. I passed out. One minute I was in Dream, having a perfectly lovely time, then boom! The next I was in Stella. And *she* had no idea who I was. Imagine that? She'd barely even heard of Asgard. Here, let her tell you herself.'

For a moment, the Goddess seemed to withdraw, allowing the host to have her say. The process was like turning down the wick of a lamp to a very low setting. Nothing changed, except that the inner fire seemed to dim; then suddenly Freyja was gone, and we were left with Stella. She blinked at us rather resentfully, then did the thing with the gum again.

'So, what's with the tattoo?' I asked.

'I told you,' she said. 'I liked the design. It's not like it *means* anything.'

'Oh, but it does,' Odin said. 'How this came to you, I don't know, but it's certainly *something*. Did you always have a close affinity with Freya? Did you read a lot about her? Pray to her in secret?'

'No, nothing like that,' Stella said.

'Well, you must have played *Asgard!*™.'

Stella shrugged. 'One time. On my phone. I don't even *like* computer games.'

'What about books? Films? Comics? Art? Could you have pulled it out of Dream?'

Stella said: 'I never dream.'

Well, I could believe *that*. Stella didn't strike me as being overburdened with imagination. Nevertheless, she had the glam – and not just any glam, either. A rune unreversed after Ragnarók, which had plunged *all* runes into darkness. I'll admit to a pang of jealousy. Or maybe that was Jumps in my mind, infecting me with her feelings.

Freyja blew another bubble of gum. I couldn't help being impressed at the way she had taken to her host. Everything about her radiated confidence and happiness. And behind it all, there was a glow; a sense of intoxication that spoke of powerful glamours at work; of powerful, untold secrets. Even I was not quite immune; I felt slightly dizzy, slightly sick, as if I had stared too long at the sun.

'Got what you wanted?'

'Not even close.'

'Too bad.' She gave me that smile, and my knees went weak. 'Got to go. Laters, haters. Bye!'

And then she was Stella once again, the glamour muted; the dizziness gone; just another pretty girl loping across the schoolyard. I watched her go, and so did Jumps, with a sudden blaze of resentment that enveloped me like a cloak of fire.

'What's your problem?' I said aloud. 'She seems cool.'

Oh, cool, now, is it? said Jumps. *You people – you all make me sick. It's all: poor Stella, she's so nice. People take advantage. It isn't her fault: she's so sensitive. She likes to adopt hopeless cases. Poor fucking Stella.* A bell rang, interrupting as I tried to make sense of her emotions. *Oh, forget it. Hurry up. Come on. We're already late enough as it is.*

'Come *on*,' she said aloud, grabbing the handles of Evan's chair. 'Or are you just going to sit and gawp at her, like everyone else?'

Ouch. That was definitely jealousy. Not one of my favourite emotions, and not one I'm generally prone to. Something to do with Evan, perhaps? Was *he* involved with Stella? It seemed unlikely, given that she was gorgeous, and that he could barely walk, but then, not everyone's as shallow as I am.

Jumps was pushing Evan's chair in the direction of the school buildings. 'Where are we going, exactly?' I said.

Odin looked at me. 'Class, of course. And I suggest very strongly that, if you want to avoid attracting unnecessary attention, you sit quietly to one side and let Jumps do all the talking.'

'But I was going to—'

'Not now,' he said. 'Look, I know you're impatient. But for now, we have to cause as little disruption as we can. That means following the lives of our hosts as closely as possible, however hazardous or unpleasant.'

'Meaning what?' I said.

He grinned. 'Meaning that school's in,' he said. 'And that if we want to live, then we're going to have to learn.'

6

O F ALL THE THINGS I'D EXPECTED from this frankly un-
settling series of developments, this was by far the least likely.
That Loki, son of Laufey, Father of Wolves and Mother of the
Eight-Legged Horse, should be reduced to sitting in a class-
room, listening to a man in a suit rambling on interminably
about something called *examination procedure*, while Jumps
made notes, and played with her hair, and sometimes drew
little pictures – of fairies, stars and the inevitable kittens – in
her English folder.

Odin had been serious about my keeping a low profile. I
sensed that Jumps was somehow even more furious at my presence than she had been previously, and rather than risk trouble
I retreated politely to a kind of mental viewing platform, from
which I watched proceedings without participating.

Gods, it was dull. Ten minutes of that and I was almost
ready to go back to my cell in Netherworld. And then, just as I
thought I was free, we had to move to another room – a much
larger room, this time – in which two hundred numbered desks
were lined up in long rows. On every desk there was a booklet
marked with the words: ENGLISH LITERATURE; PAPER 1.

Jumps sat down at the desk marked 92. The guy in the suit
came to stand at the front and waited. No one said a word.

So, what happens now? I said to Jumps.

Shut up. This is important.

I gave a mental shrug and went back to watching from the wings. I could tell she was angry, though I honestly couldn't figure out what I'd done. I spent the time going through some memories that were stored nearby – not a particularly interesting archive, mostly to do with schoolwork and exams – but I was trying to lay low. Jumps was clearly upset, and rather than cause a scene, I thought it better to keep to the sidelines.

The dog Twinkle had been left outside, tethered near the bike sheds, but Evan and Stella were both there in the hall: Stella sitting in front of me, Evan somewhere near the back. The guy in the suit (*Mr Matthews: English teacher; likes: The Smiths; tweed jackets with leather elbow patches;* Star Wars; *pretending he's down with the kids*) announced that we had two-and-a-half hours to complete the paper. Jumps turned the first page; read the questions (which were mostly about a book called *Lord of the Flies*, a play called *Julius Caesar* and some reasonably smutty poems by a fellow called D. H. Lawrence) and then began to write.

Left with nothing else to do, I allowed my mind to drift. First towards the thought of lunch, which I was rather looking forward to, but which Jumps had already written off; then towards that tantalizing verse at the end of the Oracle's Prophecy, the one that seemed to promise us some kind of salvation.

> *New runes will come to Odin's heirs,*
> *New harvests will be gathered.*
> *The fallen will come home. The child*
> *Will liberate the father.*

Well, of course, *my* child had saved me, in a manner of speaking. Without the World Serpent, Jormungand, I would never have broken free, or managed to travel as far as this world. Could that verse be referring to me? And if so, did it mean that I, too, would one day inherit those new runes? It was an attractive prospect. But one of the things about prophecies is that they tend to be rather unclear, giving out snippets of wisdom so vague as to be almost useless. The Oracle was especially so. It was bound to tell the truth, but it did so with the minimum of clarity, which meant that, in spite of having foretold Ragnarók in quite alarming detail, it still didn't give us warning enough for us to change the End of the Worlds.

Not that it wanted to, of course. It wanted to see us swept from the board. Which was one of the reasons I'd thrown the damned thing off the side of the Rainbow Bridge, hoping never to see it again. But if Odin was right, perhaps the gods had not all fallen at Ragnarók. And if the Vanir *had* survived, then maybe we still had a chance. And if the Oracle could be found, and made to divulge the New Runes—

The symbol of the conch shell is symbolic of—

I yawned. Or rather, Jumps did – in spite of her efforts, she was bored. Outside, the sun was shining. The sky was blue as forever. I hadn't seen such a sky since the Sun was swallowed by Skól the Wolf. Against it, the hill I had noticed earlier stood out like a citadel. I found myself remembering another citadel, long ago, with a fierceness of nostalgia that was almost alarming. The skyline, too, was familiar: that range of mountains that seemed to float above a layer of summer cloud. A memory, perhaps? A dream?

My stomach growled. Jumps ignored it.

I see, I said. *You're hoping to starve me out of this body – that is, if I don't die from boredom first.*

Jumps gave a little sniff. *Trust me. If I could be somewhere else—*

And then I saw it. Or she did, perhaps. A scrawl of something across the sky, glimpsed through the window opposite. A scrawl, like the words in the sky in the game of *Asgard!*™. My reaction was violent, instinctive: my heart began to pound. I stood up.

For God's sake, what are you doing? wailed Jumps.

But I was barely listening. It was a runemark across the sky,

95

invincible as the rising sun. Not a familiar rune, but one that
shone out as bright as snow.

Rune! My heart was pounding. *Rune!*
What is it? Sit down, you idiot!
But I could barely hear her. The shock was almost too much
to bear. My ears were ringing. My chest hurt. It *meant* some-
thing, I told myself. It must mean something. I stretched out
my hand to stop myself from falling. Papers and writing equip-
ment clattered over the polished floor.
Rune! Rune!
I became aware that Jumps was trying to attract my attention.
It's only a vapour-trail, she said, from what seemed like a World
away. *It's not a rune, it's a trail of hot air! Fuck's sake, Loki, please!*
Sit down!
I blinked. I seemed to be standing up. Everyone was staring.
Inside me, Jumps was apparently trying to curl up and disappear. In front of me, Stella had turned round and was watching
with an expression of mingled disgust and amusement. The
guy in the suit was looking at me as if he thought I might
explode.
'Josephine Lucas. Are you unwell?'
I hadn't felt so conspicuous since the day I was hauled up
in front of Odin's high seat for stealing Idun's apples. I looked
around. There were people staring at me from every direction. I
bent down to pick up the papers and writing things I'd knocked
off the desk.
'Er, sorry. Just stretching my legs,' I said, and sat down at my
desk again.
From a neighbouring desk someone muttered: *'Freak.'* I could
feel my face burning.
Stella gave me a knowing smirk, contempt mingled with
sympathy. I noticed that she'd tied up her hair in preparation

for the exam. Little barrettes shaped like unicorns twinkled behind her ears.

That's it, you bastard. I'm done, said Jumps. *See how you cope without me.*

Then there was silence. Jumps was gone. Not a word. Not a cry. No sign of anyone else around. It was what I'd been craving since the start, and yet somehow it didn't feel as good as I'd been expecting.

Jumps?

In the sky, the runemark was fading. Vapour from an aeroplane. Of course it was. What else could it be? Those damned human emotions again. Humiliation. Helplessness. Shame.

Hey, Jumps. You OK?

Silence. Silence from my host. She seemed to have retreated somewhere deep inside our shared space. Nothing but closed doors and shadows. And behind all the doors and the galleries, I thought I could hear her sobbing.

Hey, Jumps, I'm sorry. I didn't know.

More emotions. Fear. Remorse.

Jumps, come out. I'm sorry.

I tried to get her hands to work; to pick up the pen; to write. *The symbol of the conch shell. The symbol of the conch.* But whatever had been driving Jumps wasn't working any more. The pen stayed loosely in the hand, the phrase remained unfinished.

I tried again. I understood that this was somehow important to her; that this *examination,* for all its absurdity, was something meaningful in her life.

Come on. Wake up. Finish the test.

But Jumps, wherever she might be, was not taking calls from anyone. I had command over body and mind. I looked at the paper in front of me, with its unfinished sentence.

For a moment I was conflicted. I knew how much this mattered to her. I suppose I could have tried a few doors, copied out some details. I mean, how hard could this test be? I could probably have walked it.

But outside the sun was shining; the air was sweet; the sky was blue. Outside, there was the promise of a thousand new sensations. Inside, there was only the desk, and the hum of re-cycled air, and the breathing of the other students, and the odd stifled fart from the guy sitting next to me, a tubby kid called Steve or Dave, who kept trying to see what I was writing, which frankly wasn't much.

If Jumps wasn't going to respond, I thought, there was no reason to stay inside.

Jumps?

That distant sobbing.

Steve (or Dave) farted again. It summed up everything I felt. I looked at that necklace of mountains, with the fading rune above them.

Jumps?

Now even the sobbing had stopped. So shoot me. I picked up my things and left.

7

FREEDOM. WHAT A FEELING. For the first time since Ragnarók, I was completely myself again, alive, alert and in the
flesh. The sun shone on my face; the sky was a brilliant shield
above, and the day was spread out like a gift, ready to be
opened.

Once more I thought of that white runemark in the sky. A
vapour-trail, she had called it. The Folk are so suspicious of
signs, as if dreams and omens could *ever* be safely dismissed or
disbelieved. And yet it *was* a sign, I knew: a sign of something
momentous.

I walked through the streets of Malbry, aimlessly at first,
then with a sense of increasing purpose. Jumps' plan for lunch,
I sensed, had firstly consisted of talking to Evan about her
exams, then spending an hour in the school gym, working on
her abdominals. In her absence I changed the plan and made
for the nearest food supplier, where I found chocolate, jam tarts
and beer, and settled nearby to consume them.

I'd hardly opened the packaging when a small, angry man
emerged from the place and started to shout at me. 'What d'you
think you're doing?' he said. 'Don't think I didn't see you!'

I consulted the section marked FOOD in my mind, and
found a section on payment. Apparently, food and drink were

not always freely available. In some places, such things as jam tarts needed to be paid for.

I reached into Jumps' backpack for something she called a *wallet*. 'I'm sorry,' I said carefully. 'How much do I owe you?' The contents of the wallet were unfamiliar currency, including some paper and a plastic card, but I offered the man a handful of silver coins. That ought to cover it, I thought.

The man, who was light brown in colour, frowned. 'Are you taking the piss?' he said. 'And anyway, how old are you?'

I knew the answer to that. 'Seventeen.'

'Too young for beer, then,' said the man, taking back the six-pack. 'That'll be nine-twenty. And if I see you in my shop again, I'll call the police. Right?' And, taking his fee from Jumps' purse, he dropped the coins on the ground at my feet and marched back into the building, leaving me genuinely confused.

'Too young for *beer*?'

Jumps did not reply. An eerie, echoing silence filled the area she'd vacated. I wondered if she'd gone for good. The thought was not as appealing as I might have expected, and the jam tarts were sticky and tasteless. I finished the packet, and went on my way, feeling guilty and rather sick. Clearly, this World was less straightforward than I'd previously supposed.

Still, the bright side was that, at last, I had free access to Jumps' mind, including some of those closed doors. Perhaps I could learn something useful, I thought; something to help me negotiate the mental maze that was my host.

Jumps? Can you hear me?

No answer. Just an empty rushing sound, like the sea through a conch shell. *The conch shell is a symbol of . . .* What? I searched for the answer. But all I could find was a memory of being very small, at the seaside; of building a castle in the sand, which the ruthless waves stole away.

Wandering back through Malbry's streets, I came across another shop, this one some kind of beauty place. I could see a girl in a chair, and a woman cutting her hair. Around them, a mirror flanked with pictures of people showcasing various hairstyles. I caught sight of myself in the mirror – the lank hair falling over my eyes – and had an inspiration. I consulted the inner directory. There was a section marked HAIRSTYLES. Quite a large section, as it turned out, with some of Jumps' favourites illuminated in bright lights – styles that I sensed she coveted, without having the courage to try them.

OK, I thought. Time for a gesture. Something to show my appreciation for the hospitality she'd offered me. And maybe too because I was tired of keeping a low profile.

Welcome to the new me, I thought. Then I opened the door and went inside.

I came out some time later, feeling rather pleased with myself. I'd known I could work with this body, but I have to admit that even I was surprised at the difference. One side shaved; the other left longer; the whole thing dyed a fiery red. The hairdresser was pleased enough by my choice to offer me a discount, then, having discovered the use of the plastic card in my wallet, I decided to complete the transformation.

Jumps' sartorial tastes seemed to run to shapeless, baggy garments in black. Given that this body was reasonably workable, I decided to try for something more appealing. I went into several shops, and came out feeling more like myself. The short white dress with the pineapple print worked nicely over my *skinny jeans*, and the pink leather jacket clashed just enough with my new hair to make it cool. I was starting to look at shoes, but for some reason the plastic card had stopped working. Too bad. I couldn't wait for Jumps to see what I'd made of our shared space. Perhaps now she would understand that I was on her side, after all.

I was getting admiring looks. Before that, no one had looked at me. Now, nearly *everyone* looked at me, which suited me just fine. My profile was *far* too fabulous for me to keep a low one, and I was enjoying the attention. Sadly, most of it seemed to come from balding, middle-aged men of the type I've never found attractive. Still, there'd be plenty of time for that kind of thing later. I'd proved I could fend for myself in this World. The rest would be a piece of cake.

8

Let's face it, most problems can be solved by judicious consumption of cake. My afternoon of liberty had left me feeling hungry again, and, finding myself standing in front of a tea shop called the Pink Zebra, I checked the money I had left (the section marked MONEY in Jumps' mind told me I was still OK) and went inside for a well-deserved snack.

A pretty girl of about my own age was sitting alone at a table. I ordered (cherry coconut cake, with a side of home-made vanilla ice cream) and went over to sit next to her. Cake opens doors, and I was in need of a little conversation.

'May I?' I said.

She looked at me. 'Sure.' Her gaze was frank and humorous and open. From somewhere inside me I thought I sensed a tiny stirring of interest.

Jumps? I said.

No answer. I turned my attention back to the girl.

Yellow dress, long curly hair. Brown skin, like an Outlander's. She gave her name as Margaret, and watched me over her cup of tea.

'No cake?'

She smiled. 'No cake,' she said. 'I'd kill to be as thin as you.'

I tried to process that for a bit. Jumps had all kinds of odd ideas about her weight and body shape, but Margaret was beautiful as Jumps could never hope to be. She was plump, and soft, and brown, with golden eyes that sparkled. Just looking at her, I could tell that she would like pizza, and ice cream, and cake; and dancing, and kissing, and laughter, and sex—

I looked her up and down and said: 'We're going to need two spoons.'

'You think?'

'Totally. Cake loves company.'

That made her laugh. 'It does?'

'Oh, yes. Especially cherry coconut cake. Which, apart from jam tarts, just happens to be my favourite.'

The cherry cake turned out to be everything I'd hoped for. Margaret – Meg, to her friends – soon lost any remaining reserve. She told me she lived in White City – that's a housing estate in Malbry. She had two sisters and a cat; liked cooking and listening to music; had left school two years earlier and worked part-time in a bakery.

'I *know*. A bakery,' she said.

This may be my ideal woman, I thought.

I also learned that she liked to dance, and that there was a club nearby, where she sometimes liked to hang out. 'Do you like dancing?' said Margaret.

'Sure,' I said.

Well, to be honest, I had no idea if I liked it or not. But if Meg liked it, I was game. I mean, I had no idea of what kind of dancing people did in this world, or whether I'd be any good, but—

'Well, to be fair I've never tried, but I've always been a quick learner.'

She laughed. 'Oh, you don't have to be good. You just have to feel it.'

'I could try.'

'Maybe I could teach you,' she said. 'It's one thing I know

104

how to do.' She told me the name of the club: *The Blaze*. I made a note of the address.

'It's a date,' I told her, and smiled.

Like I said. Cake opens doors.

9

OVER THE LAST HOUR OR SO I'd been aware of an odd, intermittent buzzing sound. I finally tracked the source of the sound to Jumps' phone, which was in my jeans pocket. I pulled it out. There were several messages, most of them from Evan.

Jumps. Are you OK? Meet you at the gate at 4. E.

Jumps. Where did you go? Give me a call when you get this. E.

Jumps. I'm serious. Call me. E.

Josephine. Where are you? Mr Matthews was on the phone. He says you left early. What happened? Also, I hope you haven't forgotten that we're due to meet Grandma at the restaurant at 7.00 tonight. Please don't be late. You know what she's like. Love, Mum.

The last one was from 5:45, which I saw was over an hour ago. Not that the time concerned me much, but I sensed that it mattered to Jumps, as did many other irrelevant things, such as dress, hair, school, exams, and turning up late to dinner. I scrolled through the inner directory under EATING OUT, and found multiple references to a restaurant called The Jade Pagoda, beloved of Jumps' mother because of its relative cheapness, and liked by Jumps because the food comes in a multitude of tiny dishes and bowls which makes it easier to conceal the fact that she barely eats anything. I searched Jumps' mind, first for my host, and then, when she failed to emerge, for the address of the Jade Pagoda.

I arrived at seven-fifteen, and after a quick glance at the Book of Faces, found Jumps' parents and grandmother sitting at a table between a potted palm and a rather bad picture in bas-relief of a tea-house by a lake.

'Er, hi. Sorry I'm late.'

I was feeling a little nervous. If anyone was likely to spot the fact that Jumps was not entirely herself, it would surely be her loved ones. Jumps' mother, a wholesome blonde; her father, a fat bald man in a suit; and her grandmother, an imperious-looking old lady with fluffy white hair and snapping black eyes, all stared at me as if I were a dancing weasel, inadvertently brought to them in lieu of a dish of chicken chow mein.

'*Josephine!*' said the mother. 'Your *hair!*'

Filed under MOTHER: *Grace Mitchell. Age: 42. Spouse to Brian Lucas. Profession: Dietician. Favourite colour: teal. Favourite film: Dangerous Liaisons. Likes: fashion, sushi, shopping, Chablis. Dislikes: being surprised or wrong-footed, especially by her daughter.*

'Cool, huh?' I sat down. There was a bottle of wine nearby; I helped myself to a large glass. The grandmother gave a throaty laugh, but no one else said anything. 'I thought I could use a change. Hey, have you ordered? I'm starving.'

The mother gave me a look that conveyed both disapproval and warning. 'Well, you're here now,' she said, showing teeth. 'I'm sure Grandma would love to hear all about your day.'

Grandma. Widow. Age unknown. Possibly the only person to intimidate Mrs Mitchell. Likes: wrong-footing people; disobeying her doctor.

I shrugged. 'Well, Grandma, I flunked my exam; walked out of school; stole some stuff from a corner shop; maxed out my debit card; got a radical undercut and picked up a girl in a coffee shop. Oh, yes, and by the way, did I mention I'm a god?'

The grandmother cawed laughter. 'You always were a funny

thing,' she said, observing me with a critical eye. 'What *is* that outfit?'

I took off my shocking-pink jacket and slung it over the back of the chair. 'Too conservative?'

She smiled. 'You're still too thin, though, Josephine.'

'Yeah, well – I'm working on that.'

The food arrived. There was soup, and rice, and noodles, and fish, and roast pork, and chicken, and vegetables. There were new and exciting spices; there were rare and delicious flavours. There were dumplings and skewers of prawn and pancakes rolled around pieces of meat. We ate with something called *chopsticks* – not an implement with which I was familiar, but between Jumps' muscle memory, the wine and my own hunger, I did more than justice to the meal. The mother and father watched it all with an air of vague alarm, but the grandmother seemed to enjoy it. Charm comes easily to our kind – besides, old ladies like me.

My phone buzzed several times during the meal. Checking it, I found another raft of text messages from Evan.

FFS, Jumps, where the hell are you? E.

Call me. Call me NOW. E.

And finally, in a different tone: *Listen, Captain. We need to talk. If you think you can just step away from your responsibilities, you've got another think coming. This isn't a game. That cat can't stay in the box for ever. And if you think you can hide from me —*

I sighed. Even by mobile phone, the General had a way of making everything less fun. I dropped the mobile phone into a nearby tank of tropical fish. No one noticed, except the grandmother, who chuckled and said: 'Boy trouble?'

'Something like that.' I smiled at her. 'Listen, do you happen to know anything about a cat in a box, a cat that's both dead and alive?'

The grandmother nodded. 'Schrödinger's cat. What about it?'

'Well, what would *you* do?'

'You mean – if I were the cat?' she said.

'Would *you* stay in the box, or leave, even if it meant you might die?'

She smiled. Her eyes shone like polished jet beads. 'I wouldn't worry about the cat,' she said. 'Don't you know, they have nine lives?'

Well, as a matter of fact, I did.

'So you go out and enjoy yourself,' she said. 'Live a little – or a lot. And don't let a boy – or *anyone* – try to tell you what to do.'

I took one of her hands in mine. It felt both hot and papery, with knuckles that were swollen with age. 'Thank you, Grandma,' I said. 'You are wise. Wiser than an Oracle.' And then I stood up and picked up my jacket, and, addressing the parents, I announced: 'I have to go. It's getting late.'

The mother made a sound like an orca demanding fish. 'Go where? Late for what? Not on a school night, you don't. What about tomorrow's exams? What about your revision? And where did you want to go, anyway?'

I grinned at her. 'I have a date.'

10

THE BLAZE WAS A LARGE and shapeless hall, lit by multi-coloured lights. There was a bar at one end, and a stage at the other, upon which a group of musicians played unfamiliar instruments. The rest was a dance floor, crowded with bodies gyrating to the music. The volume was high, the hall packed full; there was an overwhelming scent of smoke, and sweat, and beer. In fact it was strangely familiar, even almost nostalgic. Memories of Aegir's hall; and of Bragi playing the lute, and of Odin passing me the cup with a gleam in his living eye.

Enough of that. The last thing I wanted was to remember Asgard. Asgard was lost, except in dreams and second-rate glamours like *Asgard!*™. I moved out onto the dance floor, keeping a lookout for Margaret. I did not see her, but a wave of bodies surged around me, and although I had no idea what kind of dancing was fashionable in this place, I found myself moving to the beat. Jumps wasn't much of a dancer. I saw this in her memory, muddied by thoughts of self-consciousness and the fear of people laughing at her. I had no such fear, of course. Even in this body, I knew I was fabulous.

Frankly, there's not much to dancing. The trick is to feel the music, barely even moving at first; to allow it to wash over you like a river of fire. Then, you can move; you let it take you, first your hands, and then your hips. It pounds like lava, sparkles like glam. It makes you shine. It makes you smile. And you dance.

For a time, that was enough. Around me, people came and went. Most of the people were young here; many of them attractive. Many young men came to dance with me; some brought me drinks. One put his arms around me and we slow-danced (he wasn't bad, but I was better, obviously); but all the time I was watching; waiting for Margaret.

Finally, I caught sight of her. She had changed her yellow dress for cropped jeans and a peasant blouse. Her hair was tied back, and she was wearing glass earrings shaped like bunches of cherries. I waved. She smiled and came over.

'You made it!' she shouted in my ear.

I put my hand on the nape of her neck.

'Let's just dance,' I told her.

I don't remember how long we danced. But her skin was warm; her eyes were bright; she smelt of vanilla and roses. At first we danced like maniacs: spinning, leaping, laughing. She was good – I was better; people watched and clapped and cheered. Then the lights dimmed; the music slowed; the crowd of people drifted away. And finally, I could almost believe that it was just the two of us, rocking gently, hands laced; her head touching my shoulder.

I know. It sounds crazy. All I can say is that I wasn't quite myself. The exhilaration of being in the flesh; the unaccustomed lights and sounds; the feel of her hair and her skin against mine – I suppose all that was more than enough to turn my head a little. And now that I was free of Jumps – her anxiety, her insecurities, her strange obsessions – I was free to enjoy the gift – this life, this day, this present.

'This is nice,' said Margaret. 'But I know something nicer.'

'You do?'

'It's a kind of dance,' she said. 'But you do it with fire.'

I could have pointed out that she was already doing precisely

111

that. But dancing with fire sounded pretty cool, and besides, I was starting to think that it might be a euphemism for sex.

'We go onto Castle Hill,' she said. 'That's where we go, where it's dark, and where we won't be interrupted. It's called fire-spinning. It's what I do. Sometimes I just go alone and practise.'

That sounded interesting. 'Tell me more.'

Turns out it *wasn't* a euphemism for sex. But I was right; it was interesting. Fire is the one deity that never goes out of fashion. And Margaret and her friends had been worshipping me – albeit in a different Aspect – through this, this fire-spinning thing, for years without even knowing it.

I listened as she told me about the fire-spinners, their batons, their *poi*, their beautiful, dangerous rituals. It sounded too alluring for words. *Better watch yourself, Loki*, I thought. *A fire-demon could fall in love.*

Draft entry for the Book of Faces: *Margaret Brown, aka Meg. Age: 21. Profession: bakery assistant. Favourite colour: lemon yellow. Favourite movie:* Chocolat. *Likes: fire-spinning; stars; the rain; otters; sunflowers; cats; the sea. Favourite food: cherry cake. Favourite fantasy—*

Meg lifted her eyes to mine. A thrill ran down my borrowed flesh, unzipping me like a bodysuit. And then we kissed, and her breasts were soft, and I thought: *Yes, a girl could fall in love—*

I opened my eyes and noticed a trio of girls staring at us. *Well, who wouldn't?* I told myself. *After all, we're fabulous.* But there was something about the way those girls were staring that made me feel uneasy. Did I know them? Did they know me? Was my mascara smudged?

A glance at the Book of Faces revealed that they were friends of Stella's. One of the adoring cliques with which she liked to surround herself. But these were special, I understood. These were part of a secret. Something that had happened to Jumps, in the days when she and Stella were friends. And now the door marked STELLA swung softly ajar, and something came out like a swarm of bees—

Omigod she never – she
Josephine – and STELLA?

There were no pictures; no faces, no words. Just a feeling of shame that ran up and down my body like an attack of hives. Something to do with girls kissing girls. Hardly a cause for shame, I thought, but the Folk can be very peculiar. When I first joined Asgard, one of the things that confused me most was all the rules regarding sex. No sex with animals, siblings, demons; no sex with other people's wives; no sex with folk of the *same* sex – honestly, with all those rules, it was hard to imagine anyone having any sex at all. And here it was again in Jumps' mind – that sense of something forbidden.

I'd assumed that this anger, this jealousy, was something to do with Evan. There was some reason to think so: I could see he was sweet on Stella, just as Odin had always been more than half-blind wherever Freyja was concerned. But this was something different: a memory of something bright, like a once-fine piece of jewellery, all snarled up with dirt and rust, all trace of its earlier glamour gone.

So *that's* what Jumps had been hiding from me. This was her big, dark secret. If it hadn't been so sad, it might have been ridiculous. Such guilt and shame and fear in her mind. So many unnecessary feelings.

My mind now, I reminded myself. Those feelings did not belong to me, but, like unfamiliar furnishings in a darkened house, I kept bumping into them, barking my shins repeatedly on the twin coffee-tables of guilt and shame. Ironic, really: that of all the things for which I might have felt genuine guilt or remorse, *this* was the one I had to endure: the memory of an incident that hadn't even happened to me, and yet which somehow affected me more than anything in my past life. I understood that this gaggle of girls were somehow connected to this incident. What had they seen? What had they said? One of them – *Pippa. Seventeen. Favourite film:* Twilight. *Favourite pastime: selfies* – a smug brunette with glitter on her eyelids – simpered and said:

'New girlfriend, Jo?'

I looked at Meg. She looked as if something had woken her from a dream. Her face was shiny and self-possessed; her eyes had lost that golden glow. Worse still, there was a *look*, a kind of resignation. As if she half expected me to turn away, or laugh at her.

'It's OK,' she said. 'I was leaving.'

Dammit, not you too, I thought.

I put my arm around her shoulders. She was trembling slightly. I understood that she, too, felt shame – though for what, I couldn't begin to guess. And then I looked at the three girls – the Book of Faces now told me their names – and said:

'That's right. New girlfriend. Meet Meg.' And in the silence that followed, I shot my brightest smile at them and said: 'You look surprised. Aw. Don't tell me you three harpies thought one of *you* might have a chance?'

And with that, the feelings, whatever they were, whoever they belonged to, just melted away into the air. Shame; guilt; jealousy; gone, like snowflakes in a summer sky. And then I took Meg by the hand and led her out into the night, where the neon stars and the real ones met in a bridge as bright as Bif-rost. I walked her home as slowly as my feet would let me, and spent as long on the porch as I could, then sauntered back to Jumps' house, where the parents had already gone to bed; and then I slept until dawn, and awoke standing naked and freezing in the bathroom, watching myself in the mirror with an open razor in my hand; and blood on my arms, and blood on the tiles, and blood spattered red on the porcelain—

I watched as my reflection lifted the razor to my throat.

Oh, crap.

Jumps was back.

Gold

All that glitters . . .

Lokabrenna: 5:19

1

P LEASE, I SAID. *Can we talk about this?* The blood – *my* blood
– was everywhere. Shallow cuts, I realized, which didn't stop it
hurting – a lot. And why in Hel would she do that? I thought.
Why would *anyone* do that?

'What the fuck did you do to me?' Her voice was no more
than a whisper. 'Get the hell out of my body, right now, or I
swear I'll kill us both.'

I considered my options, which didn't take long. Barring
miracles, I was toast. My left wrist was still bleeding freely from
a cut that didn't look too dangerous, which was more than
could be said for the blade she was currently holding against
my throat.

I said: *Put down the knife. Let's talk. I'm pretty sure you don't
want to die.*

She laughed. 'You think? What choice do I have? You've already ruined everything.'

What did I do? I said, playing for time.

'What did you do? What did you *do*? What, you mean apart
from failing my English Lit. exam, cleaning out my bank account and making me look like a—'

Like a what? You look fabulous. We look fabulous.

She gave a tortured little cry. 'You don't understand! You

don't know what it's like, being me. Having to pretend I'm like everyone else. Having to fit into a box. Having to look like my mother thinks a normal girl should look like—'

I understand this, I told her. *But . . .*

And then before she could react, I sent her her own reflection, unclouded by fear and uncertainty. I sent her the feeling of being herself – totally and completely herself, and not giving a damn about anyone else. I sent her the taste of food consumed without even once thinking about calories, and drink without fearing drunkenness, and what she might have let slip. I sent her the feeling of dancing like firelight against a wall, and the eyes of many onlookers watching her; wanting her. And then I sent her Meg's face; her golden eyes; her killer smile; the way her hair shone in the sun. I sent her a kiss still flavoured with the taste of cherry and coconut; the touch of a hand; the turn of a cheek; a dance under the neon stars. I sent her the promise of spinning with bolts of fire in both hands, of dancing on the darkened hill with a pocketful of mysteries.

'Stop it,' said Jumps. And yet, the hand clutching the razor seemed to relax a little.

'No, *you* stop it,' I told her. '*I'm* not your problem. You are. You're the one who hates herself. You're the one who can hardly even look at herself in the mirror. You're the one who's so afraid of what other people might say and think that she tries to be invisible. You're the one who would rather die than admit you might feel something for a girl like Meg – a girl who anyone else in the world would be proud to know, to want, to *lo*—'

I stopped. Jumps lowered the razor. There was silence for a while.

'You like her,' she said.

'Of course I do.'

'I mean, you really *like* her.'

I thought about that a moment. I'll admit, I haven't had too much experience in really *liking* people. I know all about desire, of course. Desires and lusts and appetites are more or less

118

second nature to me. But what I'd felt with Meg – well. That had come from somewhere else. Some*where* – maybe some*one*—

'I think that came from you, Jumps.'

'It did?' Now there was doubt in her voice: the hand with the razor dropped to her side. I turned on the cold tap and rinsed the blade, then ran cold water over my wrist. It stung, but the cut was not serious. A cry for help, I thought. That was all. A cry for understanding.

Oh, no. Those human emotions again. As if *really liking* someone wasn't bad enough, now I was learning a new one. What the hell was it? Empathy? *Compassion?* In any case, it was something that I associated with people like Idun, who believed in herbs and healing chants and channelling their inner goddess. Whatever it was, it had taken me one step further into dangerous waters. I had to be careful, I told myself: at this rate I'd be picking out penguin slippers in no time.

'Listen,' I said. 'I'm sorry. I'm sorry I messed up your exam. I'm sorry I didn't listen to you. But look at what I did for you. Look at what you did for me. Look at what else we can do if only we work together.'

And with that, I sent her the faces of those girls when I sent them packing. I sent her the feeling of being herself. I stripped off that veil of shame and guilt; I showed her young, and strong, and smart, and powerful in every way—

Her eyes widened. 'What did you do?'

'Just gave you a bit of perspective, that's all.' (Well, if there's anything I've learned – what with being dead, and destroying the Worlds, and defeating the gods – it's perspective.) 'It isn't the End of the Worlds if the popular crowd think you're a freak. It isn't the End of the Worlds if you like eating chocolate, or have a bad day, or make a mistake, or flunk an exam. It isn't the End of the Worlds if you don't look like those girls in the magazines.'

'Easy for you to say. You're old,' she said, but she sounded uncertain.

'I've had plenty of practice,' I said. 'Face it, I've been everything. What I don't know about the Worlds could fit inside a hazelnut. I've been young and old; a demon and a god; a man, a woman, a bird, a horse. I've soared over Bif-rost in falcon guise and raised the armies of the dead. I've seduced, and been seduced; killed and been killed. And, whatever else I was, *I was always fabulous.*'

Jumps gave a tearful little laugh. 'You're impossible,' she said.

'Many people have thought so,' I said. 'And yet, I survived Ragnarók. I think I can survive your World. Now, let's get this place cleaned up, bandage that wrist and get you into something that isn't expressly designed to make you look like a bag of litter.'

She took a deep breath. 'OK.'

'And then – ice cream for breakfast?'

She wiped her face and nodded.

2

B Y THE TIME WE'D CLEANED the bathroom, and dressed
in something appropriate, the sun was up, although it was
still early. The thought of breakfast was welcome, but I'd been
hoping we could leave without meeting Jumps' parents. Something told me they might not approve of my coming home so
late, or of the fact that the previous day I'd walked out of my
English exam without any explanation. Still, it was only seven
o' clock, and my inner Book of Faces reliably informed me that
Mum and Dad seldom rose till eight. Plenty of time, then, I told
myself, to hit the chocolate-cherry ice cream before sauntering
down to Evan's for cold pizza and explanations.

However, on arrival in the kitchen, I found Jumps' grandmother sitting there in front of a bowl of something that looked
like rabbit-droppings. She raised an eyebrow as I came in and
said in her dry and humorous voice:

'You're up early, Josephine.'

Leave this to me, I said to Jumps, who was starting to freak out
again. *Old people love me. Especially old ladies.*

The grandmother gave me that look again, like I was simultaneously the most hilarious thing she'd ever seen *and* possibly
the most disreputable. True, I was wearing a lime-green skirt
with a roll-neck jumper in cherry cashmere, and black tights

with little bats on them. The little bats might have been too much, I guess, but I was pretty sure my innate fabulousness could carry it off.

I gave the grandmother a grin and spooned out ice cream from the tub.

'Ice cream for breakfast,' said the grandmother. 'I suppose at your age, you still can.'

I wanted to point out that my age, as she liked to put it, was considerably greater than hers, but Jumps gave me the mental equivalent of a sharp nudge in the ribs, and I thought better of it.

'Grandma,' I said, removing the rabbit-droppings and providing her with a fresh bowl, 'I've come to the conclusion that ice cream, like so many other things, can be enjoyed at any time, and at *any* age.' And I served her a generous portion of chocolate-cherry ice cream, before attacking the rest of the tub with pleasing fervour.

The grandmother laughed. 'Wise words. Can I assume that last night's date was a success?'

'Most deliciously so,' I said.

'Well, it suits you, whatever it is,' said the grandmother, eating ice cream. 'May I know his name, or would that be too indiscreet?'

'Margaret,' I said. 'Meg, for short.'

Oh, no, wailed Jumps. *What did you tell her that for?* But it was too late. The grandmother arched an eyebrow and said: 'I see. Is she pretty?'

'No,' I said. 'She's beautiful.'

That was an odd thing to say, I thought. One of Jumps' thoughts, perhaps. I mean, it's not as if I haven't encountered beauty. I mean, I was around Freyja and Sif and Idun for centuries, which kind of puts into perspective the imperfections of the Folk. Plus, Angrboda and Gullveig-Heid, being demons, were both way more alluring than any of the goddesses. Even my late wife Sigyn – who Freyja kept by her side for the sake of contrast – was probably a four or five: more than enough for her to outshine even the most striking of humans. Which made it all the more odd that Meg should have had the effect on me that she did. I could only assume that the tingly glow I felt as I thought of her now belonged to Jumps, rather than to me.

The grandmother smiled. 'Well, I'm happy for you. Don't know what your mother will think, but—'

'It's none of her business. It's personal,' said Jumps, coming to the forefront somewhat unexpectedly. 'She wants to control everything. Putting me on diets when I was six. Telling me I was fat all the time. Look how that worked out, huh?'

'You seem to have resolved *that* issue, at least,' said the grandmother, eyeing the empty tub of ice cream.

'No,' said Jumps. 'But I'm working on it.'

'Something to do with this Meg?' said the grandmother.

Jumps shook her head. 'Not just Meg. But other people don't get to decide what I do with my body any more.'

Ouch. Was that a jab at me?

I sensed her amusement. *Asshole, relax. It isn't always about you.*

'Your mother worries about you a lot,' said the grandmother. 'So does your dad. They're both idiots, of course, but they love you. Try to understand.'

Jumps smiled. It lit up our space. Gods, but she burned brightly. The grandmother must have seen it too, because she stood up and kissed me on the forehead. I felt her papery hands on mine. She was so old, I thought, so old. And now I could feel something else – one of those human emotions not yet in my vocabulary.

Regret? Nostalgia? Tenderness?

Jumps gave me that inner nudge again. *Will you stop questioning everything? I'm having a moment here!*

The grandmother smiled and ruffled my hair. I allowed myself to be ruffled, even though I'd put effort into the styling. 'Tell them not to worry,' said Jumps. 'I'm going to sort out the exam. Everything's going to be fine from now on. Well, maybe not *fine*, but better.'

'I'm glad for you, Jumps,' said the grandmother. 'You take care now – and be good.'

'I will, Grandma,' said Jumps. She gave the old lady a hug, and I felt her bones through her old-lady cardigan. Then we were on our way again, heading across town towards Evan's place. I was feeling uneasy, although I wasn't sure what the problem was. I was glad for Jumps too, of course, though I wished she hadn't delivered *quite* such a challenge to the Norns. Those bitches – you'd call them the Fates, I guess – love to mess with folk who are feeling a little too confident. Still, we'd made a good start. I'd managed to make peace with Jumps. I'd do the same with the General. We'd find out where Freyja had got her rune, and all of us would share in the joy. All in all, I was feeling good. What could possibly go wrong?

3

I HAD DISPOSED OF JUMPS' phone, but, sadly, disposing of her friend wasn't a viable option. For a start, Jumps *liked* Evan. That ruled out most possibilities. Second, the General had to be at least as stubborn as I was myself, which meant he was un- likely to give up until I had done what he wanted. He wanted the New Runes; the Oracle; a way to escape this borrowed flesh. And, to be fair, I wanted that too: as long as it didn't mean risk- ing the skin I'd lately become quite attached to. And so I went to find the Old Man, to pre-empt any unpleasantness caused by my exploits the previous day.

By the time we got to Evan's place, I was feeling pretty good. The sun was shining, the birds were in song and the fresh air had renewed my appetite. But when we saw Evan, I started to feel that my optimism had been premature. He answered the door when I rang the bell, but he didn't ask us inside, and I saw that he was in his chair, looking pinched and delicate. I caught a spike of concern from Jumps – *One of his bad days*, she whis- pered – but as far as I was concerned, the Old Man deserved every bit of discomfort he felt.

'Didn't expect you this early,' he said. 'And what on earth have you done to your hair?'

'Yeah, sorry about yesterday,' I said. 'I got a little carried away, what with the freedom, and the cake, and the dancing – and did you know, I have a girlfriend now?'

'Never mind that,' said the General. 'You and I need to concentrate on what really matters. Which is getting our glam back and going home.'

'Yes, sir. I see that now.' I gave him my most winning smile.

'Because, however much you may be enjoying your current accommodation, you're here as a visitor, nothing else. Start thinking you can stay here, and we'll all be in danger. Remember the cat in the box. OK?'

'Cats *like* boxes,' I said.

'Not this one,' said the General.

I sighed. To be honest, I was starting to be not entirely averse to staying in Jumps indefinitely. The body was workable, and now that she had started to cooperate I was in no hurry to leave. Not so with the General. His manner was very much that of a man in a hurry. I wondered whether Evan's health was a factor in this, and if so, just how sick he really was.

'We can't discuss this in detail now,' he said. 'Jumps has another exam. But come back tonight, around six, and we'll talk. Don't be late. I'm counting on you.'

By now I was ready to move on to more pressing things, like maybe grabbing a little snack before the start of school. Odin, in his current state, seemed unlikely to provide, but Jumps' internal lexicon apprised me of the existence of something called a *Vending Machine*, which apparently handed out chocolate, and I was eager to try it out.

Odin fixed me with his one living eye. 'You'd better not let me down,' he said. 'And don't talk to Stella before we meet.'

'Why would I do that?' I said.

'Just see that you don't, that's all.'

I gave him a cheery little wave and promptly, blithely forgot him. His problems could wait until we'd fixed Jumps' English exam. And after that? Well—

Seize the day, as Jumps liked to say. We had a lot of seizing to do.

4

THE FIRST THING WE DID ON arriving at school was to seek out the Head of English. With Jumps' guidance and my silver tongue, I managed to persuade him that Jumps had suffered a momentary lapse – I had previously found that any reference to *Women's Mysteries* was usually enough to reduce most men to inarticulate, red-faced fools, and in the case of Jumps' English teacher, that wasn't much of a stretch.

After a token resistance, he agreed to write to the examination board, citing her excellent record and performance throughout the year, and asking for special consideration to be given to the test. Then he fled the room in haste, with an over-the-shoulder hunted look.

High-five, said Jumps. *Let's celebrate.*

The chocolate machine was everything I had hoped for, except that Jumps would only allow me a single small bar of the good stuff, rather than the many I craved. Still, it was a foundation upon which I meant to build, just as soon as my host's insecurities were well and truly overcome. The next thing was another exam, which I had promised to endure without complaint, as long as Jumps did what I wanted afterwards.

The exam was called Critical Thinking, which I actually found quite interesting, in spite of Jumps' deplorable tendency to give in to her feelings. Then there was something called British Politics, which was predictably dull, except for the wars, which were quite good, though not as impressive as those I had experienced. But Jumps came out of both exams feeling fairly positive, which meant that we were free to meet Meg – and if cake was involved, all the better.

I'd been hoping that Jumps would agree to accompany me on another date, and from her words to the grandmother, I sensed that she was amenable.

Meg was funny, and clever, and sweet – frankly, all the things that used to annoy me when I was someone else, and yet in Meg were somehow not only tolerable, but actually attractive. I supposed that these feelings, confused as they were, must be Jumps' influence, and yet the thought of seeing Meg again made me tingle agreeably.

I'd arranged to meet her at the Pink Zebra, the coffee-shop where we had first met. I sensed a kind of reluctance in Jumps, and yet she was somehow excited, too – an excitement that I thought had to do with the feeling that it wasn't quite real. *She* wasn't living this. It was someone else's life, someone else's dream, to her, which meant that she could enjoy it without feeling guilty, or anxious.

Stupid, I know. But it was a start.

Meg was in the corner, at the table I already thought of as ours. She was wearing a T-shirt with a picture of a shark on it. A necklace of little wooden beads shaped like flowers hung around her neck. I don't know why I noticed those things: they weren't important, and yet – those human feelings again – there was something about those small wooden beads that troubled, even moved me. I know how it sounds. But there it was. The Father of Lies, the Sire of the Wolf, the Trickster of Asgard was going soft.

Meg gave me a little wave. 'Hey, Jumps!'

I smiled and went over. Something about her calling me *Jumps* didn't quite ring right. Of course, there was no way Margaret could ever use my real name; a thought that gave me a sudden feeling of something I couldn't quite recognize. Dammit, all these feelings. They needed a library all to themselves. Why not just keep it simple? There were enough pleasures in this world to fill every hour of a human's life. Why waste so much precious time with doubt, and pain, and loneliness?

And so we ordered cherry cake, and talked about our day, and books, and British history, and the art of war, and Life in all its absurdity. And I was funny, and Jumps was sincere (which I guess is what you have to be if you can't be funny), and between us, I think we managed to make a pretty good stab at a human. Not that Meg knew *what* we were, but like I said, she was clever, and her golden eyes saw surprisingly far.

'You're so strange,' said Meg at last, when we had finished the coconut cake. 'Old and young at the same time. Laughing one minute, sad the next.'

'Sad?' I said. 'No way am I sad. In fact, this is pretty much the happiest I've been in five hundred years.'

She laughed at that. 'See? That's what I mean. I'm never sure whether you're joking or not.'

'That *was* a joke,' said Jumps fiercely, pinching the inside of my leg under cover of the tabletop.

Meg laughed again. 'Well, that's a relief. Otherwise the age difference might have presented a problem.' Then, seeing Jumps' expression, she said; 'Of *course* I know it was a joke. You're often happy. I can tell.'

She reached out her hand. I took it. For a moment I sensed hesitation from Jumps, then she gave in to the contact. I felt, rather than heard her sigh, as if some long-locked door in her mind had finally swung open. *Good*, I thought. *She's relaxing.*

Then, Meg looked down at my hands.

'What happened?' she said.

Damn and blast. I'd bandaged the razor-cut from last night, and chosen a long-sleeved garment. Even so, she must have seen the sticking-plasters on my wrist. I started to respond, but Jumps got in there before me.

'Yeah, I sometimes do that,' she said. 'I'm trying to kick the habit.'

Why the hell did you say that? I said.

Inside my mind, I felt her shrug. *Because she's nice,* she told me. *And because I'm not a liar.*

Well, excuse me, I said. *I happen to be the Father and Mother of Liars, and I can tell you right now that honesty is both overrated and, in our position, frankly the pits. So I'll thank you to keep to the script, if you don't mind, and quit with the confessions, right? Remember, we're here to have a good ti—*

But Jumps cut me short. 'Listen, Meg,' she said softly. 'I really, really like you. But I'm not sure getting involved with someone new is a good idea. Not right now, at least.'

'Why's that?' Meg lifted an eyebrow – but her eyes were still kind.

'Because I'm – not myself,' said Jumps.

I interjected. *What the—?*

'When we were at the Blaze,' said Jumps, 'I was someone different. Trust me, I'm not like that all the time. And I don't want to have to pretend around you.'

'I get it,' said Meg. 'You're new to this.'

Jumps looked at her and nodded.

'It's fine,' said Meg. 'You know, I can tell. We don't have to do anything more than talk. Or dance. Or eat cake. It's all good. I can take it as slow as you need.'

I gave an inner howl. *Ye gods. I can't believe you're doing this. I thought you were my wing-man. You're like the world's biggest gooseberry. It's like being trapped in a ménage à trois with someone who doesn't even want to watch.*

Meg went on: 'How does that sound?'

For a moment I felt Jumps hesitate. She liked Meg. I could tell. More than that, she was drawn to her much as I'd been drawn myself. There was something about her, that's all. Something warm and kind and sweet. I tried to work out what it was. She wasn't really my usual type. No make-up, no jewellery. Just that wooden necklace, and her hair in little corkscrew curls that stood out all around her face. I mean, she was OK. But I'd seen more beautiful women by far. And yet somehow this one was different. Somehow this one outshone them all.

Finally Jumps sighed. 'OK.'

'That's good,' said Meg, smiling. 'Because although I liked you last night, I like you even better now.'

'Really?' said Jumps.

Er, what?

'Last night, it was like you were putting on an act. I could tell. It was fun, but that was all. I want to get to know the real you.'

Jumps looked up and gently raised her hand to touch Meg's face.

Oh. So you're playing a deep game. Well, OK, if you think she'll —

Shut up Loki, said Jumps.

Meg's mouth was warm and sweet. Her skin smelt faintly of almonds. My own – strictly speaking, Jumps' skin – felt prickly with her closeness.

It feels weird with you here, said Jumps. *Can't you stand back, or something?*

Well, it isn't often that I'm rendered speechless. But in this case, I made an exception. It wasn't just the fact that Meg seemed to prefer Jumps to me – thought she was more *sincere*, for gods' sakes – but now that I was finally getting to see some action, Jumps was suddenly taking my place.

You're still there, said Jumps accusingly.

I sighed. *OK. Whatever.* It wasn't the time or the place for me to get into an argument with Jumps. And so I retreated as far as I could from the delicious seduction scene, with all its sensations and feelings and joys, and instead stood like an idiot in a dark corner of Jumps' mind, and tried to identify the emotions that now came rushing in on me. Human emotions. So messy, so bleak, so fundamentally unnecessary. Why did they even

131

have them? They served no useful purpose. Around me, there were directories marked LONELINESS and LONGING and LOSS. All of them seemed to welcome me like the serried ranks of the dead. A cheery thought. Very human. I turned instead to thoughts of cake, but found myself feeling slightly sick. I turned my attention back to Meg, and found that she was standing up.

'I want to show you something,' she said. 'Is that OK?'

Jumps nodded. 'Of course. Where are we going?'

Meg smiled. 'It's a surprise. Trust me, I think you'll like it.'

So far, there'd been nothing about Margaret that I didn't like. I saw no reason for this to be different. And so we followed her into the street, and through the town towards Castle Hill, where the sun was starting to set in a giant bowl of fire.

5

I'LL ADMIT IT. I'D STILL BEEN secretly hopeful that the surprise might be sexual in nature. Most of the best surprises are, which made it all the more startling when we arrived at the top of Castle Hill to find it already occupied. Three young people were sitting there around a shallow firepit. A number of metal canisters and coils of rope and bundles of wire were stacked up in the vicinity.

An orgy? I wondered hopefully.

Don't be ridiculous, said Jumps. *Just let me do the talking, all right?*

The three young people greeted Meg with smiles and hugs. A boy, a girl, and one who didn't seem to be either; two brown-skinned like Margaret, one pink-haired with dark eyes. Meg introduced them as Mossy, Alisha and Katsu, and then she said: 'This is Jumps. She's cool.'

I tried not to feel left out as everyone said hello to Jumps. I could see that they were curious, even maybe a little impressed. I thought to myself that if Jumps was cool, I was the one responsible; then, feeling unaccountably cross, took a back seat while the others got acquainted. I was bored, and annoyed, and the worst of it was, I didn't really know why. The night was warm, there was Meg, there was fire – there were even snacks, which at any other time I might have found appealing. But Jumps was the one she'd invited; not me. I was just an onlooker.

I need to get out of this body, I thought. *This World is far too confusing.*

And then finally, as Meg's friends prepared for the next part of the entertainment, I realized the purpose of the cans and wires and ropes that they had brought to the top of the hill. Meg had prepared me for this in her way. *Fire-spinning*, she had called it. It had sounded cool at the time, but I hadn't imagined how much it would chime with my especial interests.

'These are called *poi*,' Meg explained to Jumps. 'You can make them out of all kinds of things, as long as they're not too heavy. This one's made of oil-soaked rags in a cage of wire mesh. You swing it like this—' She demonstrated, starting gently at first, and then stepping to a safe distance before starting her dance in earnest.

Gods help me, it was beautiful. Meg moved with a natural rhythm, the fire moving around and beside her as if fire were her element. The *poi* moved in long lazy arcs, then in loops and circles that narrowed and widened like the pupils of a dragon's eye. I hadn't seen anything so beautiful since the birth of the Middle Worlds. Order and Chaos, in balance; dancing and moving in harmony, like a firebird in flight—

Jesus, will you stop with the commentary?

So shoot me. I like fire, I said. *Are you going to give it a try?*

Jumps said nothing, but watched the dance.

Go on. Please. I let you be alone with Meg.

Meg came a little closer, letting the *poi* swing loosely by her side. 'Wanna try?'

'Hell, yes,' said Jumps.

'OK. Swing it gently. Be careful—'

I took the reins of the fire-beast. 'Don't worry,' I said. 'I got this.'

What a feeling. What a rush. Of all the human sensations I'd enjoyed, endured, disliked or puzzled over, this was the best.

Better than sex or drunkenness, better than Sigyn's jam tarts. It was like being back in Aspect, like having my glam back, like being at the head of an army. I danced with the fire, and the fire danced back, recognizing a kindred soul. I was better than Jumps would have been: I flung the *poi* into the air, leapt over it like an animal, twisted it into a double helix that spun and spun through the glamorous air like the World Serpent with its tail in its mouth.

And when the fire had died at last, and I turned to look at Meg, wide-eyed, her pupils all pinned with reflected fire, and her friends, all watching, began to applaud, and I was almost a god again, there came from behind me the sound of an all-too-familiar voice.

'So *this* is where you got to,' it said, and there was a note in the voice that somehow raised the hairs on the back of my neck. I turned and saw Stella standing there, watching the scene as if it were the funniest thing she'd seen in years.

I was pleased to find that Jumps did not overreact. Instead she said: 'Stella? What do you want?' with a passable degree of nonchalance, even though I could tell that all her senses were on the alert.

Freyja gave a tinkling laugh, like someone's idea of a Disney princess. She was perfect. Little print dress, sunset hair, legs that went on for ever. And in the light of the firepit there was something else, something dangerous: an aura, I thought, of menace.

'New friend, Jumps?' she said.

I shrugged. 'Are you jealous, or something?'

That laugh again, like sleigh-bells wielded by an evil Santa. 'Not remotely, sweetheart,' she said. 'Because when I call, you always come. Just like a little lapdog.'

Lapdog. That made me think of Thor, and of Odin, whose warning about not talking to Stella I had hitherto forgotten. Still, what harm could it do? I thought. She was hardly a threat to either of us.

'I see you found the Hill,' she said. 'Not that you could have missed it, lit up as it was like a Christmas tree. You took your time, didn't you?'

I thought back to the previous day. The strange new rune-mark over the hill. That feeling of exhilaration. But surely that had been a mistake? Just an accidental meeting of vapours in the sky?

She must have read my thoughts. She smiled. 'That was no accident,' she said. 'That was the Hill.' She gave it a capital letter, the way the Folk distinguish their new God from the old ones. I remembered that galvanic jolt the first time I had seen the Hill. Then, that feeling of certainty at the runemark in the sky. And now, the new sensation of being more alive than I had been in over five hundred years; alive and strong and full of power. I'd assumed that the fire-dance was responsible, but now that I came to think about it, wasn't there something else in the air, a resonance that came from beneath the ground, humming like a hive of bees?

'What is it?' I said.

She smiled at me. 'Freedom. Freedom from *her*. But most of all, freedom from *him*.'

Excuse me? said Jumps, from our shared space. *What the hell is she on about?*

Just let me handle this, I said.

Freyja's blue eyes shone like stars. 'Freedom, Loki. Think of it. Isn't that what you wanted?'

I shrugged. I wasn't about to reveal how desperately I wanted it.

'And how exactly does a hill represent freedom?'

She smiled again. I thought there was something about that smile that I recognized from long ago – something I didn't associate with Freyja, or any of the Vanir. And now I could sense a *charge* in her, like a powerful source of glam. It felt good – somehow *dangerous*, like a really good bonfire. And I was drawn to it, of course. After all, it's my nature.

I looked up at the dark sky. Down in Malbry, the streetlights were on, white and yellow against the dark. The Hill loomed like a giant, rising up from a patchwork of fields. I realized that in my excitement, I'd missed the General's meeting. I didn't expect him to be pleased about that. But there was something about the Hill. Something irresistible—

I've always had pretty good instincts in the face of danger. Now my instincts were screaming. Meg and her friends were still standing there around the glowing firepit, their faces golden in the light, their eyes wide and incurious. They looked slightly stunned, in a dream – and if that wasn't some kind of glamour, I thought, I might as well hand back my demon credentials right now.

'Does the General know you're here?' I said. 'Did he send you after me?'

It was certainly possible, I thought. The Old Man was subtle. Too subtle, sometimes, for his own good. It was totally possible that this was some kind of trap to force me to cooperate. But the idea that he might be *excluded* – and by Freyja, whose esteem for me was placed somewhere rather lower than the World Serpent's nether parts – was surely an indication that said scheme was not designed to benefit Yours Truly.

I shook my head to clear it. It felt a little clouded, as if I were imperceptibly drunk, with that drunkard's confidence in his own invulnerability. My blood hummed; my head span; my arms were suddenly burning—

'You may feel a little discomfort at first,' said Freyja, seeing my expression.

I pushed up my sleeves. 'Dammit, that hurts.'

'You're bleeding,' said Meg quietly. Sure enough, the scars on my arm – the ones that formed the runemark *Kaen* – had broken open, and the blood was running freely down my wrist, blood that seemed slightly *luminous* in the dying firelight. Hot droplets fell, and spackled the ground with fitful luminescence.

And then, at last, it came crashing home. Drunk? I must

have been blind, I thought. I should have known the truth from the first moment I laid eyes on Stella's runemark. *Fé*, the golden rune of wealth – which also happened to be the rune of Gullveig-Heid, the Golden One; the Sorceress of the Elder Age; the Vanir rebel whose treachery sometimes even exceeded my own, and whose power, linked with Chaos, had brought down Asgard and the gods as easily as a house of cards—

I looked at Stella. Her face was alight with greedy anticipation. *'Heidi?'* I said.

She smiled at me. 'Oh, Loki. You used to be quicker off the mark. Or were you distracted by your new friend?'

I looked at Meg. 'You need to go. Take your friends and leave. Now.'

'She's quite attractive,' Heidi said. 'But is she really your type?' That smile again, like a flower ringed with the sharpest, whitest of teeth. My mouth was dry; my throat was tight; my arms were braceleted with fire. I was vaguely aware of Jumps protesting in our shared space, but there was no time to explain. I had to get Meg out of the way before the Sorceress realized just how much I could be hurt if any harm befell her.

'Well?' said Heidi, still smiling.

'She's nothing. No one. Forget her,' I said.

'I don't understand,' said Meg. 'Who's this? And what did she just call you?'

I cursed inwardly, trying to ignore both Jumps' protests, and the cascade of feelings my words were unleashing inside me. There was fear, and sorrow, and regret, and impatience, and something approaching dread, all of which had to be expertly hidden from the thing inside Stella, or risk exposing Meg to the kind of peril that always followed Heidi around.

Meg put her hand on my arm. 'Jumps? Are you all right?'

'We're done,' I said. 'I want you to go.'

The golden eyes flashed. 'Just like that?'

My heart was breaking. I made my voice harsh. 'Just go,' I told her. 'Fuck off. *Now.*'

6

I TURNED BACK TO STELLA, trying not to see the expression on Meg's face as she picked up her things from the firepit. Her friends, too – the people who until then might have been *my* friends – were watching me with anger and scorn.

Katsu muttered: 'What a bitch!' and although I was being noble, which ought to have filled me with pride (as well as a certain amount of surprise, it not being behaviour I was generally known for), I felt a sick kind of unfairness that I hadn't felt since my Asgard days.

Jumps was protesting. *What the hell?* But time was short, and I dared not linger. I sent her the image of a pit, lined with pieces of broken glass. The sides were crumbling and dry; a faded sign read DANGER. I felt her anger shift into wariness and anxiety.

Please, I said. *Trust me. Just this once.* I wished I could say the same thing to Meg. But Stella was watching. A flicker of doubt – a single word – would betray me.

Meg seemed about to say something. But Katsu grabbed her by the arm and led her away towards the path. 'Don't give her the satisfaction,' she said. 'There's plenty more where she came from.'

I wasn't going to turn. But I did. I saw Meg in the firelight. The flames from the dying firepit masked her face in liquid gold. The gold drowned her eyes and ran down her cheeks, and I cursed myself, and Stella, and Jumps; but most of all the General, who must have known who Stella was, but who, for reasons of his own, had chosen not to tell me.

So much for being noble, I told myself. *Remind me not to bother next time.* And then I turned back to my enemy, and saw her watching me like a cat playing with a cornered mouse, and thought: *I guess it serves me right for giving in to feelings.*

'Well. It took you long enough to work it out,' said Gullveig-Heid. 'You *really* believed I was Freyja? Even for a minute? I thought you were more perceptive than that.'

'I had other things on my mind,' I said, with an attempt at insouciance. 'And you, sweetheart, weren't exactly going out of your way to advertise.'

She shrugged. 'Call me paranoid, but I thought perhaps you might not be *altogether* pleased to see me.'

'You mean, after you lied to me and betrayed me, not to mention murdering my wife?'

Heidi laughed. 'Oh, Trickster, please. Lying and betrayal are two of your favourite qualities. And as for the wife, I don't recall you being overly distressed at the time.'

I gave a sigh. She had me there. I'd been too busy enjoying myself to think about the details. Food, drink and merriment, with a lot of demon sex thrown in and the prospect of the Worlds going *foom*. And yes, before you ask, she was very, *very* alluring. But now I was at her mercy, unarmed, bleeding and alone, now that Meg and her friends were safely out of the way, and it occurred to me that perhaps I shouldn't have been so quick to drown Jumps' phone in the fish tank.

'So, what is it you want?' I said. 'I'm guessing it's not just the pleasure of watching me bleed.'

Heidi smiled. 'No, not just that.'

Inside the mind we shared, I heard Jumps questioning me furiously. *What's happening?* she repeated. *Why did you say those things to Meg? I thought you liked her. I thought we were friends.*

140

And what the hell's wrong with my arm? Is it something to do with runes?

I sent her a picture of Gullveig-Heid at the peak of her powers: glorious, golden, filled with rage. Then I sent her Freyja.

What? I could tell she was still confused. *You're saying that isn't Freyja? But Evan said—*

What Evan said may not have been wholly accurate. Especially as his live-in pal just happens to be one of the most accomplished liars this side of Pandaemonium.

You mean Odin lied?

Well, much as it pains me to disillusion you, Jumps, it has been known for the General to tell the odd porkie from time to time. Believe it or not, I—

'Dammit, my *arm*!' I broke off to curse, and to inspect my wrist, which was still bleeding. Bright droplets illuminated the ground, and I started to wonder what purpose my blood could serve a creature like Gullveig-Heid. Of course, a god's blood is powerful stuff. Since Ymir's time, that has been true. Blood was the key to creation; blood sacrifice the key to the runes.

Blood sacrifice. That doesn't sound good.

I could feel my strength ebbing, my head growing light as my blood (or rather, Jumps' blood) drizzled onto the grass of the Hill. And now I could feel something in the air, a kind of mystic resonance.

'They're playing our song,' said Heidi. Her eyes were blue as polar ice. For a moment I was mesmerized, lost in the blue and gold of her, feeling my body draining of blood like the dying sun of a summer's day. And somehow a part of me *wanted* to die – to sink into the darkness; to be absolved of everything, and sleep at last, and bleed, and bleed—

And then there was Jumps, saying: *Hey, what's wrong? Are you going to bail on me? Are you going to just lie down and let her take what she wants from you? Just the way she did before?* Except that it didn't sound like Jumps, but some other Loki from long ago, a Loki from before the time of Odin and the Aesir. And she was persistent, and she was strong, and she grabbed my bleeding wrist and wrapped the sleeve of her sweatshirt around it like a tourniquet, and all the time her voice in my head was repeating: *I've had enough of this. I've had enough of people like her. People who think that all they have to do is click their fingers to get what they want. People like Stella. People like you. Now pull yourself together and run!*

'Where to?' I said. 'There's nowhere.'

The ground at my feet was shining now, illuminated with my blood. I could see it on the grass, splashes, almost like runelight, shaping itself into patterns I knew.

'Look,' I said dizzily. 'Look, Jumps.'

But Jumps wasn't paying attention. She pushed to the forefront of our space, overrode my resistance. I could feel her energy, the fire that lived within her, the thing that lives in all of the Folk, but so seldom shows itself.

'Runes,' I told her. 'Look, runes—'

'Fuck the runes,' said Jumps. *'Run!'*

7

WE RAN BETWEEN THE GLOWING runes and made a dash for the firepit. Heidi came after us hard and fast. I heard her footsteps behind me. As we reached the pit I jumped, scattering embers around me, and in the confusion of sparks and ash I managed to gain some distance.

I'd deliberately chosen an escape route that would lead us away from Meg and her friends, as well as putting Stella at a disadvantage. Heidi's host favoured high-heeled shoes, and the footpath that led to the road was both muddy and treacherous. But Gullveig-Heid was quick and strong. She soon made up the lost ground. And I was weak with loss of blood; I could feel the sticky warmth on my arms, my fingers.

What had she done to me? Was it glam? Certainly, that rune-mark of hers suggested she had the power. Those runes on the ground – runes that had formed somehow through the shedding of blood – were only a part of a net of glam that I sensed closing around me.

And now I could feel her in my mind, as if an invisible fish-hook were dragging at my consciousness. *Naudr*, the Binder, slowed my steps; *Isa*, the Ice rune, froze my spine and filled my brain with needles—

Who the hell is this? said Jumps.

I explained Gullveig-Heid more fully, using a series of (somewhat alarming) snapshots, both of Ragnarók and what came before.

So fight her! said Jumps. *Turn round and fight!*

Great idea, I said. *Let me just get my magical sword. Oh, wait —*

I thought you knew how to do this, said Jumps. *I thought you fought at Ragnarók.*

I'm sorry? Did you not understand? I don't have a thing to fight her with. No weapons, no glam. What do you suggest? A quick game of Asgard!™?

The fish-hook was dragging me back now. I could feel Jumps starting to panic. I wasn't far from it myself – I knew Gullveig-Heid from the old days, and the word *mercy* wasn't in her vocabulary. Whatever she wanted from me, I was pretty sure that, as the gratuitous blood-letting suggested, it wasn't something I was going to enjoy giving up.

I had almost reached the road when Gullveig-Heid caught up with me. My head was spinning; my legs were weak; there was no strength left in me. To one side stood the dark mass of the Hill; to the other, the road, with its distant spray of orange lights, seemed a thousand miles away.

Heidi, still looking like springtime, gave me a pitying kind of smile.

'Don't be stubborn, Loki,' she said. 'You can do this the hard way if you like. But the hard way's going to hurt, and you know I'll win in the end.'

I stopped. My feet didn't work any more. My head was filled with fireworks. Jumps was trying to tell me something, but her voice seemed far away. Only Heidi mattered now. Heidi, smiling like the sun and shining like Otter's Ransom.

'Come on, Loki,' she said. 'We used to be good together. We used to trust each other. Don't you remember what Odin did? Promised you godhood, betrayed you and then sacrificed you to himself? Do you think you're here by accident? Do you think he's forgotten Ragnarók?'

144

Jumps' voice, from far away: *What the hell are you doing? Run!*

But running was out of the question. Where would I run to, anyway?

Heidi has a point, I said. *Odin doesn't want me. And to be honest, maybe he's right – I betrayed him at Ragnarók. So there were faults on both sides, but yeah. I basically brought down Asgard, destroyed the Nine Worlds and opened the way for Chaos to rule. I mean, who am I fooling? There's no coming back from that kind of thing. I thought that we could start again. Put Ragnarók behind us. But all he ever wanted was to use me as a sacrifice.*

I suddenly felt exhausted by this world, this body, these *feelings*. What did I think I was playing at, trying to be human? My head hurt; my arms hurt. All I wanted to do was surrender.

Er, what? Jumps said. *Surrender?*

You don't know what she can do, I said.

I don't give a crap about her, said Jumps. *You're supposed to be a rebel. So stop talking like an emo kid and show some guts, for Christ's sake!*

That stung. Jumps had no idea of what Heidi was capable. I turned down the volume of her tirade so that she was no more than a nagging whisper at the back of my mind. Then I fell to my knees on the path.

'That's right,' said Heidi softly. 'I'm not going to hurt you, or your host. I liked you, you know. I was sad when you fell. But I knew that one day you'd find an escape. You can't keep Wildfire a prisoner. That's what Odin wants, you know. To keep you under his control. To use you, as he used you before. To make you serve his purpose.'

Fuck's sake, Loki! Stand up!

I tried to ignore the nagging voice. But Jumps was difficult to ignore. Her presence in my mind cried out in protest at my weakness. But Heidi was irresistible. I looked up. She was smiling. From Stella's face, the full glamour of the Sorceress shone, like a shield of burnished gold.

'You don't have to be a sacrifice,' she said. 'We can be

145

partners. You and me, like the old days: drinking and fighting and making love. Don't you remember the old days?'

'I remember,' I told her.

'So come with *me*.' She reached out her hand. 'All you have to do is take my hand, come with me, and *dream*—'

In a dream, I held out my hand. Our fingers were almost touching. Her face, so bright, so radiant, was barely twelve inches from my own. I could feel the heat from her, like the heat from a glowing furnace.

'Oh, sweetheart,' said Heidi tenderly. 'This is going to be *such fun*—'

Suddenly I felt a jolt – as if someone had pushed me roughly aside. Jumps had wrested control from me and was back in the driver's seat. I found myself lurching to my feet. The glamours lifted from my eyes. Gone was the shining face of Desire, and in its place was Gullveig-Heid, in all her ancient malice. The one who had saved me from torment only to use me for her own ends. The one who had ordered the death of my wife – not that I cared much at the time, but Sigyn had been harmless, and innocent, and if I had a conscience (which luckily, I don't), her death, among all the other deaths I caused, might weigh on it more than a little. I won't pretend I wasn't afraid. But Jumps was oddly exultant. Couldn't she feel it? How could it be that I was weak, and she was not?

'Loki?' said Heidi.

'Fuck you,' said Jumps. 'Loki isn't available.'

Heidi raised an eyebrow. 'Oh. Think you can fight me, little girl? Loki knows better. Calm down. There's nothing for you to be afraid of.'

'Loki's afraid of you,' said Jumps. (Yeah, so shoot me. Maybe I was.)

Heidi smiled. 'Let's not talk about him,' she said. 'Let's talk about you. You want him gone. That *is* what you want, isn't it?'

'Maybe,' said Jumps.

'Then give him up.' The voice was soft, seductive as only

Gullveig-Heid knew how. 'Just let me take him back to the Hill. There's something there I need him to do.'

'And after that?'

'Go back to your girl. Forget all of this ever happened.'

The charm was working. I knew it was. I tried to beg for mercy. But I was frozen, helpless, mute; encased in a burning capsule of ice.

Jumps sighed. I could feel her resistance giving way. I should have known, I told myself. She was, after all, only human.

She said: 'Is Stella watching this? I mean, she's still in there, isn't she?'

'Of course she is,' said Gullveig-Heid.

'Then there's something I'd like to say.'

Heidi leaned forward. Jumps did, too.

Please, don't. I'll do anything, I whispered from my hiding-place.

I'm going to hold you to that, said Jumps.

And at that – don't ask me how – my host, my helpless, human, teenage host somehow summoned the fire-rune *Kaen,* swung it like a flaming *poi,* and flung it into Heidi's face in a shearing arc of runelight.

Heidi screamed. Her hair was on fire. Spikes of runelight speared the sky.

'Bitch. Don't fuck with my friends,' said Jumps. And then we turned and ran down the hill, and into the streets of Malbry.

8

HEIDI'S RAGE WAS A PSYCHIC blast that blossomed over Castle Hill. But this time, there was no pressure, no pain. Just a warning – *Trickster, you're toast* – and then Jumps' voice in my mind, shouting: *Whoooooo, I did it! Whoooooo!* as we raced through the back streets of Malbry.

We'd done the impossible, I thought. We'd somehow evaded Gullveig-Heid. Those high-heeled shoes of Stella's must have given us the edge. And I was wearing sneakers, which meant—

What do you mean? I kicked her ass!

I had to concede that indeed, she had. What I still didn't get, was how. I mean, I don't want to brag, but Jumps was only a human, and yet—

'You used a rune.' I said it aloud. It didn't make any more sense that way.

Whooooo! I kicked her aaaaaassss!

'You used a rune. You used *my* rune. *My* rune, the runemark *Kaen*, that Odin put on me back in the day. *You*, a human, used *my* rune, and—'

Relax. I found it in your mind. I thought it might be useful. And it was. I kicked her ass. Whoooooooooo! Whooooo!

'You're high,' I said.

Yes, said Jumps. *I'm high on Life.*

148

'Well, enjoy it while you can. Because she's gunning for both of us now, and trust me, what she doesn't know about suffering isn't worth knowing. In fact—' I paused for breath, and because something was nagging in my mind – something that Jumps had said, which in the heat of the moment and the excitement of using glam I hadn't wholly taken in—

'Er, hang on a minute,' I said. 'What did you mean, *don't fuck with my friends*?'

Oh, that. Nothing, said Jumps.

'No, it was something,' I told her. 'Wait, did you mean to imply that – maybe – *I* was your friend?'

No. Of course not.

'You did, though,' I said. 'I can read your mind.'

I doubt it, said Jumps. *It's in joined-up writing.*

I could have argued further. But I sensed that something had shifted – some balance of power, some pendulum-swing – and I wasn't sure in whose favour the mechanism was working. I started to think that maybe I should at least mention the fact that she'd saved my life – or rather, saved me from something a whole lot worse than dying – but I wasn't quite able to find the words. Yours Truly, the master of flattery and silver-tongued lord of deception, was suddenly short of things to say.

I took a deep breath. 'Er, Jumps,' I began.

It's OK, said Jumps. *You're welcome.*

Oh. 'Oh.'

I read your mind. Forget it. It's not like it's complicated, or anything.

We walked the rest of the way in silence.

9

B y the time we reached Evan's place, it was late. Heidi's enchantment was down to the dregs; I felt only a little light-headedness now, and a reckless kind of relief. I took the lift to Evan's flat, knocked on the door, and waited.

Evan was standing, but only just. He looked exhausted and in pain. His wheelchair was by the window. The dog Twinkle was eating something in the corner of the room. Otherwise, we were alone. His mother must be at work, I thought. He looked at me darkly for a moment, then beckoned me to enter.

'You idiot,' he said.

'Who, *me*?'

'I can smell it,' Odin said. 'I can smell the glam on you. What did she promise you? Power? Gold? Freedom from responsibility?'

I gave him a hard stare. 'So you knew? You *knew* that wasn't Freyja? You knew it was Heidi all along, and you never thought to tell me?'

'That's why I told you to keep away. I should have known you wouldn't.'

'By pretending Heidi was Freyja?'

He frowned. 'To be honest, I thought she *was* Freyja at first.

She led me to believe she was. And she had that runemark, of course. I guess I just saw what I wanted to see.'

What Evan wanted to see, said Jumps, with a touch of bitterness. *He's always been crazy about Stella. And Stella always let him believe that maybe, one day —*

I had to laugh. The General's soft spot for Freyja had cost him dearly, back in the day. Now it had blinded him again, allowing Heidi to slip through the net and work her plans against us.

Odin gave me a keen look. 'Care to tell me what happened?'

'You mean apart from almost bleeding to death?'

'Apart from that, yes,' said Odin.

'I was lucky. I got away,' I told him with heroic restraint. 'No thanks to you, apparently. And it never occurred to you to warn me, or trust me, or anything?'

He gave an oddly familiar shrug. Strange, to see the Old Man's face behind that of the young man: stranger still to hear his voice so clearly from another's throat.

'I did warn you,' he said grimly. 'Look how much attention you paid. And as for trust, it'll take more than five hundred years and a body change to make me trust you again. Wildfire burns; that's its nature. Isn't that right, Captain?'

'There were faults on both sides,' I said. 'Besides, if you need me, you'll have to try. I'm not going near Gullveig-Heid again until I know what she's up to.'

'Do *you* trust *me*?' said the Old Man.

'Not even a bit,' I told him.

He laughed at that. 'I've missed you,' he said. 'I never thought I'd say that, but it's good to have you by my side.' He sat down in his wheelchair. Beckoned me to join him. 'Sit down,' he said. 'I'm going to tell you something I've never told anyone before.'

'So, why would you tell me now?' I said. Knowledge is power. The Old Man, I knew, wasn't the type to give it away without an ulterior motive.

'Because, if I'd told you this from the start, when I first recruited you, we might have avoided some bloodshed.'

I raised my eyebrows. It wasn't often the General admitted to making a mistake. He must need something quite badly, I thought. I looked down at my bloodstained hands. The blood was mostly dry now that the wounds had closed again, but I was still feeling jumpy. I didn't know what Odin knew of the events on Castle Hill, but I was reluctant to ask him, for fear of losing the element of surprise. And yet I was buzzing with questions. Why did Heidi want my blood? What – or who – was under the Hill that made my sacrifice necessary?

The answer was unlikely to be straightforward. The queue of people after my blood had always been a long one, and even allowing for the carnage brought about by Ragnarók, the list was still extensive. One name did suggest itself, though. A name as familiar as my own, and someone almost as devious.

'Could this be about the Oracle?'

His silence suggested that maybe it was.

'Do you know where it is?'

'Not quite.'

'But it's something to do with that Hill. Right?'

Odin smiled. 'You're getting warm. I've been watching that Hill for some time.'

'Why?'

'Because there's something hidden there. Something that might mean a great deal.'

'Not the cat in the box again.'

He laughed. 'The box is a metaphor. The thing under the Hill is real. Although, like the cat, it can be several conflicting things at once. The problem is how to get to it.'

I thought of those runes on the grass of the Hill, and the way my blood had illuminated the thirsty soil. And then I thought about Mimir's Head, and how the General had sacrificed his friend for the sake of the Vanir runes.

'Why?' I said. 'What's under there?'

'Patience, Captain.' Odin smiled. 'Let me tell you my story.

It's a story you haven't heard before, which might explain a thing or two.'

And as the Old Man told his tale, I started to feel a sensation – a slow and creeping coldness running down my (*Jumps'*) spine. A feeling of discomfort – one more of those human sensations – that, after some uncertainty, I finally identified.

Fear? No; something colder.

Weltschmerz? I had to look that one up, but it didn't seem quite right either. It was only when Odin fell silent at last that I realized what it was. Not fear, or even anxiety —

The word I was looking for was *dread*.

Desire

Beware most of all your heart's desire.
Lokabrenna: 2:24

1

'At the start of the Elder Age,' said Odin, 'there were two warring tribes. The first were the Aesir, sons of Bór, led by Odin, Vili and Ve. The second were the Vanir, keepers of the Fire – or, as we call it, the Elder Script – the runes that make up the fabric of the Nine Worlds. But the Vanir kept their knowledge close, and would not share their powers.'

'*Quelle surprise,*' I murmured.

He smiled. 'And so Bór's youngest son set out to take the runes by stealth. He was young; he was naïve; the Vanir saw him coming. They took him captive and flung him into one of their dungeons. Then they sent word to Vili and Ve to demand a ransom in gold.'

My eyes were starting to widen. The legendary Vili and Ve were nothing but names to the Aesir. No one knew what had happened to them. No one alive remembered them. Oh, I'd had my suspicions, of course. But that's all they were. Suspicions.

'Gold, huh?'

He nodded. 'The Vanir always liked gold. So did Odin's brothers. So much that they were reluctant to pay the ransom the Vanir demanded.'

'I'm starting to see where this is going,' I said.

Odin ignored me and went on: 'Alone and afraid, Odin

157

waited for his brothers to answer the call. But Vili and Ve were oddly slow in coming to redeem him. Finally, Odin realized that he had been abandoned. A coldness came upon him, not of fear, but of anger. He may have been young, but he was no fool, and he started to look for a means of escape. In the dungeons, there was another prisoner whose ambitions had led to his fall. This prisoner was called Mimir.'

'Mimir the Wise?'

'The very same.' Odin's mouth twisted a little. 'Mimir promised to help him, in exchange for a place by his side. Odin agreed, and together they escaped and returned to the Aesir stronghold. From that moment, Mimir became Odin's closest counsellor. As for Vili and Ve, they soon succumbed to a fatal sickness, which killed them both, along with their wives and children, and all of their supporters.'

I grinned. 'I like this Odin,' I said. 'I wonder, what could have happened to him?'

The Old Man gave his blandest smile. 'With Mimir by his side, he became the architect of the Elder Age. The rest of the Aesir came to believe that Mimir was his uncle. And when, years later, Gullveig-Heid came to challenge the Aesir and to issue her ultimatum, no one suspected Mimir the Wise. You see, he had omitted to mention that he knew the visitor. Knew her rather well, in fact. Gullveig-Heid was his daughter.'

'His *daughter*?'

Odin nodded. 'Mimir was not originally from the tribe of the Vanir. He was one of the Rock Folk; a man of great wisdom and learning. But his ambition to master the runes led him onto a dangerous path. He married one of the Vanir, hoping to learn their secrets from her, but was caught out by her people before he could achieve his desire. But now he had a daughter, and she was all he had hoped for. Powerful, ruthless, clever and as ambitious as he was himself.'

'Did she know about Mimir?'

He shrugged. 'I never knew for sure,' he said. 'But after she

158

left, Odin began to question Mimir's loyalty. He would vanish for days at a time, with no explanation, giving only evasive answers to Odin's questions. He had some dubious connections among the Rock Folk and the Ice People. And he spoke increasingly of an alliance with the Vanir: of an exchange of hostages; of our chance to possess the runes. And so at last I conceived a plan to keep him for ever by my side, and yet which would curb his ambition for good.' He shrugged. 'Well, you know how that ended.'

I did. With Mimir's severed head, kept alive in a cradle of runelight. A slave to Odin's ambitions; a sacrifice; an Oracle.

'You planned that from the start?' I said.

He sighed. 'Oh, don't sound so surprised. Mimir was a piece of work. I used him when it suited me – but don't think it wasn't mutual. If I hadn't caught him in time, that might have been *my* Head, not his, prophesying Ragnarók.'

I let that one go. It made my head ache. Mimir, as Allfather?

'It's what he wanted,' Odin said. 'He'd always been ambitious. And he'd been so certain the Vanir wouldn't suspect or recognize him when he returned to their camp as my ambassador. To be fair, he was right. He'd left their camp as a young man. He returned as an old one. But all it took was a word or two, delivered by my ravens, to put them on the alert again. They sent me his head as a token – and of course, by then, the runes were ours. The Aesir–Vanir alliance was born.'

I thought about that. It explained a few things. And I'd always known Odin was sneaky. In fact, if I'd known just *how* sneaky he was, we might never have ended up enemies. But however interesting all this might be, it didn't explain what Gullveig-Heid wanted from me in particular. Revenge against Odin, yes, I got that. Even though Mimir had hardly been much of a parent, it went some way to explaining her rage, her split from the rest of the Vanir. What it didn't explain was why she wanted Yours Truly.

'Because she wants the new runes. The runes the Oracle

159

foretold. They are the key to a new World. And she will do anything to possess them.'

The dread I mentioned earlier was starting to kick in by then. 'Why me? I don't have them,' I said. *'New runes will come to Odin's heirs.* Am I Odin's heir? No. Did anyone ever give her the impression I was *likely* to be Odin's heir?'

'No,' said Odin gently. 'But you were the one who had Mimir's Head on the day of Ragnarók. You were the last one to speak to it. Gullveig-Heid may think you know where it is.'

'I threw the damn thing off Bif-rost. It could have landed anywhere.'

Well, I knew that wasn't *quite* what had happened. This tale (which rang true enough in terms of Odin's sneakiness) was, I suspected, some kind of ploy to get me on his side again. Possibly to make me divulge any knowledge I might have of the whereabouts of Mimir's Head, and thereby of the New Runes. Of course I hadn't told him about the scene on Castle Hill, and the way my blood had cast runeshapes on the thirsty ground at my feet. So shoot me – I haven't survived this long by trusting folk like the General.

Odin looked sceptical. 'A pity,' he said. 'While I believe your story, I suspect Gullveig-Heid will not.' *Which doesn't look good for you,* he meant, although he didn't say so. He didn't *have* to say so: his eye gleamed with quiet menace.

I said: 'I don't know where it is. And even if I did know, we left that Head in another World, a World that you and I have no means of reaching.'

That gleam again, like a firefly in the eye of a marble. 'I wouldn't say that,' said Odin.

'What?'

'There may be another way out of this World. A way to return to the one that we left.'

That sounded *far* too attractive to be entirely straightforward. 'How?'

Odin smiled. 'In every World, there have been places of

power. Places where lines of energy cross. A place where such lines of power converge might possibly also exist, in some form, in any number of other Worlds.'

I thought of that vapour-trail in the sky; the one that looked like a runemark. 'Let me guess. You mean the Hill?'

'You saw it yourself; you felt it.'

'I did.' Once more I almost considered telling Odin about the scars on Jumps' arms, and the fact that she'd thrown a rune-bolt, and the way my blood had summoned runes on the open hillside, then I decided against it. I still wasn't sure what he wanted of me, and knowing Odin, I guessed he wasn't telling me everything he knew.

'So, what you're saying is, keep away from the Hill. Because only an idiot would risk facing that kind of power. Right?'

Odin shook his head. 'No, Captain. That's *not* what I'm saying.'

'Oh.' I wasn't really surprised. Give the Old Man a choice between an easy, if restricted, life of jam tarts, cold beer, sleep and shopping, with the promise of sex with Meg thrown in, and the likelihood of being torn apart by intersecting lines of force, he'd take the peril every time. That was the thing about Odin: he could never resist a gamble. And if he was risking my life with his, all the better. My life, plus the lives of our hosts, which I assumed they valued almost as much as we did ourselves.

Hang on a minute. What was that?

That was Jumps, who until then had been immersed in some kind of distant reverie, and now snapped to attention. I sought a reassuring lie, but she sensed it before it could take shape.

Don't lie!

I—

Yes, you were!

'OK. I admit, I was going to lie. I was going to say not to worry. And you shouldn't, because I'm going to keep as far away from that Hill as I can. Because I don't have a death wish. So your lines of power can jolly well do one, because there's no

161

way I'm risking what we have for anyone, or anything.'

Odin raised an eyebrow. 'Your host?'

'My host believes, quite rightly,' I said, 'that the life we share should not be a pawn or gambling-chip. I happen to concur, by the way.'

Odin looked impatient. 'Don't think that you or your host have a choice. If you don't go after what's under that Hill before Gullveig-Heid comes after you—'

'I'm not afraid of her,' said Jumps.

'You should be,' Odin said grimly. 'Because she, too, is short of time. Every moment she spends in her host's body is a risk. She's here for the runes of the New Script. And she's not taking any prisoners.'

Prisoners. The word clanged alarmingly in my mind. At the same time, I felt Jumps tense, as if she'd had the same as yet unspoken thought. We'd escaped Heidi's clutches on the Hill, but there was someone else out there, someone Heidi knew about—

'Oh, shit,' I said.

In our shared space, Jumps echoed the sentiment.

'Jumps, I'm sorry,' Odin said, and suddenly he was Evan again: Evan, as sincere as the General was sneaky. 'You were never meant to be a part of this, but I promise, you'll be totally fine. You know I'd never go along with anything that could hurt you. You might not understand that now, but—'

Then his expression flickered, and he was the General again. 'Enough of that,' he said briskly. 'Let's leave this to those who know. Castle Hill is a passing-place, a crossroads between many Worlds. We know that there is power here; maybe the kind of power that could take us back to our own World. It is vital that you and I harness this power before Gullveig-Heid unlocks its secrets for herself. And that's why there is no time to lose. We have to—'

Just then, the phone began to ring. A shrill, persistent trilling.

Odin picked up. 'Yes? Hello?'

He listened for a moment. Then he put the receiver down and turned to me with a twisted smile. 'That was Gullveig-Heid,' he said. 'She tells me to tell you Meg says hi.'

2

THERE WAS A LONG AND rather fraught silence, in which I felt a little awkward, Odin sat in his wheelchair, and Jumps bounced around our shared space like a cat in a baking-oven, shouting *Meg, she's got Meg,* as if the thought hadn't occurred to me; as if it wasn't obvious; as if it wasn't already twisting my guts like a wet rag.

'What exactly did she say?' I said, when I managed to form the words.

'She's holding your friend,' said Odin. 'Meg is unhurt, and will remain so as long as you meet Gullveig-Heid at Castle Hill within the hour.'

For a moment I joined in the bouncing act. '*Me?* What does she want with *me?' Apart from blood, of course,* I thought.

'Possibly something to do with the fact that you were the last to see Mimir's Head—'

'So *what?*' I started to pace. The dog Twinkle looked up hopefully.

'So,' said Odin. 'Perhaps she thinks that you might know how to find it.'

'Well, she's wrong,' I told him. 'This is where you should have said: *Who, Loki? Don't be absurd. Besides, I have no idea where he is. He might have left the country. In fact, I'm pretty sure I saw*

164

him heading for the airport on his way to somewhere warm—'

Odin shrugged. 'This is your fault,' he said. 'You were the one who went off-piste. You disobeyed my orders. You were too busy having fun, going on dates, eating jam tarts—'

'Excuse me,' I said. 'If asked to describe this learning curve, *fun* isn't the first word I'd choose. There might have been small pleasures, yes, but there were also feelings, exams, parents, teachers, mean girls, a grandmother and something called yoghurt—'

Odin gave me a quelling glance. 'Also,' he said, 'the weapon I was *planning* to use in our defence against Gullveig-Heid has been rendered useless, thanks to your paranoid antics—'

'Who, *me*?' I was indignant.

'Well, this is the point at which we could probably have used the Thunderer, in some Aspect other than that of a fluffy white dog.'

In the corner, Twinkle barked. Even his bark sounded harmless. I put my head – Jumps' head – in my hands. 'This isn't my fault!' I wailed. 'I never asked for any of this!'

'You threw Mimir's Head off the bridge. You involved Meg. You lost us Thor. You partnered up with Gullveig-Heid. Just whose fault *is* it, then?'

I racked my brains for an answer. For some reason, there wasn't one. Inside our shared space, Jumps was still bouncing around, repeating: *Meg, she's got Meg!*

'*Do* shut up. I'm trying to think. It's hard enough being trapped in here – which, to be perfectly frank with you, is hardly the mind palace I have been accustomed to – without having you climbing the walls like a sackful of squirrels,' I said.

I don't suppose she realized the severity of my words. With her love of small animals, I suppose she might even have taken it as a compliment, whereas anyone who knows me knows that next to snakes, and possibly lutes, I detest squirrels most of all. Anyway, she ignored the gibe, but mercifully stopped the bouncing.

'Now to think of a plan,' I said. 'Preferably a plan that includes saving Meg, whilst keeping as far away from Gullveig-Heid as possible.'

You'll have to do as she says, said Jumps. *You'll have to give her what she wants.*

'And what if what she wants is my blood? And yours?'

Odin shrugged. 'I'm sure you'll think of something. After all, if she wanted us dead, she would have killed us already.'

'Good point,' I told him gloomily. 'Death's probably too good for us.'

Odin gave his twisted smile. 'There's only one way to find out,' he said.

'You mean, you've got a plan?'

He said: 'You'll have to get to Mimir's Head before Gullveig-Heid gets her hands on it.'

'That all?' I said. 'Oh well, that's fine. I thought you might be asking for something *really* difficult.'

'That sounded like sarcasm,' Odin said.

'Really? I can't imagine why.'

I could feel Jumps getting impatient. *Is there a way of doing that?*

'Oh, there's a way,' I told her. 'Unfortunately, the way involves my crossing between Worlds, which option is sadly unavailable, Bif-rost having fallen, and my own powers being, shall we say, somewhat depleted?'

But the General thought otherwise. I could tell by the way he turned to me, a gleam in his single living eye. I felt a lurching sensation somewhere in the region of my solar plexus, as if in anticipation of a blow.

'You're right, of course,' he told me. 'And yet, there may be other ways to cross between the Worlds. Your offspring, Sleipnir, had that skill.'

For Jumps' benefit, I sketched a new entry in the Book of Faces. *Sleipnir: Eight-legged horse with a foot in all Worlds, except for Pandaemonium. Unnatural offspring of Loki and Svadilfari. So*

166

shoot me, yes: I'm a mother. Likes: grass, oats, hay, sugar lumps, trav-
elling between Worlds. Dislikes: the usual. You know: giants. demons,
snakes, the dead. And squirrels. Bloody squirrels.

I looked at Odin. 'So?' I said. 'Sleipnir fell at Ragnarók.'

Odin shook his head. 'Not quite. You know how I mentioned energies? Places where lines of power converge?'

I nodded. His one living eye gleamed.

'The Hill is one of these places. A place that exists very close to *our* World. Perhaps it's even the *same* place, built on some tributary of Dream, linked by something as powerful as the gods themselves—'

'Please tell me you're not suggesting we try to cross between the Worlds, without glam, riding an eight-legged Horse that might not even be there?' I said.

'I *could* say that,' said the General. 'But that would make me a liar.'

'You *are* a liar,' I told him. 'You're almost as good a liar as me, and I do mean that as a compliment.'

He smiled again. There was nothing warm in that smile: just a kind of brightness, like the sun on treacherous ice.

'As you are aware,' he said, 'Sleipnir was at Ragnarók, inasmuch as a being with a foot in all Worlds can ever be in a single place. I gave him orders, in case I fell. I told him to wait for my return. And during my time in Netherworld, I scanned all of Dream for signs of him, or traces of his passage.'

'And you think he's here?' I said.

'I sensed his presence from the start, the first time I saw Castle Hill. Just as you sensed him yesterday, when you saw that sign in the sky. Some places are attractive. Places where the Worlds connect, like the cells in a piece of honeycomb. Castle Hill is one of these; a place that exists in more than one World, connected by lines of energy. And yes, I believe that by following it, we can get back to our own World.'

'So why haven't *you* followed it?' I said.

He shrugged. 'Believe me, if I'd had the glam, I would have

done that long ago. But without a functioning runemark—'

'Well, I don't have one either!' I said.

'That's not quite true, is it?' he said. 'Jumps, if you'd kindly show me your arm.'

'I'd rather not,' I told him.

Jumps scowled and pushed up my sleeve, exposing that ladder of silvery scars, almost obscured now with fresh blood. No, not quite a runemark, and yet I could see the shape of *Kaen*, bastardized and broken. And was it my imagination, or was the scar slightly *luminous*, as if, under the skin, something were trying to make itself visible?

Odin smiled. 'Well, would you look at that. The force of the energies under the Hill is already starting to work on you.'

I shook my head.

He smiled again. 'No time to waste. This is your cue. Remember, Gullveig-Heid has your friend.'

Jumps was getting impatient. She turned towards Odin in his chair. 'I suggest,' she said aloud, 'that we go find this Mimir's Head, use it to ransom Meg, then *you* get out of my life for good, taking your friends – *all* of them – with you. OK?'

I tried to convey how totally *not* OK all of that sounded. But Odin seemed not to see me. Instead Evan leaned forward, once more addressing Jumps. 'You'll trust me?' he said. 'I promise you, I never meant to involve you in this. You were never meant to be Loki at all. But now that you *are*—'

Er, no.

Once more Evan's face reflected his inner conflict. 'I *had* to go along with it,' he said in a low and earnest voice. 'Because of Stella. You know that, right? And yes, I know I let you down—'

Behind that door marked STELLA, I felt a kind of mental surge, as if of feelings held in powerful check. But her voice was calm as she said:

'Don't worry about that now. I'm fine. And as for Loki—' She paused for a moment. I sensed her determination. Then, addressing Odin, she said: 'If he won't help, then I'll do it myself.

I know him now. I can read his thoughts. I don't need him to cooperate.'

Odin smiled. It was the same damn smile he'd worn when he called me out of Chaos, promised me the Nine Worlds, then proceeded to mess me up from Asgard to the End of the Worlds.

'Looks like we've got a plan,' he said.

No, please. You don't understand—

But Odin was already moving his chair towards the door of the flat. 'It's really very simple,' he said. 'All you need to do is trust me.'

3

T RUST ME. IF I'D HAD A JAM TART every time Odin told me that, I'd be the size of Jormungand. And I had no intention of trusting him – or indeed his host, whose feelings for Stella seemed as complicated as the Old Man's for the erstwhile Goddess of Desire. I get it; those feelings are treacherous, and so are the people who feel them. I made a note to myself to ensure that Odin was nowhere near Gullveig-Heid when whatever was under the Hill finally revealed itself. His host was a liability in more ways than his physical state: his feelings for Stella made him weak, which made the General equally so.

But Odin wasn't looking good. He – or rather, Evan – was even paler than usual. His hand on the wheel of the metal chair shook like that of an old man. He looked exhausted, with the fatigue that comes from enduring chronic pain. I happen to know that sensation well. It isn't one of my favourites.

I felt Jumps' concern for Meg shift again sharply to her friend. 'Are you OK?' she said.

Oh, I'm great. Apart from being hunted by Gullveig-Heid, the most ruthless and unpredictable demon this side of Netherworld —

'I'm talking to Evan, idiot.'

Evan smiled. 'I'm fine, Jumps.'

'No, you're not! I can *tell* you're not! He's been pushing you too hard. You shouldn't even have been in school, the way you've been for the past few days. And now, with all this—'

'Relax. All I need is a bit of fresh air, and maybe a couple of Tramadol—'

'How do I know you're even *here*?'

I caught a glimpse of her thoughts, like a thread of smoke from behind one of those doors. An image – not a flattering one – of herself and Evan, marionettes in the hands of giants.

Hey! I protested.

Bite me, said Jumps. *Your General needs to understand. Evan isn't like other people. He sometimes overdoes things. He doesn't always tell you if he gets tired. He needs to rest. Your General seems to think he can just find another host if this one breaks down.*

To be honest, I hadn't really thought all that much about the condition of Odin's host. But now the Book of Faces opened to give me the details – far more than I could possibly need – of Evan's good days, his bad days, the days when even to breathe was an almost impossible burden; and worse, the days when no one really believed he was ill, because he looked fine, and could walk, and run—

But it was always there, she said. *That thing that was hiding inside him. Waiting to steal whatever it could, whatever joy it could take away. Not unlike the thing that's inside him now, feeding on his energies.*

She turned back to Evan. 'You can't go now. It'll kill you,' she said.

Evan waved aside her concern. 'Pain is boring. *Dying* is boring. *This*, on the other hand, is interesting. *Important*. Don't worry. Trust me, I'm fine.'

I was just about to retaliate with a finely crafted epithet when there came the rattling sound of keys in the door. I turned, the dog Twinkle set up a joyous barking, and there was Evan's mum at the door, looking surprised and not too pleased.

'What's going on in here?' she said.

I searched through the Book of Faces for details of Evan's mother. *Name: Jan. Profession: nurse. Favourite colour: sky-blue. Favourite film:* Dirty Dancing. *Divorced, now seeing a married man, a doctor, who keeps promising to leave his wife, but never will.*

I cursed, finding little of use.

Meanwhile, Jumps took over, smiled, and said: 'Hi, Mrs Davis.'

Davis. That's what I needed. This filing system could do with some work.

Jumps ignored me. Evan said: 'Just playing a game, Mum.'

Mrs Davis gave him a look. 'You know my shift,' she told him. 'I have to be up at six-thirty.'

'Sorry, Mum. We got carried away.' Evan gave a cheery smile. That's how I knew it was Odin's smile, and trusted it accordingly. 'Let me make you a cup of tea before you go to bed. OK? And maybe a toasted sandwich?'

Mrs Davis nodded. 'Thanks.' She took off her shoes and sat down on the couch. 'That's better.' She turned to me. 'Sorry to snap at you, Josephine. But maybe you should be getting home? Do your parents know where you are?'

I said: 'It's fine, Mrs Davis. I was just leaving anyway.'

Odin gave me a piercing look. 'I'll walk you back.'

'Oh no, you won't!' Mrs Davis gave him a look. 'And what have you been doing? Why are you in your chair again? Did you eat? Did you take your meds?'

'Mum, I feel fine, honestly.' But Mrs Davis could see it now. He looked ready to collapse. The last couple of days must have taken it out of him more than I'd expected. I felt something odd and unprecedented, almost like compassion —

'It's fine,' I said. 'I promise. Don't worry. I'll be back in the morning.'

And so we left, Jumps and I, into the mild and starry night, in search of something I had lost centuries and Worlds away. And frankly, it should have stayed lost. I knew that, just as Odin did. But that damned bauble had a way of coming back, against all odds. And this time, I had to find it: for myself, for Meg, and now for Jumps, whose life was now inextricably linked with mine – or at least until parted by Death, Dream, Damnation or maybe just Desire—

4

Now here's the thing about Desire. It never goes out of fashion. War, Famine and Pestilence can sometimes be kept under control, but Desire is only one step from Dream, and as such can never be far from our hearts. I'd wondered more than once since my arrival in this World why Freyja, rather than Frigg, or Sif, figured so prominently in the game that had provided my means of escape from bondage into this borrowed flesh. It's not that she wasn't a warrior – in spite of her airs and graces she could be as savage as Gullveig-Heid in the heat of battle. And Freyja was *popular* in this World – although her representation in various books and movies of Jumps' failed to take into account her basically treacherous nature.

But she was one of the Vanir – the tribe that gave us Gullveig-Heid. The tribe that gave us the original runes. And although the plot of *Asgard!*™ was absurd in many ways, I couldn't help remembering that in *this* version of Ragnarók, some of the gods had survived the War, and waited, sleeping, under the ice. Could this have happened in *our* World? Could the Vanir be under the Hill?

Stop it, said Jumps. *You're making my head ache. And besides, what does it matter? We're going to the Hill anyhow. Because you can't not do it.*

174

She was right, of course. The Hill had an undeniable appeal. That runemark, scratched against the sky. The Hill itself, like a treasure mound. And now that scar, like a runemark, shining out from Jumps' wrist as she had flung the runebolt. I'll admit, it excited me. The thought of gaining my power back; of being in my natural Aspect; of once more seeing the World I had shaped, the World in which I'd been worshipped—

Actually, I was thinking of Meg, said Jumps.

Well, duh. So was I. And yes, there was Meg: Meg, whom Heidi had rightly identified as the chink in my armour. *That's why it's a mistake to start caring about people*, I thought, although just *how* I had managed to do that was still as much of a mystery as ever. I blamed Jumps, and her feelings, and the fact that they had somehow infected me.

But they were *supposed* to infect me, I knew. Gullveig-Heid had seen to that. And Gullveig-Heid, I also knew, was the mistress of deception and greed. That's why I was on my guard as I approached the Hill from the far side, keeping under cover of gorse bushes and fallen rocks. My precautions were unnecessary. Arriving at the summit once more, we found it deserted and silent. The firepit had died to a glow. There was no sign of Heidi or Meg, or any remnant of glamour. Gone were those runes on the ground; even the blood that I had spilled had been absorbed without a trace.

Below us, in the valley, the lights of Malbry twinkled and shone, looking very far away, although it was only a couple of miles. I checked my arms. They seemed fine. No burning sensation; no bleeding. In the dim light, my scars just looked like scars again, all luminescence vanished.

'There's no one here. What a pity,' I said.

No you don't, said Jumps. *You're not going anywhere until you've found whatever it is you're supposed to find. You're doing this for Meg. And me. And Evan. And your General.*

I sighed. *I liked you better when you were neurotic and insecure. There's something here. Evan said so. Look for a sign!*

175

'Whatever.'

I looked. The Hill was a kind of dome, rising from a gentler slope. Below, mostly fields and woodland, with a path leading down to a country road. A five-day moon was rising, casting only a thread of light, but I saw that the top of the Hill was bare, except for the ruins of the castle from which it apparently took its name. As castles went, it was nothing much. Just a line of earthworks, a trench and a single squat tower was all that remained, and yet, now that I came to look, there was energy in the place: a charge that seemed to run through the air like a seam of something combustible.

What is it? said Jumps. She could feel it too. That silvery edge in the air, like a blade. That deep and mysterious energy.

'I don't know. But there's something here. I think it's to do with the castle.'

Go closer.

I followed the earthworks. The trench was a line of spilled ink along the crest of Castle Hill. I could easily imagine something asleep under the ground: a serpent with its stony spine coiled around a giant head —

Uneasily, I wondered how long Jormungand would take to escape. *Asgard!*™ was a fortress, but even so, it wouldn't take much for him to find a way out of the game. Jormungand, like Sleipnir, was able to travel between the Worlds. I wondered whether he'd come after me. It seemed depressingly likely.

I shivered. It was cold up there. In the sky, a scatter of stars. I looked for the Dog Star. It wasn't there. Not that I'd really expected my star to be visible in this alien world, though it might have been nice to have seen it. But there was nothing familiar in the bleak and scuddy sky. Just that yellow slice of moon, like something you'd find in a gin-and-tonic.

Slowly I became aware that my arm was hurting again. I gritted my teeth and continued to search along those lines of energy —

'Ouch! *Dammit!*' My sleeve was wet. Warmth soaked once

more through the fabric, sticking it to my cold skin. I pushed up my sleeve to look at my arm. Sure enough, the runemark was back, and with it, that dim violet glow. The blood, which in moonlight should have looked black, was subtly, darkly luminous.

It's working! said Jumps.

Oh, joy, I said.

But she was right. Whatever it was had started to gather momentum. Blood has power – she knew that. Even such common blood as hers. But the blood of a god was something more. Mimir's blood had bought us the runes. Ymir's blood, spilled by Odin's hand, had created the oceans.

But why did it have to be you? said Jumps. *Why couldn't Heidi have done it herself? Or Odin, for that matter?*

I took a breath. My arm still hurt. The violet glow intensified: it seemed to be lighting up my veins. I could feel Jumps, in our shared space, questioning me persistently. But now my head was filled with light. My wounded arm was sleeved in light, dripping slowly to the ground. And now, at last, at my feet, I could see something shining out from a crack in the earth – the familiar shape of the Chaos-rune *Kaen* – the rune that Odin had given me.

And now I could feel a response from the Hill, like a giant stirring from sleep. Something had been given life – I hoped at not too great a cost to Yours Truly, pain and self-sacrifice not being two of my favourite pastimes.

What is it? Is it Sleipnir? Jumps was bouncing around in my head.

'I don't know. Maybe. Yes.' I said.

The truth is, a mother never forgets giving birth to her first-born. The blood, the mess, the suffering – frankly it was appalling, and I'd hoped never to do it again. No doubt this was the reason why Odin had sent me in his place: his host was weak, and might not survive the trauma of birthing Sleipnir. The runemark *Kaen* shone out with a light that seemed to come from deep in the ground. And now I could see a cluster of hair-line cracks around the mark, as if something under the skin of the Hill were straining to be released —

'Runes,' I said. 'Or maybe *reins.*'

Reins?

'As in riding a Horse,' I said.

5

LIKE I SAID, THE BLOOD of a god is potent stuff. Even one such as I – half god, half demon, all renegade – must carry some of that power, and when the god in question happens to be the parent of a being that can travel between the Worlds, his blood can suddenly acquire an unexpected value.

This must have been the plan, I thought. To bring me into proximity with my eight-legged offspring; to harness his power to spill my blood, and use our close connection to bring Sleipnir out of his long sleep; and then to use him to hunt for the Oracle. But Sleipnir was born to obey no one but his master – and, of course, Yours Truly, although I'd never been much of a parent. Heidi knew that she'd never survive awakening Sleipnir without me, which was probably why I was still alive, rather than lining the interior of a cistern somewhere deep in World Below. Once she had what she wanted, however, all bets were likely to be off, which was why I was thinking furiously as I searched for the reins to Odin's Horse.

Now that I knew what to look for, the second rune was easier to find. The General's Horse has a foot in each World, except for Pandaemonium, as the runes that controlled it would reflect. *Bjarkán*, for the world of Dream, shone dimly at my fingertips:

then three feet away came the runeshape *Yr*:

then *Raedo, Logr* and *Naudr*, shining out of the ground like gold . . .

I sensed Jumps' impatience, and tried to explain as best I could, although my own impatience was almost too much to contain. There was still no sign of Gullveig-Heid, and yet I could feel her presence there, waiting for me to uncover the thing that currently slept between the Worlds.

'The runes,' I told Jumps, 'were originally given to the Aesir by Odin, long ago, in the Golden Age. They were the marks of knowledge, the language of Creation. Not even Surt understood what they were, although they were from his element; volatile and adaptable. The gods in those days each had a runemark of their own, though Odin had knowledge of them all; a knowledge he bought at the price of his eye, and the life of his oldest friend. My own Aspect was governed by the rune *Kaen*, which means Wildfire or Chaos. And when I fell, it was broken, just as I was, on Ida's plain. Just as all of us fell, and were lost, and our power was shattered and dispersed.'

So why do you have it back? said Jumps.

'Good question. Of course, I *don't* have it back. This mark is reversed, which means that it has only a fraction of its glam. But that was enough, in this World, to lead me to the honeypot. Sleipnir's presence did the rest, awakening this runemark, weak and broken as it is.' I flexed my mental muscles. 'Well, a broken rune's better than no rune at all. Why look an eight-legged horse in the mouth?'

You think Sleipnir's really in there?

I sensed her doubt – I'd shared it. But the runes were there to confirm the tale. *Hagall*, the Destroyer, and Ós, the rune of the gods of Asgard, shone out brightly from left and right.

I counted eight of the runes in all, I thought; a rune for each of the eight legs of a being that straddles all of Eight Worlds—

But didn't Sleipnir fall with the gods?

'One Aspect of him, maybe. Nevertheless, one part of him is always in Death: just as another part of him is always in Dream. That's how the General could cross between Worlds. That's how we can do the same.'

But something had occurred to me. Something was making me nervous, and had since I arrived here. Odin's pursuit of the Oracle. Odin's knowledge of this World. And the fact that Odin had already *known* that Gullveig-Heid was in Stella—

What *else* had he known? What plans had he made? What had the Oracle told him, before the darkness of Chaos fell? What runes had he cast, supplies laid by for the long, long winter? And, if he already *knew* how to find Sleipnir under the Hill, then why the hell hadn't he done it himself?

For a moment, I tried to marshal my thoughts. My mind was a snarl of barbed wire. From the first, I'd struggled with the thought that my presence here was simply a happy accident; that Odin had wanted Thor, not me; that I was never a part of his plan. But that didn't sound like the General. What if Odin had known from the start that summoning me would set this chain of events into motion? What if everything – my presence here, my close escape from Heidi, even my friendship with Meg – had been part of a long con to bring him what he wanted?

The Oracle? said Jumps. *The runes?*

'That's what I believed at first. But remember the game of *Asgard!*™? Remember the sleeping Vanir? What if those sleeping gods were buried somewhere in *our* World – a world linked to this one by this Hill, this castle, these lines of energy? What if Odin did a deal? The Vanir in exchange for the New Runes? *New runes will come to Odin's heirs.* That's what the Oracle prophesied. But what if the runes were his bargaining-chip, his way of controlling Gullveig-Heid? What if he sold his inheritance for a greater, more valuable prize?'

Like what? said Jumps. *It doesn't make sense. What could be more precious to him than the New Runes?*

I let her work it out for herself. 'What's the thing that doesn't make sense? How did Odin connect with his host? What's the thing, that, apparently, makes the whole of this World go round?'

Love?

Jumps was silent for a beat. Then she said aloud: 'Oh, fuck.'

'Well, quite,' I said softly. My mind was already racing; making connections, imagining things too dreadful to articulate. I told you, Odin has never been rational where the goddess of Desire was concerned. Imagine if the General's plan had been to liberate Freyja from Dream. Imagine if the plan had gone wrong; that Gullveig-Heid had taken her place. Odin had already told me that he had at first *thought* she was Freyja. Imagine if Odin and Gullveig-Heid had come to some agreement. Perhaps the Head of Mimir in exchange for the rest of the Vanir? And imagine if Yours Truly – and, by close connection, Jumps – had been a pawn in their game from the start; a pawn, intended for sacrifice?

Evan wouldn't do that, said Jumps.

'Why ever not?' I told her. 'After all, there's a precedent. The Runes of the Elder Script came at a price. Odin sacrificed his friend to gain the knowledge he needed. And then he used his new-found skills to bring him back, as the Oracle. Now we're not exactly *friends* nowadays, but I *can* deliver the New Runes.

And when he has them, what's to stop Heidi from doing to me – to *us* – just what was done to Mimir the Wise?'

For a moment Jumps was lost for words. *But that would be—*

'That would be Odin,' I said.

And yes, I thought; that would be Odin. Odin, who called me out of Dream to do his bidding one last time. Who knew my bond with Sleipnir. Who knew that my presence on the Hill would release what lay beneath, and open the way to another World—

Odin, maybe. Not Evan, said Jumps. *Evan would never hurt me.*

'Not even for Stella?'

I sensed her doubt.

'It's OK,' I said. 'I've got a plan. All we need to do is make sure that Heidi's never alone with the Oracle. That way, the New Runes – and therefore Meg – are safe until I figure out a good way to get Heidi out of her human host, and Odin out of his, although I'll concede that it sounds like a juggling act, rather than an *actual* plan, but, trust me—'

'You're babbling,' said Jumps. 'What plan? You don't have a plan.'

I shrugged. 'Of course I do,' I said. 'I'm naturally inventive. That's why the Old Man enlisted me from Chaos in the first place. That's why he brought me to Asgard, to do the things that no one else could do. That's why he let me live, when all the others were after my blood. And that's why I'm always one step ahead, in spite of all his scheming, because everything the Old Man knows about lying, conniving and trickery, he knows because I taught him. I'm Loki, son of Laufey. And I *always* have a plan.'

A pretty rousing speech, I thought, which ought to reassure my host. I could tell that Jumps was impressed. I gave myself a little bow.

And then, just then, from behind me, there came the sound of clapping. A fairly innocuous sound, you'd think, except in the context of that deserted Hill, with the river of stars above me and that runemark shining out from my arm. I turned, and saw Odin, in his chair, with the fluffy dog Twinkle beside him.

'Ah,' I said, and closed my eyes. I wasn't even surprised, somehow; just incredibly tired.

'Always so modest,' said Odin, and I could hear the smile in his voice. 'Always so self-effacing.'

I kept my eyes closed. It didn't really help, but that way I could still pretend that my worst fears hadn't been realized.

And then I heard another voice, as troubling as incense: 'I warned you, Loki, didn't I? I *said* he wasn't on your side.'

'Yes, Heidi. You did,' I said. 'Please tell me Meg isn't with you.'

Heidi laughed. 'Of course she's here. Would I leave her out of this? Say hello to Loki, Meg.'

'Hello to Loki,' someone said.

I opened my eyes, and there she was, standing behind Odin's chair. The Golden One in full Aspect, unveiled, and as full of poison as a spitting cobra. And next to her was Margaret, looking like a sleepwalker, staring at me with no sign of recognition in her eyes. I guessed at once that she had been charmed – only Heidi's glamours would have given her such tranquillity – but inside me, Jumps was bouncing like a squirrel piñata covered in firecrackers. For a moment I was lost for words. To my shame, my silver tongue had turned to paper in my mouth.

Odin looked at me and smiled.

'How well you know me, Captain,' he said. 'How well you divined my intentions. Of course, it's what I expected from you; and rarely do you disappoint. So tell me,' he said in a silky voice. 'What *exactly* is this plan?'

6

T HE MOMENT SPUN OUT LIKE the threads of our lives in the hands of the blind Norns. It was humiliating to say so, but, caught as I was, I had no choice.

'Yeah. I don't have a plan,' I said.

'I thought as much,' said Gullveig-Heid. 'You're as much of a liar as ever. But congratulations on working out so much of ours. Odin thought you might figure it out,' she went on. 'That's why we followed you here. Just to make sure you didn't try anything – *unpredictable.*'

I narrowed my eyes at Odin. 'I thought *you* were having a bad day.'

'Oh, I was,' said Odin. 'But I had some help.'

Inside our shared space I could feel Jumps climbing the walls. 'Send Meg home. You don't need her,' I said.

'You know I can't do that, Captain. But as long as you do what I tell you, I promise nothing will happen to her.'

I thought he looked weak behind his smile; weak and unconvincing. I wondered how much energy just climbing the Hill had cost him. Enough for me to try to escape? But then, if I did, what would happen to Meg?

'You're looking peaky, Odin,' I said.

'Not looking so good yourself,' he replied. 'I may have omitted to mention the effects of the energies under this Hill on your current Aspect.'

He was right: come to think of it, I wasn't feeling all that great. My arm still hurt, and violet light was bleeding out onto the grass. In this corporeal Aspect, at least, the return of my glam was accompanied by a growing physical weakness. *Terrific*, I thought. *Just what I need.*

'And what might these effects be?'

'Wildfire burns. You know that. And when you combine Wildfire with something even more volatile—'

'*Poof*,' said Heidi, helpfully.

'Not that it matters any more,' Odin went on. 'Because very soon, we'll both be out of here and in accommodation more suited to our status.' He gave a very Odin-like wink that did nothing to reassure me.

'The last time I let you choose my accommodation,' I reminded him, 'the bed was too hard, the décor stank and the snake *motif* was decidedly *de trop.*'

'Oh, *that*,' said Odin dismissively. 'I was a different person then. But you – you should be saving your strength. After all, it's a while since you last gave birth, and—'

'Since I last did *what*?'

He smiled. 'Of course, I never explained that part. But maybe now's not the time, eh? You need to concentrate. It's close. You only get one chance at this.'

'This?'

'Why, birthing Sleipnir, of course. Just as you did when the Worlds were young. Except that you had your Aspect then, and all the power of your glam. And now all you have is a single charge; but it should be enough for what we need. Just take the reins and think of home.'

'Just like that?' I said. 'And then? Let me guess. First, we defeat the enemy. And then, we free the Vanir, of course, and then we rebuild Asgard—'

For a moment I thought he looked shaken. 'What makes you think that's even possible?'

I shrugged. 'Dude, relax. It was a joke. Remember that stupid computer game?'

Odin gave me a look. Five hundred years after Ragnarók, and he still wasn't ready for Asgard jokes.

'So what about Heidi? What does *she* get?'

'She gets her father's Head, of course, and any information she can persuade it to divulge.'

Oh, please, I thought. *And what if the first thing it wants is to put an end to us, once and for all, using those New Runes you gave her?*

But the General was in stubborn mood, and I knew he wouldn't listen to me. Besides, there was Heidi, with Meg at her side, and there was no escaping *her*, not without making a sacrifice I couldn't bring myself to make. I'd have to find the Oracle. For Odin, for Heidi, for Margaret, for Jumps.

And so I gathered the runes with my mind, and closed my eyes, and thought of home, which somehow looked more like Jumps' World than Asgard as it used to be. There came a grating, rumbling sound, as if the whole Hill were coming alive, with rocks surging out of the dry ground, and that violet light emerging in spikes. I felt it go through my body like a hundred burning spears – I fell to my knees, crying out in pain—

'Now!' cried Odin. 'Take the reins! And push, for gods' sakes! Push! *Push!*'

Dream

In space, no one can hear you dream.
Lokabrenna, 9:12

1

I HAVE TO SAY THAT GIVING birth was a whole lot easier the first time. But this birth was beyond flesh: it was a kind of chemistry.

Odin had described it as a meeting of volatile elements. I have to admit, that's how it felt: as if I were being consumed by fire. Bit ironic, come to think of it, fire being my element; but still the pain intensified, blooming like a sunrise, becoming something greater than the sum of my nerve-endings. Blood drizzled onto the ground from my broken runemark; the humming, like a swarm of bees, seemed to encompass the whole sky.

Inside our little cell of flesh, I could feel Jumps' anguish and disbelief. Of course, I was forgetting: she was new to *real* suffering. Those cuts on her wrists, the odd grazed knee or persistent headache – that was nothing next to this. I wanted to tell her there was worse; that she might even experience it before this escapade was over, but I didn't want to frighten her more than she was already.

'You'll be OK. Hang in there, Jumps,' said Evan in a low voice. 'Soon he'll be gone, and you can go home and forget that any of this happened.'

What does that mean? said Jumps.

'It means that this is where we part company,' I said, from

between clenched teeth. 'There's Nine Worlds of hurt out there, and you're not built to survive them.'

Part company? No way, said Jumps. *Not until Meg's safe, you don't. I'm not letting you go off alone.*

The gridwork of luminous runes on the ground shone with hectic energy. I reached for them and *pushed* with my mind, seeking the Fire within me. All around me the forces that had lain for so long under the Hill responded; sang like telephone wires; arced like bolts of lightning.

The fluffy dog Twinkle was barking. I wondered why Odin had brought him. I couldn't imagine him being of much use, even as a guard-dog. But something about the energies under the Hill inflamed him; I saw him cavorting over the grass, his shadow grown suddenly monstrous, like the hound at the gates of Hel—

Still, there was no time to think of that. The Hill shook. The air hummed. The runes at my fingertips shivered with glam. Then suddenly, there was silence. The pain that had racked my body was gone. The sky lit up. The air grew still. And there it was above our heads: a sprawl of colour that spanned the sky eight ways, like a giant spider—

That's supposed to be a Horse?

Jumps was apparently unimpressed, both by Sleipnir's ethereal Aspect and by the fact that I had single-handedly birthed him out of Castle Hill, with nothing but runes and willpower.

'That's my boy,' I told her.

But it's nothing like a Horse. It's – I don't know what it is.

I grinned. 'Did you expect it to look like those rainbow ponies from the cartoons?'

No, but—

I looked back at Odin. 'I've done what you wanted,' I told him. 'Now it's time to let Meg go.'

'Not yet.' That was Heidi, looking like Hel incarnate, with one side of her face alight and the other side deep in shadow.

'Little Margaret stays with me until *you* deliver my father's Head. And just to make sure you don't decide to simply keep the Head for yourself, we're sending a friend. For security.'

'*Whose* security, exactly?' I said, glancing back at the dog Twinkle. Sure enough, the mutt was cavorting around my ankles.

Heidi smiled. 'Oh, *ours*,' she said. 'And we knew you'd be happy to see Thor again, in his natural Aspect.'

I winced. 'But he's so *cute* as a dog.'

'You'll love him even more,' she said, 'now you've seen his fluffy side.'

I suppressed an anguished howl. The Thunderer. Back in full Aspect. Odin couldn't have asked for a more effective means of keeping me under control. Loyal, strong, but not too bright, Thor would obey without question. Which, even without the threat to Meg, reduced my chance of escape to nil.

Jumps read my thought. *Escape?* she said. *No way. I'm coming with you.*

I tried to protest. 'You can't do that. Didn't you hear what I just said? There are *things* between the Worlds. Things that can bring down even a god. You could lose your mind, or worse; never find your way back home.'

'Loki's right,' said Evan. 'Stay. There's nothing you can do to help.'

Within our shared space, I felt her push back. 'You let that – *creature* kidnap Meg. And for what? Because of Stella?'

Evan started to reply, but Jumps had already dismissed him. I could feel her stubbornness, her refusal to face facts; her anger; her guilt; her fear for Meg; and behind it all, the childish hope that she could be a hero, like the heroes of the books and games and shows she liked so much, and save the day against all odds, and be back home in time for tea . . .

Stop it, I told her. *This is no game. You won't be the hero. You'll just die quietly in the wings, and life will go on without you.*

I sensed her disbelief. She was young, and the young really

don't believe that death could ever happen to them. I know. I used to be like that myself.

You don't know anything about me, she said, sensing my thoughts in her turn. *Just because you're like, five hundred years old, or something—*

I happen to have a certain amount of, shall we say, experience?

Says the guy who didn't even know what pizza was until last week.

Pizza is unlikely to leave you stranded for ever in Dream, or to suck out your soul like an oyster, or tie you naked onto a rock with a massive big snake spitting venom into your face—

Whatever. I'm coming.

Whatever. You're not.

Odin fixed me with his one living eye. There was no sign of Evan. 'No time for arguments,' he said. 'Your steed awaits. It's time to go.'

He was right. The eight-legged Horse was now a luminous arch reaching far across the sky. Marking all points of the compass, it looked quite a lot like the sky-trail I had seen the other day. And, if I had read the signs aright, it was a trail that would lead me home.

I turned my attention once more to Jumps. In spite of all she'd put me through, somehow I didn't want to leave her now without at least saying goodbye. After all, I might never make it back into her flesh – and the thought of that exile made me feel suddenly, queasily, starkly cold.

Listen, I said. *I may not have been the easiest person to live with. But I want you to know—*

I told you, she said. *I'm coming.*

I thought we'd discussed that, I told her. *This is Dream we're travelling though. It's not like a day trip to Bognor.*

I don't care. I'm coming.

Listen, I said. *Leave your body to travel through Dream, and you may never find it again. Come in your current Aspect, and you run the risk of being torn apart by forces beyond your comprehension.*

Shit happens, said Jumps. *Are we leaving, or not?*

Well, faced with that level of stubbornness and stupidity, what could I do? I had more on my mind than safeguarding the well-being of a human with a death wish. The eight glowing runes on the side of the Hill had merged into a silvery rope – a glamorous harness for Sleipnir. The dog Twinkle was barking furiously, and Odin was smiling at me as if all his birthdays had come at once – all fifteen hundred or so of them.

'Whatever,' I said. 'Your funeral.'

And with that I grabbed hold of the silver harness – the thing that Odin thought of as *reins* – and with one final effort of will, I hurled myself right out of the flesh and into the turbulent vastness of Dream.

2

DREAM, AS I MAY HAVE MENTIONED BEFORE, isn't a
wholesome element. Filled with the debris of human minds, it
is a sink of feelings, aspirations, subconscious urges, forbidden
passions and broken taboos, with fantasies and hopes and fears
thrown into the blender to make a kind of emotional soup, in
which the sharks of Otherworld circle and lurk in the shadows.
It had almost consumed me the last time I had entered it, and I
wasn't looking forward to taking another dip.

Of course, riding Jormungand through Dream was different
to riding Sleipnir, but even so, the ride was not what you'd call
enjoyable. Sleipnir's Aspect shifted constantly from the abstract to
the monstrous – one moment a giant spider; the next a ship with
wings for sails; the next a train of camels with legs that reached
like ladders to the stars. I turned to see how Jumps was doing.

Behind me, Thor, in his natural Aspect, was watching me
much as the dog Twinkle might have watched a pizza slice
casually left on the floor. Massive, red-bearded, and with more
muscles than any being really needs; his disapproval was pal-
pable, his silent hostility unnerving.

'Ah, Thor,' I began cheerily.

'Keep your eyes on the road,' growled Thor. 'Or I'll break
your spine.'

So much for pleasantries, I thought. I turned back to the task in hand. And now, through the rushing of the night and the starkness of the light and the roaring of the dreamstuff that surged around us from every side, I could hear Jumps' voice in my ear:

'Seriously, you call this a *horse*?'

She had used my momentum to follow me out of the body we shared, and was currently in her dream-Aspect, dressed in her penguin pyjamas and looking scared and determined, borne along by the river of light that was Sleipnir's current manifestation in this very liminal World.

'Oh, *now* you're asking questions,' I said. 'Sleipnir isn't just a Horse. In Dream, he can take any Aspect – a horse, a car, a flying machine—' I gestured vaguely at our steed, which had assumed the shape of a string of red birds, dragging a kind of sky-sledge that bounced across the ridge of clouds. 'Never mind. Just hold on.'

'What *to*? What *with*?'

I gave a shrug, or what passed for one in the space between the Worlds. My own Aspect here was familiar – that of a young man with fiery hair and a certain louche charm, with the rune-mark *Kaen* on his arm – but in the corporeal World, I knew, I was no more than the stuff of dreams. Jumps, however, being alive, was still connected to her corporeal self by means of a gossamer-fine silver cord, which spooled out in the Horse's wake.

I indicated the silver cord.

'What's that?'

'That's your lifeline. The string that connects you to your physical Aspect. Don't let anything break it. You'll need it where we're going.'

Then I returned to my mission, which was searching Dream for traces of Mimir's Head in the turbulence: a signature; a vision; a thought; a fragment was all I needed. Mimir's Head was a powerful glam. *Someone* must have seen it. Seen it, held

197

it, dreamed of it. If I could find even a *glimpse* of it, then I could follow the money.

Behind me, the Thunderer gave a growl. 'Less talking. More looking. Unless you want me to choke you with your own tongue.'

Which concluded the chat for a while, and left me to my unquiet thoughts. Why hadn't Odin told me the truth? Apart from the obvious fact that he was as much of a liar as I was myself, why had he thrown in his lot with Heidi, rather than trust me? Surely it couldn't just be because I'd turned my coat and ended the Worlds. He had to have a better motive than that. I mean, you can always rely on me. At least, as long as you bear in mind that I'm naturally unreliable.

'Freyja,' said Jumps, and I was sure she had somehow read my mind, even though that was impossible, given the space we no longer shared. 'Is she worth it, do you think?'

I turned to look at her, and saw that she had swapped the penguin pyjamas for a dress of some kind of silvery stuff, split at the knee over high-heeled boots. Her hair was blonde, tied up in a bun, and fastened with a diamond clasp. I said:

'Don't tell me this is your idea of what a goddess looks like.'

Jumps looked down at herself in surprise. 'I didn't mean to—' she began. 'Why do I keep changing?'

'Everything changes here,' I said. 'This is Dream, remember?'

Jumps took a moment to look abashed, and then returned to the subject in hand. 'Odin must really care for her, to risk our lives to get her back. You, me, Evan, Meg—'

I cut her short. I couldn't bear to leave her with the delusion that Odin was a hero. 'You're mistaking Desire for Love,' I said. 'Love may be crazy and volatile, but Desire is all-consuming. A man in its clutches would burn the Worlds rather than give up what he wants.'

Jumps gave a wistful little smile. She was back in the penguin pyjamas. 'I just wish it hadn't been Stella,' she said, and even though we no longer shared the same inner space, I could feel her sadness. 'Evan doesn't have a chance. He never did, he should have known. Stella wouldn't be seen dead with anyone who was – *damaged.*'

By that I wasn't sure whether she meant Evan or herself. But she was looking at her arms, still braceleted with the silver scars that mirrored my violet runemark. How odd, I thought, that she should choose to reveal to me now what she had kept behind those secret doors in her mind.

'That isn't damage,' I said to her. 'It's proof of what you can survive.'

And at that I went back to the task in hand, while my monstrous child span its webs in eight Worlds, and we rode through the many lands of Dream in search of the Head of the Oracle.

3

DREAM IS A RIVER IN PERMANENT FLUX, made up of countless islets. Some are no more than bubbles of time, while others may contain whole worlds. The challenge was trying to find what amounted to a grain of sand in a world consisting of nothing but beaches. But Sleipnir had feet in every World, which made our task at least possible, although communication with our steed was still something of a mystery. And gods – even fallen ones – tend to dream more brightly, more fiercely than the Folk. If Mimir was there, I would find him. That is, if nothing found me first.

'So – why didn't Odin come himself?' said Jumps, still clinging on, her Aspect now that of a child of nine, wide-eyed and in pigtails.

'Maybe it was too risky. Maybe he doesn't trust Heidi. Or maybe he has some other plan that involves being in human Aspect.' I didn't say that I hoped he might be playing some kind of double game; partly because I didn't want to give false hope to Jumps – or to myself – and partly because Thor was there too, and listening to every word.

Thor as a small fluffy dog had been cute – if you liked that sort of thing. But Thor in full Aspect was fearsome. The Meta-Thor of the *Asgard!*™ game had come close to conveying his strength and size, but for bristle, and rage, and sheer muscle, there was nothing like the real thing. And currently, the real thing was looming over my shoulder with a look of tremendous suspicion.

'*Boundaries*,' I told him, trying to nudge his bulk aside. 'What do you think I'm going to do? Swallow the Oracle whole, then vanish into thin air?'

Thor growled, although his expression remained that of a small dog guarding a very large bone. 'I wouldn't trust you to find a cat that wasn't even lost,' he said. 'But if you *do* find the Oracle, I'm here to make sure that it goes to the General, and no one else.'

'The General, who's working with Gullveig-Heid?'

'Odin knows what he's doing.'

I raised an eyebrow. '*Do* tell.' But as I'd suspected, the Thunderer was only following orders. His perspective – such as it was – was limited to an unshakeable belief that the General knew best, and that I was not to be trusted. Which frankly made the business of speeding through Dream on one of my monstrous children even less fun than it would have been otherwise.

Time works differently in Dream. Years in Dream can often amount to the passing of mere seconds in the corporeal World. Great for Odin and Gullveig-Heid, waiting for us on Castle Hill, but not so fine for those of us clinging to that silver cord. Every moment we spent in there was a risk to our sanity – well, maybe not Thor, whose imagination wasn't of the highest calibre, but Jumps had never encountered Dream outside of her own little bubble, and I knew how easy the Folk were to break. And yet Jumps had inner resources that belied her youthful exterior. I hoped that they would serve her now.

'Hang on. It's about to get bumpy,' I said.

'You mean it gets even *worse*?' said Jumps.

'Trust me, I wouldn't do this if I didn't have to,' I said. 'But the Oracle works through Dream, and the dreams of those who encounter it are likely to be – disturbing.'

Well, *that* was an understatement: but I didn't want to frighten her any more than she already was.

'Do you have a favourite memory?' I said, above the roaring of Dream. 'Remember it now; hang on to it; never let it out of your mind. These waters lead to Madness. They will drown you if they can. So think of something warm and good, and cling to it as hard as you can—'

She nodded, her eyes as round as the Moon. Her Aspect had changed again: now she looked no more than seven years old, dressed in yellow shorts and a blue sweater with a penguin on it. I hoped her chosen memory was strong enough to carry her through – but in a way I envied her, too. My tolerance may have been greater than hers, but I had no warm, good memories. Except, perhaps—

Cherry coconut cake, and a scoop of vanilla ice cream; and the way her eyes shone as we danced; and the arc of the fire on the hillside—

And thus armed, I entered that part of Dream that the Folk call Madness, hoping for a fugitive gleam of the thing that had once been Mimir the Wise.

It was the very worst of Dream: the cesspit of the subconscious. Here there were lakes of lethargy; bottomless pits of depression. Here was the fear of never being well; the certainty of never being loved. Here there were dreams of small blades driven beneath the fingernails; and of committing terrible acts; and of being drowned beneath black ice. Here, there were murdered loved ones, and dreams of being stifled by clouds of gas, and colourless pockets of terrible despair where even dreams could not enter.

Behind me, Thor was growling, and I could hear Jumps sobbing steadily. Even I had begun to feel bitter, nauseous, afraid. But finally, after a timeless interval, I caught it – not more than a glimmer in the slipstream of the General's Horse – but those colours were unmistakable.

'*There*. Right *there*!' I urged Sleipnir after the Oracle's reflection. Quicksilver-green, it winked at me from one of the floating islands of Dream: a World that owed its existence to the fleeting mental processes of an unknown dreamer.

'Are you sure that's a sign of the Oracle?' That was Thor, scowling over my shoulder.

I gritted my teeth. 'Oh, I'm sure.' I'd know those colours anywhere. That bauble had brought me nothing but woe from the very first moment I'd seen it. Spreading discord wherever it went, it had lured us with its prophecies; severed my bond with Odin; brought about the End of the Worlds; and was even now conspiring to mess with my mind, even after I'd thrown it from Asgard's highest parapet. The Oracle had a habit of leaving its mark on people. And that mark was reflected in the dreams of those its presence had touched – in this case, clearly a strong one, from the substance of the world contained within the dreamer's thoughts.

'Hang on, Jumps. We're close,' I said.

The sobbing behind me seemed to subside.

'We're going into a bubble of Dream,' I told her. 'No one can hurt you physically there. Just remember you're spirit, not flesh. And try to stay close to Sleipnir. We may have to leave in a hurry. Can you do that?'

Jumps nodded. Her hands tightened on the lifeline. I saw that she looked older now, closer to her physical age, although she still had the pigtails. Quickly, I urged Sleipnir towards that thread of bottled lightning. I could already see where it led: into one of the bubble-worlds that shimmered along the banks of Dream. How long that world would last, I could not tell. Some dreams of the Folk last minutes, others only seconds, and if I lost the Oracle's trace, we would be back to square one. There was no time to check the terrain; no time to identify the dreamer, or even to check if they were sane. Instead I guided Sleipnir towards the Oracle's colours. For a moment I saw the reflective curve of the dream-bubble surging towards me. Then, we crashed through the bubble's side and into the World of the dreamer.

4

I'D ALWAYS THOUGHT THAT IF THE Folk could somehow harness the power of dreams, then there would be no need for gods, for they could shape the Worlds as they pleased. Their imagination is boundless; the breadth of their vision as vast as the sea. And yet they choose to live as they do, constrained by petty little laws—

I'll never understand them.

The dream was ambitious, even for such grandiose dreams as the Folk can sometimes build. It was a hall of tremendous size, perhaps even large enough to rival Asgard in its heyday. There were columns of marble and ebony, elaborate mosaics on the floor, sculptures and gilding and coloured glass, and at one end a giant organ, all swagged with velvet and gilt, its largest pipes as thick as the most ancient of oak-trees. Ten thousand wooden benches were lined to face a massive altar: the aisles stretched as far as the eye could see, and the whole thing was topped with a massive dome of cut-crystal and glass, bright with the light of a thousand suns.

'Nice,' I said.

In this world, the Horse was just a horse, vaguely roan in colour. Holding the lifeline in one hand, Jumps got down to look around.

'What is it?' she said.

'A grand design,' said a voice that seemed to come from everywhere. 'My great Cathedral, built to bring Order out of Chaos.'

That must be the dreamer, I told myself. In this dream, he or she might take any shape – a useful way of determining what kind of person they might be. I looked around, and saw a tall man of middle age dressed in a workman's tunic; a belt of tools wrapped round his waist; a tasselled cap upon his head.

Of course, this might not be the dreamer as he was in his physical Aspect. In life, he might be a different man, or even a woman, or a child. But this was how he saw himself – at least in this particular dream – a master craftsman, secure in his work; humble, yet authoritative.

'*Your* design?' I enquired.

'Aye, the good gods willing.'

That sounded promising, I thought. In this man's world, the gods were still, if not an active force, at least alive in memory. I looked around for a trace of the colours I had glimpsed in the slipstream. They should have been pretty easy to see, but in that dazzling bowl of light no signatures were visible.

I turned to the dreamer. 'What's your name?'

He looked at me, but did not reply. Dreamers rarely give their true names, although you can often tell more about them by what they call themselves in dreams than by the names their parents chose.

'I am – the Architect,' he said at last.

'And this?' I indicated the great glass dome. 'A palace? A cathedral? A pleasure dome?' I had learnt this last term from Jumps' interior lexicon, in one of the subsections marked ENG-LISH LITERATURE, and I thought it sounded pretty cool.

The Architect gave a little smile. 'It *was* the Cradle of the gods,' he said, 'in the time of the Golden Age. Now it is the Cradle of the Folk: its completion will mark the beginning of a new Golden Age of learning, wisdom and Order.'

That was the second time he'd mentioned Order. Worthy, I thought, but rather dull. Order is overrated: Odin spent centuries trying to establish it in the Middle Worlds, and look how fast we lost it all. From Asgard to mudguard in one fell swoop. It hardly seems worth the energy. And yet I was sure there was something I'd missed.

Jumps had followed me as I moved towards the base of the great glass dome. I sensed that she was about to speak, and signalled for her to be silent. The less attention she drew, I thought, the safer she would be in this dream – which, if my suspicions were correct, might turn out to be very dangerous.

Once again, I looked around. The place was divided into five halls: the central dome, plus four smaller chambers, one for each point of the compass. At the far end of each chamber, a window of colourful and glorious design, detailing scenes from Ragnarók – the World Serpent rising out of the sea; the fall of Bif-rost; the General, falling to the Fenris Wolf. In a distant corner of the northern window, I could even see Yours Truly, tumbling from the parapet, with Heimdall hanging on to my arms – a tragic scene that in my view deserved a larger canvas. Still, there was no time to spend on mourning my demise. And now I saw, along the great aisles that linked the chambers to the dome, a shimmer of something more than just the gilding on the mosaic tiles: a pattern that ran along the ground to form a design I'd seen before.

It was the same sign I'd seen in the sky; the thing Jumps had said was a vapour-trail. I'd been so certain at the time that it was some kind of a rune: now the certainty returned. I moved to the point where the two lines crossed – in Dream, distances are meaningless – and there beneath the gleaming dome I saw, fixed into the ground, a black stone, carved with runes down one side, and with that crossroads shape engraved on top—

'What is it?' I asked the Architect. 'What does this symbol here mean?'

The man who called himself the Architect shook his head. 'I do not question the patterns,' he said. 'The Whisperer desired it there.'

'The Whisperer?'

'He speaks to me.' The Architect's voice was hushed with awe. 'He watches. He operates the Machine. He tells me I'm going to build for him.'

That sounded promising, I thought. This Whisperer – or was it an Oracle? – seemed to be a big influence. Had the man seen it? Glimpsed it in Dream? Could he even have *found* it somewhere in the real World?

'What Machine?'

The dreamer smiled. 'The Machina Brava. Over there.' He indicated the organ. It looked – if that were possible – even bigger than it had before, its golden pipes like columns of fire, thick as Yggdrasil itself. I noticed that the dome, too, was bigger than it had been a moment before; impossibly high, its crystal vault refracting the whole of the blameless sky.

'What's happening?' whispered Jumps. Her whisper, grotesquely amplified, filled the hall with hidden snakes.

'I think the dream is beginning to change,' I said. 'Jumps, Thor – get ready to ride.'

Jumps took hold of Sleipnir's mane. Thor just looked suspicious.

'It's OK,' I said irritably. 'What, did you think I might try and escape? Where *to*, for gods' sakes?'

'Wouldn't put it past you,' growled Thor.

'Bite me,' I said. But my heart wasn't in it. The danger of staying in a dream that might be ready to collapse was outweighed by the fact that I needed to know more about this Whisperer. The whole of the sinister setup sounded all too familiar to be a simple coincidence; and if the Whisperer *was* the Oracle, then maybe here I could find a clue as to its physical whereabouts.

I turned to the Architect, whose Aspect had shifted slightly. Now he was a younger man, maybe thirty years old or less, wearing a kind of dark robe and a three-cornered cap with a tassel. I wondered how long after Ragnarók this was, and what the dreamer's World was like in the wake of the gods' demise.

'Tell me about the Whisperer,' I said, addressing the Architect. 'Is he here? Can you see him? What's his name?'

'I speak of One who is Nameless, and yet his name is Legion. He will bring Order to the Worlds, and bring about a Cleansing. From the Cradle to the grave, he lives in rage and malice. And his parting gift to you will be a poisoned chalice.'

That was odd. It sounded almost as if the dreamer were reciting something. A verse, perhaps a poem. Maybe even—

A prophecy?

I looked at the dreamer. 'What was that?'

'I speak as I must, and cannot be silent.' The Architect gave a dry little laugh. 'Oh, Loki,' he said. 'I'm disappointed in you. I thought that you, at least, would appreciate what I'm trying to do here.'

'Oh, *no.*' I turned to Jumps. 'Get on the Horse.'

'What is it?' said Thor.

'Get on the bloody Horse.'

The dream was changing faster now; expanding to fill every horizon. The cathedral; the windows; the glass dome; even the organ were starting to shift; the colours, already dazzling, to intensify even further. The Architect was smiling; his Aspect, now grown to monstrous size, loomed over us like a giant.

No wonder I hadn't been able to see the Oracle's signature, I told myself. The Oracle was the World itself; shining out from every piece of glass, and gilt, and marble. A World that, if the Oracle chose, might at any time collapse, with all of us still inside it—

'I SPEAK AS I MUST,' said the Architect, his voice as loud as an avalanche. *'I SPEAK, AND THE NINE WORLDS WILL LISTEN TO ME, FEAR ME AND OBEY ME.'*

Thor was still standing by Sleipnir, his massive brow furrowed, his red beard bristling. As I started to mount the Horse, he put his hand on my shoulder.

'Not so fast,' he said. 'I want to know. Did the dreamer prophesy?'

I glanced at the Architect. 'Kinda.'

'How?'

I cursed inwardly. Thor's mental processes were never fast at the best of times. Here, they were even more sluggish than in a game of *Asgard!*™.

'I don't have time to explain,' I said, trying to shake off Thor's grasp. 'Just trust me. We need to get out of here, and fast. Before all Hel breaks loose.'

Thor looked around suspiciously. 'Why would it do that?' he said.

I tried to keep calm in the chaos. It felt like being the only immovable object in a world of projectiles. I began, very dimly, to understand what it might have been like for the General, back in the Elder Age, trying to bring Order to Asgard.

I took a deep breath (even though in Dream I didn't need to). 'We're not in the Architect's dream,' I said. 'I think we're in the Oracle's.'

5

THERE USED TO BE A SAYING, back in the day: *What is it that the slave dreams? He dreams of being the master.* And now, as I urged Sleipnir towards the wall of the bubble-world, I turned my thoughts back to that saying with a whole new sense of perspective.

How scarily apposite it was now. *The slave dreams of being the master.* And now, after so many centuries in the service of the gods, the Oracle's dream – a bubble-world of unusual breadth and potency – reflected its powerful longing to build, to inspire, and to rule. I wondered just how far that desire reached. To be a ruler in Dream is one thing; but what I knew of the Oracle suggested that it meant to rule not just a bubble-world in Dream, but a World filled with dreamers; a World in which, with the right kind of help, one could even be a god—

Behind me, Jumps said: 'Will we make it?'

'Of course,' I said.

'You liar,' said Jumps.

The Architect – now as tall as the World Tree itself, his head encircled by the dome like a massive glass corona, beamed down at the three of us, his monstrous smile spanning the sky.

'I SPEAK AS I MUST,' it thundered, 'AND YOU WOULD BE WISE TO LISTEN TO ME. A NEW AGE APPROACHES.

THE AGE OF THE GODS IS FINISHED.' There was a pause, then the Voice spoke again, not without amusement: 'WHY ARE YOU TRYING TO RUN?' it said. 'DON'T YOU KNOW WHO I AM YET?'

I glanced at the enormous sky. 'You know, I thought you'd be taller, somehow? And maybe more impressive?'

Laughter from the Oracle, like hail across a field of glass. 'You always were amusing,' said the Oracle in a more normal voice. 'I wonder, would it amuse me more to see you suffer, or let you survive?'

I did not reply, but kept going, urging Sleipnir towards the receding horizon.

Behind me, I could hear Jumps singing to herself in a small, childlike voice. I hoped this didn't mean that her mind was giving way, but there was nothing I could do, except try to reach the edge of the dream before the bubble finally burst.

Thor was looking mutinous. 'Why are we running away,' he said, 'if this is what we were sent to find?'

I tried to explain, as Sleipnir shifted to his travelling Aspect. His eight legs arched into the air like pieces of a rainbow. The three of us clung to his fiery mane as he started to gain momentum, racing down the gleaming aisles of the great cathedral, as stained glass cascaded around us like rain, and the laughter of the Architect echoed all around us.

But even though we made for the wall of the bubble-world as fast as Sleipnir could carry us, it did not come any closer. The aisles seemed to stretch into coloured mist; the sky to expand as we advanced. And all the time, it was losing form, like a watercolour in the rain, its substance becoming smoke, cloud, rainbow in the rapturous air—

Once more Thor repeated: 'What are we running away for?'

'Because this is a trap,' I said. 'The Oracle isn't some human dreamer that we can quietly interrogate. It *knows* us. Knows our weaknesses. And in this world, it has all the power.'

The Oracle laughed again. Looking back, I saw him sitting

at the keyboard of the great organ he had referred to as the Machina Brava. The organ now seemed the only thing in the dream that was not losing substance: it gleamed as golden as ever before, and its voice was like that of an erupting volcano.

'I see *you* understand,' he said. 'You always were the clever one. How did you escape Netherworld?'

'Oh, this and that,' I said, clinging fast to the mane of Sleipnir.

'And of course I know the Thunderer, even though his Aspect appears to be linked to that of a fluffy white dog. But who's that with you?'

'No one,' I said, squinting into the watercolour mist.

'That isn't quite true, is it?' said the voice of the Oracle. 'I can see her quite clearly, you know, even at this distance. Who is she? One of the Folk?'

Jumps was still clinging to my back, her Aspect now that of a small child, no more than five or six years old, still singing that little wordless song. Something about it reminded me of a tune I'd heard in her mind, but there was no time to think about that, with the Oracle's voice all around me.

'No one. Just a friend,' I said.

As soon as I'd said it, I wished I hadn't. But it was too late. The Oracle laughed. 'A *friend*? Oh, dear. Are you sure this is Loki? The Trickster I once knew was too smart to have friends.'

'Loose term,' I muttered. 'I should have said—'

'*Host*, perhaps?'

Dammit, that was no better.

'So, you managed to find yourself a human host,' said the Oracle. 'Well done. But it must be draining to have to adjust to your host's needs. Her feelings. Her incessant demands. The limitations of her flesh.'

I said nothing, but concentrated on reaching the boundary of the dream, which seemed now to have receded beyond the limits of my vision. The three of us hung in the coloured mist, while the Architect, at his organ, seemed suspended in amber, an aeon away.

'I could perhaps help you with that,' suggested the Oracle, his voice as close and intimate in my ear as if he were sitting behind me. 'But if you want to keep riding, I can wait.'

I cursed.

'What does that mean?' said Thor.

'It means that we're in trouble.'

I should have known, really. The Oracle was an ancient, powerful glam. Its knowledge of runes was peerless. And its malice was unknowable, its hatred unassailable, its guile as deep as —

Gullveig-Heid?

Of course. It runs in the family. I'd wondered why Odin had told me about the relationship between Mimir and Gullveig-Heid; now I wondered if he had known that this was a possibility. Had he sent me into Dream in the knowledge that he was delivering me into the hands of his enemy? But if he had, what could he gain?

Beneath me I could feel Sleipnir still straining to escape the pull of Mimir's world. I laid a hand on the Horse's flank, signalling it to rest. At our back, the Oracle's deep and resonant laughter.

'Oh, Loki. I always liked you,' it whispered, in a voice only I could hear. 'You always were reassuringly selfish and predictable. Whatever else you did, you could always be counted on to look after your own self-interest. What if I did you a favour? Freed you from the demands of your host? Allowed you to walk away from all this, and into a future of your own devising?'

'I'd say that sounded very out of character,' I said.

'Well, obviously, I'd need something from you,' said the Oracle softly. 'But, given my trust in your sense of self-preservation, I think we can maybe do business.'

'Really?' I said.

'Oh, yes,' said the Oracle.

'So – what do you want me to do?'

'Well, for a start, I suggest we play a little game,' said the Oracle.

'What kind of a game?' My experience of the Oracle's little games was not, on the whole, I thought, positive.

'This is one I think you'll like,' said the Oracle gently. 'The prize is your freedom, if you do exactly what I ask of you.'

'What about the others?' I said, with a glance at Jumps and Thor.

The Oracle smiled. 'We'll see,' it said. 'Besides, since when did you care?'

'Good point.'

Ten seconds later, Sleipnir and I were galloping across the landscape of Dream alone and unencumbered: a million opportunities stretching out below us like stars; the surface of the bubble-world gleaming faintly, far below, like one of those marbles Jumps had as a child, with a twisted strand of colours inside; played for and lost in a game of chance, long ago and far away.

6

FREEDOM. YOU CAN'T IMAGINE HOW that felt for Your Humble Narrator. Even in Asgard, I'd been no more than a slave to the gods; a dog that could be trained to serve, but who never got more than the table scraps. A prisoner in Asgard; a prisoner in Netherworld; and then a prisoner in Jumps, subject to all her little demands, her silly little urges.

And now I was free, and in Aspect – Dream being the medium in which even Death has no purchase – and, with the aid of Sleipnir, could travel to any one of ten thousand Worlds, taking from them what I could—

Which made it all the more incomprehensible that I now found myself back on Castle Hill, inside Jumps' body – now strangely cavernous without her personality inside – and facing my enemies with a not entirely-unreasonable quiver of fear as I announced:

'I have good news and not-so-good news. The good news is, I have located the Oracle. On a slightly less positive note, I may have temporarily mislaid my passengers.'

'*You lost Jumps?*' Evan said, just as Odin said: '*You lost Thor?*'

'I didn't *lose* them, precisely,' I said. 'But I may have had to leave them in Dream.'

I shan't go into the details of the unfair and unfounded

recriminations that followed my announcement. I just waited for Odin to simmer down and for Heidi to stop laughing, then said: 'I *did* find the Oracle, though. And if we give him what he wants, I have his word that they go free.'

'And what *does* he want?' Odin's eye was like ice.

I shrugged. 'What else? *You*, of course.'

Heidi gave me a narrow look. 'I hope you told him that his only daughter was alive and well, and working to free him.'

'Of course I did,' I said. 'But understand that Mimir isn't what you'd call the most trusting of personalities. He wanted certain assurances. And I don't think I can deliver them.'

'So who can?' said Heidi. 'And who in Hel's this?'

I smiled my sweetest smile. 'Let me introduce you,' I said. 'It's rather a funny story.'

7

SCROLL BACK A WHILE WITH ME, if you can. I may not have revealed all the facts. The fact is, the Oracle's offer *had* tempted me a little bit – I mean, who wouldn't jump at the idea of total freedom, physical autonomy without the drag factor of Jumps' mind in my body *and* the bonus of the Wanderer's Horse at my command, to carry me between the Worlds whenever I felt like a change of scene?

All I had to do was deliver what Mimir wanted. The General, at his mercy. And I could have done it, too, except for one thing – one *person*. Jumps. Even in Dream, the link we shared was enough for her to guess my plan, and what she had to say wasn't nice.

'I can't believe you're considering this,' she hissed at me, as we fled. She had changed from her child-Aspect, and now she was seventeen again, and filled with teenage attitude.

'Considering what?' I said.

'Oh, please,' said Jumps. 'I can tell. You're seriously considering leaving me and Thor in here, prisoners in Dream, and gadding off on Sleipnir, never to return. Am I right?'

'Thinking isn't a crime. Is it?' I was suddenly unsure.

'You weasel. And to think I thought that you might have

changed, a little bit. Not miraculously, but enough to make you a little bit human.'

'Human?' I was revolted. I mean, there's only so much abuse a demon can take.

'Oh, what's the use?' she said. 'I should have known better than to think you could ever be anything more than just a free-loader, user, liar, cheat—'

'Those are my best qualities,' I protested.

'Just *go*,' said Jumps, sharply. 'I'd rather be trapped for ever with the Phantom of the bloody Opera over there than spend a single minute more listening to your excuses—'

I shrugged. 'Well, of course, I *could* do that. I *could* just run away from the problem, which, by the way, would still leave me with three powerful enemies out for my blood. Or you could maybe remember that (a) I'm Loki, and (b) I've always got a plan. Are you cool with that, Jumps?'

'You haven't got a plan,' said Jumps. 'You said as much to Odin.'

'I lied. So shoot me. That's what I do.'

For a moment, Jumps said nothing. I felt the weight of her disbelief slipping from my shoulders. Then I heard a little voice behind me whisper: *What plan?*

8

'THERE'S AN OLD RIDDLE AMONG THE FOLK. It's about a ferryman. This ferryman needs to transport three cargoes across a lake: a wolf, a goat and a cabbage. Don't ask me why – that's his affair. There's no one at the far side of the lake to look after the goods, and both the goat and the wolf are hungry.

'But his boat is very small: he can only carry one thing at a time. The thing is, if he takes the wolf first, the goat will eat the cabbage. If he takes the cabbage first, then the wolf will eat the goat. And if he takes the goat first, then the next thing he brings to the far side of the lake will either be the cabbage, which the goat will eat as soon as he leaves, or the wolf, which will eat the goat the minute the ferryman is out of sight. So what does he do to keep all of them safe?'

'Er, tie up the goat? Cage the wolf?'

'No. The guy doesn't have any rope.'

'He has a ferry, but no rope? So how come the wolf and the goat don't run away as soon as he paddles off?'

I sighed. This was beginning to sound a lot like one of Odin's tales. Not as bad as the one with the undead cat, and yet the animal motif was irksome. Still, I'd thought it might appeal to Jumps, what with her love of furry things.

'Just take it from me,' I said. 'They'll stay where the ferryman puts them.'

'Well, if they're that obedient, why doesn't he just tell the goat not to eat the cabbage, and the wolf not to eat the goat?'

I sighed again. 'That's not the point. The point is solving the riddle, which to a certain extent reflects our current predicament. I'm the ferryman, of course. The river is Dream. You and Evan need to be safely on the waking side. Heidi and Odin need to be taken to the *far* side – *our* World. And Mimir's Head – the cabbage – needs to be kept as far away from either of them as possible.'

There was a rather long silence. 'I don't think that's a riddle,' said Jumps. 'More of a lateral thinking problem.'

'Never mind what it is,' I said. 'You know I have a plan, right?'

I looked at her. She smiled and said: 'Loki always has a plan.'

'And I promise I'll be back, right? On my name, I promise you.'

Again, that nod. I don't know why it made me feel anxious, as if something – a roll of wire, perhaps – had suddenly tightened around my heart. It was a troubling feeling – especially as this time I couldn't attribute it to anyone else – and it made me wonder just how much Jumps had managed to corrupt me during the short time we had shared together. That tightening sensation. That tremor of something deep inside. It felt too much like caring to me. It felt too much like weakness.

'Jumps,' I said, fearing the worst. 'Do you trust me?'

Jumps nodded.

I put my head in my hands. 'Did you learn nothing from me at all? Trust *no one*. Understand?'

Jumps looked puzzled. 'But you said—'

'Oh, just forget it,' I told her. And at that I urged Sleipnir back into Dream, leaving the Architect's bubble-world behind me in the darkness.

9

AFTER THAT, I MADE A SMALL DETOUR, following the colours that had led me to the Oracle. But this time I followed them not into Dream, but into the corporeal World in which its counterpart remained.

Linked to its Dream-Aspect by the finest of cords, Mimir's Head slept – though for how long I could not hope to speculate. Jumps had one of those cords, too: at least until the bubble-world failed and the Oracle returned to its conscious self.

Time in Dream works differently, allowing the dreamer to travel and drift for hours, even sometimes days or weeks, while in the waking world only a matter of seconds might pass. But now, I was travelling into the physical World again, which meant that every second would count, every breath make a difference. Jumps' survival depended on how long the Oracle stayed asleep, how fast I could retrieve the Head, and whether or not I could persuade Odin to come with me.

I know. Put that way, it sounds as if I didn't really have a plan. But while I might have led Jumps to believe that my plan was fully formed, I *hadn't* lied to her, except perhaps in allowing her to believe my riddle had a solution. The ferryman's problem – and mine, of course – lay in never allowing the wolf to be alone with the goat, or the goat with the cabbage. But my version of the riddle was further complicated by the fact that I had *multiple* goats and wolves, all of which needed to end up on their respective sides of Dream, not to mention – *ahem!* – the ferryman, whose survival in all of this was still of some small importance.

But what did I hope to achieve, you ask, alone and without a physical form? Well, one thing I've learnt in my time is that you can tell a lot about someone by the way they dream. And Mimir's dream had given me much to reflect upon: especially its depiction of that vast cathedral; the cross-shaped symbol carved into the stone; the organ with the odd-sounding name; the figure of the Architect. These things, added to the fact that, within the millions of criss-crossing signatures that ran through Dream, the Oracle's colours seemed closely linked to *another* set of colours, suggested a human connection. Had one of the Folk unearthed the Oracle from its burial place? Had he, too, fallen under the spell of the thing that had cost the gods so dear?

On Sleipnir, I followed the signature. The Oracle's trail was very bright, cutting through the tangle of lesser, muted colours. But that second trail continued; sometimes crossing the Oracle's, sometimes winding around it, until, as I'd expected, it led me into a World I could almost recognize. Green and gold and ice-blue; a place of valleys and mountains, a frozen North, a fruitful South, with the One Sea all around them—

It had been a long, long time since I fell from Asgard's parapet. At that point, the World of the Folk was dark, and cold, and fiery. The Sun and Moon had been engulfed; the glaciers had marched down from the hills; and the armies of the living dead had poured from the tributaries of Dream to gather in frozen Ironwood. All right, I'll admit I wasn't in any position to pay much attention to climate change. But the Winter War had ravaged the land and decimated the people, making them into little more than scavengers on the decaying corpse of the world. Into this cesspit of darkness and ice I had thrown Mimir's Head, hoping that it would be lost for ever – and yet, I told myself, it would seem that the Head had not only survived in this World, but had managed to find itself a human host to work on.

Of course it had. I'd expected no less. Mimir was always resourceful, even in the old days. But as the General's Horse and I emerged from the misty chaos of Dream, I found myself blinking in disbelief at the change to the World as I'd seen it last – the place between Ida and Ironwood, where we had brought that World to an end. Instead of a dark and smoky sky, I saw a blameless stretch of blue, dotted by little fluffy clouds. And instead of a barren, blasted plain, I saw a large and vibrant settlement: wooden two-storey houses; narrow little cobbled streets leading towards a river; and beyond, a series of towers and spires, built from sooty golden stone and rising above the rooftops.

Ironwood had receded – its trees most probably cut down to build those wooden houses – and the river, once a maelstrom of wild and torrid water, had been dammed and bridged and tamed, with rowing-boats and ferries and boardwalks and dykes all along the waterfront.

I took a moment to understand that our World had not ended with Asgard's demise. Of course I knew that already – but all the same I couldn't help feeling absurdly surprised. How long had it been since Asgard fell? In this World, I guessed it could only be two hundred years or so. But where were the ruins? The monuments? The shrines to our people, lost too soon?

From Netherworld, I'd watched through Dream as all trace of our occupancy was removed. But here, on the ground where I'd fallen, it was still a shock to see how completely we had been erased.

I glanced down at Sleipnir, whose Aspect in this World had shrunk to that of an ordinary horse, vaguely reddish in colour, wearing a runemarked bridle. My own Aspect was so hazy as to be almost invisible, being little more than a fragment of Dream, but if I kept hold of Sleipnir, I knew I could take a more visible Aspect if required. I had no corporeal privileges – eating, sex and other pleasures were out until I was back in the flesh – but Sleipnir kept me in the World, which was all I really wanted.

The clock was ticking now for Jumps. In Dream, her time was running out. I had to find the Oracle, and all I had was the memory of that building: the columns, the stone, the glass. Of course, it might not look at all like the building I'd seen in Dream. But if I could find the original Architect; the man who'd dreamed it into being—

Looking around, I became aware of the sound of hammering on stone. It was some distance away, but rising above my steed for a moment, I could see a building site, beyond the labyrinth of streets. Something was happening back there; something a good deal more ambitious than those wooden houses, or even the stone towers beyond. I urged Sleipnir forward, and in due course we found ourselves watching a work-in-progress: a half-completed structure of unusual size and scope, around which lay a number of lesser buildings, positioned geometrically to form the rays of a six-pointed star.

Rising invisibly above the scene, I could see the grace of the design; the courtyards, gardens, avenues. Asgard itself might not have been as fine as this was shaping up to be, and I guessed that an Architect of extraordinary talent and vision must be behind the project.

No shit, I thought. *I wonder who?*

Once more disembodied, I rose to explore the scene from the air. Stonemasons; labourers; sculptors; scaffolders; great wagonloads of timber and marble and stone. And right in the centre of it all, like a spider in its web, I could see those colours again: the Oracle's colours, its silver-green mingled with those of someone else—

I urged Sleipnir onwards, keeping him to his most mundane Aspect. Following that signature-trail, I finally found myself by a thick canvas tent, in which a man of the Folk seemed to be contemplating diagrams, away from the dust of the building work and the noise of the workers.

The man was not asleep, and yet Dream seemed to cling to him like a cloak. Some artists are like that: existing only half in the corporeal World and half in the World of their imaginations. I'd met such people before, but never one whose inner life felt as tangible as this. This was why his signature had been so closely connected to the Oracle's dream. This was why at first I had failed to see them as two distinct entities. In essence, the vision belonged to both the human and the Oracle. Both of them were the Architect. Both were joined by the same dream.

I took this as a good sign. It meant we could communicate. More than that, it meant that as long as the man remained in this state of enhanced creativity, the Oracle's dream, too, was secure, and Jumps had an extra lifeline. I banished Sleipnir's corporeal form and together we passed through the canvas of the tent. The man looked up, as if a draught had disturbed the papers in which he'd been absorbed, but the dream-haze around him remained intact.

'Who's there?' he said. 'Is anyone there?'

I took what hazy form I could, and saw his eyes widen in sudden alarm – though rather less astonishment than I'd been expecting.

'No!' he said. 'I'm not ready! You promised you'd leave me alone until my work was finished!'

I said: 'We seem to have a case of mistaken identity. I've never met you before, and I mean you no harm. Quite the opposite.'

The man seemed to relax a bit. He extended a hand to touch the mane of the General's Horse, and seemed relieved to find that it was corporeal. 'Who are you? An angel, a demon, a ghost?'

Actually, a bit of all three. But I didn't want to waste time in formalities. That timepiece was still ticking in Dream.

'A traveller, from the future,' I said, which had the dual advantage of being both absolutely correct, and sounding nicely mysterious.

The man's eyes widened again. I had the chance to study him

a little more closely, and I realized that he was a version of the man I had seen in the Oracle's dream. Red-lined robe, tasselled cap, blue and slightly sleepy eyes: he seemed a gentler, kinder version of the Architect I'd seen through the grandiose lens of the Oracle's vision. Best of all, his colours revealed no guile, no malice. It looked to me as if the Oracle's tool was an innocent: a man whose sole love of his art was enough to sustain him.

His eyes had lit up at my words. 'Is it there?' he said. 'Is my great cathedral there? Did I finish it? Is it as great as my visions foretold?'

I thought back to the Oracle's dream. 'I saw a dome of crystal glass,' I said, 'with pillars that seemed to reach into the very firmament. I saw a great organ, the voice of which seemed to fill the Nine Worlds.'

His eyes were like stars. Keep it coming, I thought.

'I saw great alleys of golden stone. I saw gracious archways of breathtaking height. I saw statues, and panels of multicoloured glass.' I took a breath (even though, disembodied, I didn't need to.) 'And I saw a disembodied Head, hidden away in the darkness, a thing that spoke and lived and dreamed, and showed me things from years ago—'

His colours shifted uncomfortably. 'How do you know about that?' he said.

'Never mind. I know,' I said, giving the performance all I had.

The man looked still more uneasy.

'Tell me,' I said, 'how it came to you.'

The man seemed to hesitate for a time, then nodded, his colours clearing. 'I was a mathematician,' he said, 'a Master at the University. I had no ambitions beyond my work. I liked to study number squares. They were so neat, so elegant. I was even writing a book – on the architectural properties of multiplicative squares of complex numbers. And then, on one of my walks, I found the stone, half-buried in a pile of ash.'

'And then the dreams began,' I said.

'How did you know?'

I shrugged. 'Go on.'

'At first I thought I had become too absorbed in my work,' he said. 'I dreamed of numbers and number squares more complex than any I had previously created. Sequences that seemed to explain everything in the known Worlds, from the smallest to the greatest. I abandoned my book on number squares and began to work on my great Theory of the Known Worlds, in which I ventured to speculate that there might be more than the Nine we know – perhaps a great many more, existing alongside our own, in which many possibilities might be played out and tested, like complex equations waiting to be solved.' The man gave me a wan smile. 'I know it sounds insane,' he said, 'but I began to imagine a sequence of Worlds, interlocking like honeycomb, built from the magic of numbers; complex equations expressed as symbols – the symbols we still think of as *runes*—'

'This theory of yours,' I said. 'It didn't happen to feature a cat in a box, did it?'

The mathematician looked confused. 'Er, no.'

'Thank gods for that,' I said. I'd heard enough. I could guess the rest. The Oracle had found itself a foothold in the Architect's mind, though what it hoped to achieve there was a mystery to me. The cathedral was clearly important to it, as it was to the Architect, but I couldn't for the life of me see why a building, however fine, could serve the Oracle's purpose.

My mind went back to the words it had spoken to me in Dream. I'd had time to consider them carefully as I tried to find my way back, and the more I thought about them, the more they sounded like a prophecy.

> *I speak of One who is Nameless*
> *And yet his name is Legion.*
> *He will bring Order to the Worlds,*
> *And bring about a Cleansing.*

From the Cradle to the grave,
He lives in rage and malice.
And his parting gift to you
Will be a poisoned chalice.

Nothing I'd encountered so far had been designed to make me change my mind on the subject of Oracles and prophecies. *Never trust an Oracle*, so the saying goes, and the plan as far as I was concerned was to get as far away as I could from anything that prophesied or spoke in verse (even unaccompanied by a lute). But the words of the Architect of the dream still continued to trouble me; especially the last line:

And his parting gift to you will be a poisoned chalice.

What gift was this? It sounded like a warning. Could this be a trap? Could the Oracle have foreseen my arrival, somehow? Could it even have lured me here? I pushed aside the troubling thought.

'Where is it?'

The architect seemed to hesitate. 'Safe,' he said at last. 'Held safe in the Great Library of the University.'

I didn't know this University, but I guessed it must be linked to those towers and spires I'd noticed. 'Why not keep it with you?' I said. 'Isn't that how you dreamed this place? Isn't that what inspires you?'

His eyes grew dark. 'It *whispers*.'

'It does?'

'At first it was only good things,' he said. 'It told me how to solve problems, and how to bring mathematics into a more practical context. It showed me how an arch could stand much stronger than a doorway; how to plan the crossing where the axes of the nave and transepts meet. It told me how to use the runes to build things I'd never conceived of. But then, it started to *want* things.'

'What kind of things?' I said.

The man shook his head. 'I fought it at first. But it had grown

228

so much stronger. I promised I'd do what it wanted as soon as my great work was finished. And so I threw myself into the building of my cathedral. The work that would ensure my fame, rivalling even Asgard itself.' He paused. 'Is that what it is?' he said. 'The Head of one of the Aesir?'

'Not quite, but pretty close,' I said.

'Have you come to take it back?' His voice was almost pleading.

'Would you like that?'

He nodded.

'Then it's your lucky day. But I'll need you to come with me. I can't manage it on my own.'

That nod again, as if he feared to speak aloud. 'But what if it awakes?' he said, his voice barely more than a whisper. 'What if it awakes and knows that I mean to send it away?'

I summoned a reassuring smile. 'Just do as I tell you,' I told him, 'and I promise everything will be all right. By the way, what's your name? I want to make sure that the Future remembers you as clearly as your great work deserves.'

The architect looked at me and nodded. His eyes were the cold bright blue of the sky on a winter's morning. 'My name is Gift,' he said. 'Jonathan Gift, Professor Emeritus of Mathematics at the University of World's End.'

'Then take my hand, Jonathan Gift,' I said, with a gesture of welcome. 'Take my hand and come with me. We're going to be very close, you and I.'

10

THE UNIVERSITY OF WORLD'S END was a fine building of yellow stone, accessible through an archway that led into a green courtyard, then a set of stairs that took us through a wood-panelled hall and a series of sunlit cloisters towards the Great Library.

It not being the most natural place for a horse, we had left Sleipnir out in the yard. If only Jumps had been with us, we might have dispensed with Jonathan Gift, but we needed someone corporeal to give us access to the Head. And so I entered Jonathan Gift – easy to do, with Sleipnir channelling Dream as he did – and investigated my new surroundings.

I'll admit, I'd been half expecting Jonathan Gift to freak out at that, as Jumps had done when I entered her. But I sensed no alarm at my presence. In fact, I sensed very little reaction. I guessed that Jonathan Gift was used to feeling an alien presence in his mind.

I cast a cursory glance around. Jonathan was more learned than Jumps: his inner space was filled with maps and graphs and equations, and formulae and charts of the sky. There were whole rooms filled with number squares; directories filled with symbols and runes; chambers filled with theories and dissertations and papers and graphs. And while Jumps' mind was filled with people and relationships, Jonathan Gift seemed to have no friends, or family. A section marked *Colleagues* catalogued the Masters in his department at the University; a section marked *Craftsmen* listed the woodcarvers, builders, stonemasons, glassworkers, journeymen, enamellers, tilers and labourers that made up his daily interactions. There were no closed doors in his inner space – except for one restricted zone, cold as Hel, dark as Death. There was no sign of what it might contain, but I sensed that there might be trouble if I tried to explore it.

And his parting gift to you will be a poisoned chalice.

The name couldn't be a coincidence, I thought, as I considered that cold space. Gift, the poisoned chalice – but what kind of poison, and how could it be? There was no guile in Jonathan, no sign that he knew the answer. It made me deeply uncomfortable to think that the Oracle might know a part of what I'd been planning. I wondered what would happen if it awoke to find me in Jonathan's mind. Not that I thought Mimir would deign to stay in the head of a mortal with no runemark and no power. Perhaps that was why the Oracle preferred to spend its time in Dream, conducting grandiose plans instead of experiencing the joys of the flesh. I wouldn't have chosen that option myself, but I guess there's no accounting for taste.

Instead I turned my attention to our surroundings as Jonathan passed through the cloisters. Students in their robes and caps bowed to the architect as he passed; a couple of elderly Masters, recognizable by the red trim on their robes, nodded affably in greeting. Jonathan greeted them in return – his version of the Book of Faces gave me their names and Departments, but nothing more elaborate. Did this man have no friends at all? Was there no one important to him?

But then we entered the Library, and I had eyes only for the books. Books had never been part of my life when I was in Asgard, and in Jumps' world they were commonplace, even sometimes disposable. But, watching the Worlds from my cell, through Dream, I had learnt to respect the written word, as well as those who valued it. And I wondered how this orderly world, this place of books and scholarship, could have sprung from the chaos of Ragnarók. How long had it been since then? Time works differently across the Worlds, but I sensed that this climb out of Chaos had been unusually fast, and shaped at least in part by books, and by the people who wrote them.

Looking around at the Great Library of World's End, I could tell that the people of this World valued books. There must have been over ten thousand of them, lined up on bookshelves twenty feet high: leather-bound books as big as house doors, vellum books as small as your hand; some illustrated in coloured inks; some bound in precious metals. The Library was divided into several sections, each headed in ornate script: *History, Alchemy, Poetry, Philosophy, Astronomy, Geometry, Ars Mathematica*. I noticed the section marked *History* was cordoned off from the rest of the room, and that the books were contained within a glass-fronted cabinet, fastened with a large golden padlock.

Why the padlock?

Jonathan shrugged. 'The History Department is notoriously secretive about its work. I've heard they're working on a definitive Chronicle of Tribulation, and they don't want the other departments interfering in their research.'

Tribulation? I searched Jonathan's mind for more details, and discovered, to my surprise, that it had been no more than two hundred years since Ragnarók, which the Folk now preferred to call *The Tribulation*.

'We thought the Worlds had ended,' said Jonathan in a low voice. 'But out of adversity comes progress, and out of Tribulation comes strength. The Worlds did not end, and out of the long winter there came a new beginning. Books and learning carried us through. The University of World's End was created to study the lessons of the past, and to make sure that never again would we suffer that descent into barbarism.'

Two hundred years seemed a very short time for such a rapid ascent, I thought. I wondered what had inspired it. Someone hunting for treasures in the ruins of Asgard, perhaps? A drily whispering voice from Dream?

It whispers, had said Jonathan Gift.

Just how long had the Oracle been secured in the Library? How many people had heard its voice? What had it whispered in the dark, as it formed its dark dreams of freedom? More importantly, how long ago had the Oracle made the connection with Jonathan Gift?

He gave an inward sigh. *Too long.* I felt a coldness from that restricted area, a place I sensed held memories – or maybe just *one* memory. What memory, what act could be so terrible that he would want to hide it away, even from himself? What crime had this dreamer committed? What secret had the man suppressed in his years of serving the Oracle?

'Please,' said Gift. 'We need to be quick. I'm not supposed to be here.'

He was probably right, I thought. The longer we stayed here, the more risk to those I had left behind in Dream.

Where is it? I asked, trying not to linger over the spines of the books, books with names like *A Historie of the Nine Worldes* and *Asgard – the Myth of Order*.

Jonathan gave a nod in the direction of a cabinet on the far side of the room. It was standing against the wall, in the section marked *Geology*. We walked up to the cabinet, which was labelled *Obsidian fragment: pre-Tribulation*. And there was the Oracle's stone Head; a little chipped, but essentially much as I remembered it.

I felt a shiver go through me, even in Jonathan's body. That damned bauble had never brought good luck to anyone who touched it; and even though I knew it slept, I didn't want to touch the thing.

Jonathan shared my reluctance. Looking around him, he quickly unlatched the glass door to the cabinet, then, picking up the stone Head using the folds of his long robe, he slipped it into the satchel slung across his shoulder. A red-robed Master, sitting nearby, gave a disapproving grunt, but Jonathan ignored him. Carrying the satchel, we left the Library in haste, and, crossing the cloister, went back outside to find the General's Horse cropping grass.

'Will I be free of it now, at last?' said Jonathan in a low voice, looking at the satchel.

'Do you *want* to be free of it?' I said, once more resuming my Aspect as I took my place on Sleipnir's back.

Jonathan nodded.

'How long has it been?'

'Twenty years,' said Jonathan. 'Twenty years of hearing its voice, of having it give me orders. Twenty years of feeling it watching me, questioning me. Twenty years of working for it, of trying to please it, and now—' He stopped abruptly.

'Now what?' I said. 'Why now?'

He paused. I could sense his uncertainty; the same cold and hidden thing that I'd sensed when I was inside him. But I was no longer inside his head, and the hidden thing was still out of reach.

'I made a promise, long ago. It was wrong,' said Jonathan. 'But the Whisperer offered me something I thought I could not refuse. My dreams, made real. My vision, fulfilled. I was young, ambitious: I would have done anything to satisfy my ambition. But now my Cathedral is almost built—'

'You don't want to pay the price?'

Silently, Jonathan shook his head.

'What did it want?' I was getting increasingly curious. But Jonathan just shook his head again, as if even speaking the words might make him guilty of a crime. 'I just want to be free,' he said.

'Free?' I said.

He nodded. 'Free. Free of this life; free of this place; free of the man I have become.'

'Well, I can help you with *that*,' I said, feeling the germ of a plan begin to formulate at last in my mind.

'What must I do?' he said.

I smiled. 'All you have to do is dream.'

Runemarks

By his Mark shall ye know him . . .
Tribulation, Book of Words

1

A ND SO WE FLED ONCE MORE INTO DREAM, with Jonathan in corporeal form, clinging on to Sleipnir's mane with one hand, and holding the satchel containing the Oracle with the other. In Aspect once more, with Sleipnir spanning the sky with his spidery legs, we crossed over what had been Ida's plain, towards the distant mountains.

'You've travelled into Dream before,' I told him, noting his lack of surprise as we left the rooftops of World's End.

Jonathan nodded. 'But not like this.'

'The Oracle's powers are more to do with vision and communication than travel,' I said. That was true; the bauble was certainly talkative enough when it wanted to be. And that explained why it had chosen a visionary as its human contact – a dreamer, whose inner World was almost as real as the World outside. Just how strong that World might be was something that interested me particularly.

'Tell me,' I said.

He looked away. I sensed that he was uncomfortable even remembering the event. 'Twenty years ago,' he said. 'Hard to believe I was ever so young. I was out searching for specimens of pre-Tribulation rock fragments.'

I raised an eyebrow.

'The Winter War,' explained Jonathan Gift, 'was accompanied by a number of interesting geological events. Volcanic eruptions of cinder and ash, which may explain the stories of wolves devouring the Sun and Moon. Of course, nowadays no one believes that those stories were ever literally true. But there's usually a core of truth in stories, whatever the History Department might think. And I had always been curious to know how such primitive warlords as the Aesir could have built something as grandiose as the Sky Citadel of Asgard.'

'*Primitive?*' I said.

'Well, yes. What else do you call a people who made conflict their way of life, who lived for nothing but conquest, who exacted a barbaric revenge on those who dared to defy them?'

Well, I wasn't arguing with *that* one, anyway. I said: 'You seem to have made a study of this.'

He smiled. 'It was my passion. I had a secret theory that behind those stories of magic and runes, the Aesir must have had knowledge of complex engineering and advanced mathematical formulae. Those pieces of cinder that littered the plain were all that was left of Asgard. I wanted to know what properties those pieces of pulverized rock might have had; what secrets I might learn from them to aid my own research.'

'And so you found the Oracle,' I said, imagining the scene. Ida's plain, still littered with the fragments of fallen Asgard; still strewn with the splintered bones of those who had fought alongside me. Maybe even my *own* bones, smashed upon the battlefield—

Damn, that was gruesome, even for me.

But Jonathan Gift was still talking. 'At first I thought I'd found a piece of obsidian-bearing igneous rock. But when I put my hands on it, and felt its presence enter my mind—' He stopped. 'It was unlike anything I had ever felt before. It was like discovering a new kind of equation. I felt power beyond anything I had ever known; I felt the potential for great deeds, great and important discoveries. The thing in my mind seemed to bloom, to expand, to explore every contour of my brain – and then I felt its terrible rage, its terrible disappointment.'

'Disappointment at what?' I asked, although I had a few ideas.

'I wasn't who it wanted,' he said. 'I didn't have what it needed. But I was all it had, and it was not about to let me go. It made me bring the rock sample home. It made me tell it everything I knew. And then it took me into Dream, and showed me what it would do for me – and what it expected in return.'

'And what *did* it expect?' I said.

For a moment Jonathan Gift seemed to hesitate again. Then, finally, with averted gaze, he told me of his deal with the Oracle.

'Of course.' I should have known. It made sense. It was the final piece in the puzzle; the way in which Mimir the Wise could escape his fate and be reborn – not into flesh, but into the Aspect of a god, and wielding the powers that he had always coveted in life—

'I understand,' I said quietly. 'I see now why you were ashamed. But you were brave enough to resist. Few men of your World would have done so.'

Jonathan looked at me hopefully. 'Do you really think so?' he said. 'For twenty years I resisted. But when you found me I was close – *too* close – to fulfilling my promise.'

I felt a little sting of hope. 'Just *how* close exactly?'

He sighed. 'I had what it needed. I could have had it brought to me – to *it* – in only a matter of days.'

'*Brought?* You mean, there's someone else? Someone else who knows about this?'

'Someone. Some*thing*,' Jonathan said.

He started to explain, and I began to see what had happened here; and how, with luck, and a certain amount of deception, I might be able to turn it to my own advantage.

'And if something were to happen,' I said. 'Is there a way of contacting this – *individual*?'

'There's a word,' said Jonathan Gift. And he spoke a word – a *name*, in fact – in a language I hadn't heard spoken for many years: the language of the Elder Age, which now survives only in cantrips and fragments of ancient kennings.

I smiled. Names can be powerful things. *A named thing is a tamed thing*, as the Folk of my World used to say. And this one might just hold the key to my continued survival.

I made a mental note of the name. If I survived the next few hours, I might even get to use it. And then I fled with my passenger back towards the World I had left, in which Jumps' body, connected to her ethereal Aspect by the thinnest of silver cords, was (I hoped) still waiting for me to bring her back to life, like the Vanir in *Asgard!*™, or one of those sleeping princesses from her childhood storybooks.

2

'YOU LOST *JUMPS?*' EVAN SAID, showing more animation than he had since I'd first encountered him. 'But how can you still be—' His face fell. 'Oh. I see.'

I let him figure it out. Corporeal Aspect is better than hanging around as a fine mist, even when that Aspect happens to be someone else's. I wished, for Jumps' sake, that I could explain to him what was going on, but with Odin and Heidi watching me, that wasn't exactly an option.

The silver cord that linked Jumps to her Dream-self remained unbroken, through very faint, almost invisible, even to me – I guessed that Odin and Heidi probably wouldn't work out what that meant, especially as my passenger was taking up all their attention. Of course the dog Twinkle had no such cord, though its behaviour was just as it had been when the Thunderer was in charge, and it capered happily around my legs as I introduced my new friend.

'Folks, meet Jonathan Gift,' I said. 'He's quite appropriately named.'

Less than fifteen minutes had passed in this World while I was away. That translated into almost an hour in Jonathan's World; and in Dream, where Time has no meaning, it might have been hours, even days. I tried not to think too hard about what Jumps might be doing: whether or not she was still sane, or had drifted off into that part of Dream the Folk call Madness. But no, that silver cord was intact, which meant that the link between body and mind was still theoretically viable. But time was running out, and my plan, never a dead cert from the start, needed only for one thing to go wrong before everything came down in pieces.

For a while there was confusion. Odin and Heidi both wanted to ask their questions at the same time, Evan was crazy concerned about Jumps, and I was trying my hardest not to look at Meg at all, not even to see if she was OK, because that might have revealed the plan that was forming in my mind.

Forming, you say? So shoot me. No, I wasn't yet totally sure of the possible outcome. I've always been better making things up as I go along than sticking to a strategy. My ferryman, with his single wolf and goat and cabbage, had it easy. Yours Truly was trying to juggle not only the thrice-damned cabbage, but a whole infernal menagerie.

And besides, I was dealing with Odin here – never a predictable guy, though in this case I guessed that the thought of facing the Oracle on its home ground was unlikely to appeal to him.

Meanwhile, Jonathan Gift, wide-eyed, descended from the eight-legged Horse – now in a humbler Aspect once more, and starting to crop grass. He looked around at the orange lights of Malbry town below us. He looked at Evan, at Heidi, at Meg. He looked at me in Jumps' skin, trying to work out what had changed. And then he saw Twinkle, and started to smile—

'Oh,' he said. 'A little dog!'

I gave an inward sigh. Of all the marvels of this new World upon which he might have chosen to fix his attention, he had to choose the damn dog. Still, Twinkle seemed to like him, and capered happily around his legs. I tried not to look at the satchel slung across his body – I hoped that its humble appearance,

244

as well as the fact that the whole Hill was already alight with glamours, would serve to hide what it contained.

Instead I addressed Heidi. 'Jonathan Gift,' I explained, 'is the Oracle's current toy. He rescued it. He knows where it is.'

Heidi gave me a cold look. 'I thought I made it clear,' she said. 'You were to bring me my father's Head, not some random human.'

'He isn't a random human,' I protested. 'I told you, the Oracle has a plan. This man has been putting that plan into action. And much as I long to please you, my discorporate Aspect might have given me some difficulty when it came to, er, *collecting* it—'

Heidi's eyes narrowed. 'You're talking too much. It's a sign you're up to something.'

'He's always up to something,' said Odin. 'And he always talks too much.' He turned his attention to Jonathan Gift, who by then had dropped to his knees, leaving the pack with the Oracle's Head lying beside the firepit, and was asking Twinkle who the good boy was.

'Who are you?' said Odin.

'An architect,' said Jonathan Gift, reluctantly looking up from the dog. 'Once a mathematician. Now trained in the art of construction.'

'Really?' said Odin. In Evan's skin, I couldn't tell what he was thinking, but knowing the Old Man as I did, I guessed he was thinking deeply. Thinking about whether I was planning to betray him (I was); about whether I had a ulterior motive (I had); about whether to trust me anyway. He did, of course. He had to. When it came to it, in the end, I was still a safer bet than Gullveig-Heid.

'Jonathan Gift is the man,' I explained, 'who will lead us to the Oracle.'

Odin's gaze speared me. 'I see,' he said thoughtfully, and, still looking at me, took the architect by the hand.

Gullveig-Heid had not noticed the look that passed between

245

us. Instead, she spoke to Jonathan, without trying to conceal her eagerness:

'Tell me about the Oracle. Where you found it. What it said. Did it make a prophecy?'

The architect gave a little shrug. 'It was so long ago,' he said. 'It spoke in some kind of poetry. I don't remember the exact words, but—'

'It *prophesied*?' said Heidi. 'It prophesied, and this idiot doesn't *remember*!'

'It mentioned runes,' said Jonathan, looking aggrieved. 'New runes for the gods – which doesn't make sense, as the Aesir all fell at Ragnarók. I can only suppose that it must have been some form of metaphor—'

'*What runes?*' said Gullveig-Heid, her expression growing dangerous.

Odin saw it and intervened. 'It doesn't matter,' he said. 'We need to find it.'

'And by "we", you mean yourself and—?' I said.

'Oh, don't think you're getting out of this,' said Odin in his grimmest voice. 'You're coming too. And so is *he*—' He gestured towards Jonathan. 'That way at least we'll have *someone* with a physical presence.'

Heidi broke in. 'No, not Odin. *He* can stay here, in his human host. If the Oracle makes a prediction, I want to hear it first-hand.'

'So do I,' said Odin.

Heidi laughed. 'You don't say? You're staying here until my father's Head is in my grasp. And after that—' She looked at me. 'I will fulfil my part of the agreement.'

I raised an eyebrow. *My part of the agreement.* That sounded interesting. The whereabouts of the Vanir, perhaps? I should have known Odin wouldn't throw in his lot with Heidi unless she had something he wanted. And I knew Odin well enough by now to understand that what he *wanted* wasn't always what he *needed*.

'You don't need me, either,' I said. 'Leave me here. I'll be fine.'

She laughed. 'Not a chance, Trickster. You're not getting away until I have my father's Head, and the new runes. After that, you'll be free to go.'

I feigned chagrin. 'Is this necessary?'

'Oh, yes. I think it is.'

I gave an exaggerated sigh. Then I grasped the Horse's mane. Looking at Evan, I said: 'All right. See you on the other side.'

Preparing to leave, I took one last look at Meg there on the hillside. If my plan worked, I would probably never see her again. In fact, if my plan worked, I would probably never see *any* of them again, which, to be fair, was fine by me. Being human might have its perks, I thought, but in the long run, what with the feelings, the angst and the existential confusion, I much preferred to be myself: disloyal, uncaring, selfish; pure and unconflicted.

Evan was standing beside Meg, looking into the bright air, his face upturned in livid stripes that radiated from the Horse as it prepared to cross over once more into the maelstrom of Dream.

For a second, our eyes met. No question of speaking my thoughts aloud; and without the special intimacy that had linked me with Jumps in our shared space, all I could conjure was the very simplest of messages. So, across the glamorous air, I sent him a distant memory of himself and Jumps, aged seven, on their first day of junior school. Jumps was wearing yellow shorts and a blue sweater with a picture of a penguin on it. Evan was wearing dungarees and a Spiderman T-shirt. And Evan took out his glass eye and put it into Jumps' hand, where it gleamed like a marble—

Here. You can hold it.

Can it see?

No. But it once scored twenty points in a game of ringer.

There. I thought I saw him flinch. I hoped I'd managed to get it across. A small and unrelated thing, which hopefully would fail to attract the attention of my companions. His gaze flicked to Stella, who, freed from her passenger, was blinking prettily (if somewhat vacantly) at the scene. Then he looked at me again, and I thought – I hoped – he'd understood.

Here. You can hold it. Keep it safe.

'Good luck, Captain,' Evan said.

'Thanks. I make my own, you know.'

Then we were tumbling through Dream, I still clad in Jumps' skin, Gullveig-Heid discorporate, Jonathan Gift clinging on for dear life, and the next thing I knew was Heidi's voice in my ear, saying:

'Right. So what's the *real* plan?'

3

I ASSUMED AN AIR OF INNOCENCE. My being in the flesh meant that Heidi could not easily see the thread of deceit in my colours.

'What d'you mean, the real plan?'

'I mean, I don't buy your story,' she said. 'Why aren't you in your true Aspect? Why have you brought this useless human body with you instead? You're up to no good, and you're hiding it. And where's Thor?'

I shrugged Jumps' shoulders. 'He got left behind.'

'Or maybe you ditched him in Dream. Maybe he was on to you. Maybe you're playing a double game. What's the plan? Divide and rule? Or are you working for Odin?'

'You should know me better,' I said, glancing back at Jonathan Gift. 'Why should I want to help Odin? I haven't got where I am today without two things: self-interest and self-preservation. Would I really risk my skin (to which I'm rather partial, even though technically it belongs to someone else) to help anyone other than myself?'

'You came in corporeal Aspect,' she said. 'I can see only one reason for that. You mean to take the Head for yourself. It's impossible, but clearly you think it's an option. You think that in your borrowed flesh, you can outwit the Temptress.' She smiled, and it was like looking into a golden furnace. 'Coming from somebody else,' she said, 'that would look stupid and naïve. Coming from you, I'm thinking maybe you have something up your sleeve.'

I shrugged. 'If I'd wanted the Oracle, I wouldn't have thrown it off Bif-rost. And as for Odin – I don't owe him a thing. He betrayed me. Remember? And on that subject, I'm curious. How did you manage to draw his teeth? I've never seen the Old Man so compliant. What have you got that he wants so much?'

Heidi said: 'Wouldn't *you* like to know?'

I grinned. 'I'm always up for ways to score one off the General. Whatever it is, you've got him good. What is it? His spear? His ravens? His hat?'

Heidi gave a girlish laugh. Out of her human Aspect and in her natural form, the sound of her laughter was terrible, like a cascade of molten gold pouring down onto my head. 'Something far more important,' she said. 'He was always sentimental. And when I told him my people hadn't fallen at Ragnarók, but instead lay sleeping under the ice, awaiting their true destiny—'

I feigned surprise. '*Your* people?'

She shrugged. 'The Vanir were never his folk,' she said. 'That alliance was born of treachery. Odin used my father simply to help him steal their runes. But the Vanir were never his to command. They followed him out of self-interest. And if a *real* leader had come along – a leader who was one of them, with the strength and the vision to lead them, instead of that perennial con artist who calls himself the General—'

So, I thought. The story was true. *Asgard!*™ had predicted as much; along with the rise of the old gods and the rebuilding of Asgard itself. A strange, but compelling thought began to formulate in my mind. If *Asgard!*™ had been right about the Vanir, what else might the game have foreseen? What other predictions might be contained in that strange little virtual World?

'The Vanir?' I said. 'You mean they're alive? Njörd, and Idun, and Freyja, and Frey? Bragi? That bastard Heimdall? The guy who killed me at Ragnarók? You're telling me he's still *alive*?'

Heidi smiled. 'I have no reason to doubt it,' she said. 'Although I believe Odin's interests lie in another direction.'

'Let me guess,' I said. 'Freyja.'

Heidi looked amused. Here, in Dream, her true Aspect was both glorious and disquieting. All black and gold, with eyes like flame, and skin like smooth obsidian. And yet, if you'd put her side by side with the Goddess of Desire, you might have imagined them to be twins. Both of them had that dangerous gleam, a glamour that went far beyond mere physical attraction. I'm not immune to it myself, but Odin was worse: he knew what Freyja was like, and yet he couldn't keep away from her.

'That's Desire for you,' she said. 'Blind in one eye and unable to see from the other.' She smiled her golden smile. 'And yet, it's ironic, isn't it, that the man who built the Worlds could still be so weak, so fallible as to fall for the oldest trick in the history of trickery?'

I shrugged. 'It's a good trick. I've used it myself.'

'And fallen for it, too,' she said, with a gleam of amusement.

'Whatever,' I said. 'That's all in the past. Unless—' I gave her a sidelong glance. 'Unless it isn't. *Is* it? No.' I shook away the thought of us together again, as we had been in those dark and glorious days. That was her glamour talking, and I wasn't about to be suckered the way Odin had been.

'Tell me Odin's plan,' I said. 'Seeing that he doesn't seem to have felt the need to share it with me.'

'I don't suppose he did,' she said. 'He only wanted to use you. All he needed was your blood, to awaken Sleipnir. After that, he was planning to pull Thor and Freyja out of Dream, via the funny little World contained within a computer game. Of course, that's how I was able to make him think I was Freyja – at least for long enough for me to find myself a host body suitable for my needs. After that, he was easy enough to seduce. With my father's Head, and the new runes, and with the awakened

Vanir back under his command, I let him believe he might have a chance to regain what he'd lost – to build a new Asgard, to rule once again.' She gave her tinkling, terrible laugh. 'But that won't happen. I'd rather see the Vanir dead than under his command once more. And, of course, I know where they are.'

'You do?'

'Because I put them there.'

Of course she did. It made sense now. Heidi, working for Chaos, casting a final web of runes as Surt's shadow fell on the Worlds, locking her people under the ice that fell in the wake of the Winter War. Had she meant, even then, to revive them some day? Was this part of her greater plan? Or had it been some unexpected sentimental impulse?

Heidi smiled. Her Aspect was now less terrible, closer to the Aspect in which she had seduced and betrayed me. In this form, with her jet-black skin and hair as gold as the sunrise, I could remember why I had been so ready to join the renegades, so blinded with lust and rage that I had failed to see how she was using me.

'We were so good together,' she said, touching my corporeal lips with her ephemeral fingers. 'We could be good together again. I was sorry you had to fall. It wasn't my decision. But with my father's Head, and the runes, and the Vanir awakened and under my rule, maybe we could be friends again. Maybe even more than friends.'

There's a reason they called her the Temptress. And I'd be lying if I said I wasn't briefly tempted. But I could see what she meant to do: to lure me out of my borrowed flesh, perhaps to glimpse my colours. And this time, I wasn't playing her game, although she *was* still alluring. I said:

'I know how you treat your friends. I'm not about to go there again.'

'Oh, did I hurt your feelings? Did poor little Loki think that I would give up my ambitions for him?' She laughed. 'You're so sentimental. You need to lighten up. We had fun, didn't we?

And I never promised you eternal loyalty. In fact, my dear, as I recall, I never promised you *anything*.'

That was true, I told myself. I'd been so grateful for my release from torment (plus there was the delirium of corporeal sex, wine, jam tarts and all the pleasures she offered me) that I'd somehow omitted to engage my natural defences. I'd made an assumption – a mistake that I had paid for dearly.

'Bygones,' I said. 'No hard feelings.'

'No?'

'Well, maybe a few,' I said. 'But you have the advantage of being a lot smarter than Odin – as well as being far more attractive. Let's dance.'

She gave me a look that in the corporeal World would have ignited paper. She said: 'I'd trust you a whole lot more if you slipped out of that body. Why are you wearing it, anyway? You'd look a lot better without it. I mean, I like you as a girl, but as a boy you were fabulous.'

'I will,' I said. 'Just as soon as you tell me where that bastard is sleeping.'

'You mean Heimdall?'

'Who else?'

She looked at me. 'And why would you want to know that?'

I laughed. 'Maybe I want to wake him up with a runny egg and some toast soldiers.'

'You'd kill him in his sleep?'

'Well, *duh*. What, did you think I'd leave him there? After all he's put me through?'

Heidi smiled. 'No, I don't think you would.'

'So tell me. Better still, *show* me. Show me, and I'll finish him. Odin's right-hand man, the one person who would have challenged you. Let me finish him for you, and the rest of the Vanir will follow you.'

She gave me a supercilious look. 'I don't need your help,' she said. 'I can deal with him myself.'

'Yes, of course,' I told her. 'But if you kill Heimdall, you'll always be the one who killed one of your own to take power. That's what Odin did, and look how it worked out for him. Odin knew that, sometimes, a god has to keep the moral high ground whilst controlling the moral low ground. That's why he enlisted *me*. And that's why you're going to do the same.'

For a long time, Heidi looked at me. Then she said: 'You may have a point. I'll give you Heimdall as soon as you give me my father's Head. Is that a deal?'

I nodded, secretly gnashing my teeth. I could see clearly now why Odin had been so reluctant to tell me the details. He must have known I'd feel strongly about the prospect of my old enemy snoring away under the ice while the Aesir suffered in Netherworld. But Heidi knew my value, I hoped – at least for as long as it suited her. After that, I sensed that she might wish to reconsider my continued survival.

We were approaching the bubble-world in which I had left Jumps (and Thor). The Oracle's colours were brighter here, shooting vivid bursts of luminescence into the turbulent current. I held on to Sleipnir's bridle, guiding him, and then we were back in the Architect's dream: the cathedral; the Machina Brava; the crystal dome that engulfed the sky—

I reined Sleipnir to a halt and climbed down onto the mosaic floor.

'What are we doing here?' Heidi said. 'Is my father in this World?'

But I was already looking for Jumps. I found her curled up at the base of one of those giant columns of stone; but tiny now, no more than four years old; tucked into herself like a flower bud, as if she had made every effort to make herself as inconspicuous as possible.

Thor was there, too, in Aspect, though dwarfed by his surroundings. On seeing me, his face did a number of things, most of them contradictory.

I took a moment to acknowledge that Thor wasn't having the best of times. Trapped – first of all in *Asgard!*™, then in the

Aspect of a small dog, and now in the dream of a creature who should have been dead when the Vanir cut off his head nearly a thousand years ago. Well, that kind of thing puts a strain on a man, and Thor was not the most patient of men. He looked like a thunder god desperate for something to hit, and from the look in his eyes, I could tell he wanted it to be me.

Of the Oracle, there was no sign.

I bent down to try and awaken Jumps. She looked fast asleep, but as I moved closer, I could hear her singing, very softly, the song I had once pulled from her mind:

Land whale, land whale—

'Jumps?' I said. 'It's Loki. Jumps?'

The little girl looked up. I could see confusion in her face, and then, at last, the beginnings of recognition. 'Loki?' she said.

I was relieved. That little song had troubled me. 'Why *that* song? You were supposed to choose something warm and good to carry you through the worst parts of Dream.'

'I chose something I could fight,' said Jumps. Her Aspect was more familiar now, closer to her true self. 'You showed me I could fight back. But you—' She looked at me blurrily. 'You look different. Did you bring—' Then her face brightened and she said: 'Loki. You brought – you brought *me*!'

I had to smile at her trust in me: her automatic assumption that I had brought her body through Dream for *her*, rather than for any nefarious purpose of my own.

I held out my hand. 'Welcome back,' I said.

She flung her arms around me.

For a moment we were together again, at one and filled with power. In that moment I sent her everything – a plan, a warning, a riddle and a set of instructions – and then I stepped out into Dream and gave her control of her body. It felt like taking off a coat moulded to my contours. I doubted I'd ever wear it again, and, given what she had put me through, the thought was surprisingly painful.

Jumps looked at me with a brilliant smile. I'd thought her

pretty enough, but the smile made her suddenly beautiful, and I wondered if she'd ever smiled like that when I was in her.

'I knew you'd do the right thing,' she said. 'I knew you wouldn't leave a friend.'

Which made me feel even worse, as I knew precisely what I was planning to do – it didn't feel great, but what choice did I have? My options weren't what you'd call endless.

Gullveig-Heid gave me a sideways look. '*That's* why you brought the body?' she said. 'To bring your host with you into Dream?'

'So shoot me,' I said. 'I've grown fond of her.'

Heidi looked contemptuous. 'It seems like self-indulgence to me. But each to his own. If you want to be absurd, don't let me stop you.'

I shrugged my ephemeral shoulders and kept my expression neutral. I knew I was under scrutiny, and that here in my natural Aspect, Heidi would notice the slightest disturbance in my colours. But I hoped that the agitation of learning that Heimdall was still alive, as well as the hellride through Dream, would account for any unusual activity in my coloration. Of course, if it didn't, I was toast. But I counted on my expertise in all forms of deception to keep the game up for just a little while longer.

Jonathan Gift dismounted and looked around at the great glass dome. 'Gods,' he said. 'I had no idea my plans could be so beautiful.'

Heidi gave him a look. '*Your* plans?'

Jonathan nodded happily. 'I used to read about the old gods. I read of their adventures, their wars – but what I really wanted to know was the secret of how they built it.'

'Built what?'

'The Sky Citadel. Of course, it fell long before I was born. But there were so many stories. Bif-rost, the Rainbow Bridge. Valhalla, the Hall of Heroes. Every god and goddess with their own hall.'

'Not *all* of us had a hall,' I said, but Jonathan Gift wasn't listening.

'I knew that their secret lay with the runes. But runes are just equations. Mathematical symbols. Symbols, that with the right knowledge, can reveal the secrets of the Nine Worlds.'

'Did my father teach you this?' said Heidi. 'Is my father here?'

But before Jonathan could answer, suddenly we were no longer alone. At the far end of the great hall, by the Machina Brava, stood a figure I had seen before, standing taller than Ymir himself, its head in the silvery haze of the dome, its great feet cracking the floor-tiles.

I heard Thor give a low growl. Jumps moved closer to Sleipnir. But Gullveig-Heid was staring, transfixed, at the apparition; her colours brightening, her face shining with anticipation.

The Oracle looked down at Heidi with no apparent interest or recognition.

'Father. It's me,' said Heidi.

I noticed her Aspect had changed in this dream: like Jumps, she looked younger, more vulnerable. Could this be the Oracle's influence? Could it be that Gullveig-Heid was intimidated by a fatherly presence?

'It's me. Your daughter. Gullveig-Heid,' she said, with an edge of impatience.

The Oracle, however, continued to ignore her.

'Where's Odin?' it said in a voice that seemed to come from every dark space in the Nine Worlds, all the while scanning our party for what it sought. Flesh is in no way a perfect disguise, but I felt naked without it; fully aware that my unease was visible in my colours.

But Heidi wasn't watching me. Instead, she addressed the Oracle, now with a combination of impatience and what might have been pique. 'Father,' she said. 'I seek guidance. I have sought you for so long. I have made such plans for us. Will you give me your prophecy?'

257

For a moment the Oracle looked down at the tiny figures at its feet. Then it laughed, and waved a hand around the giant cathedral. 'All *this* is My prophecy,' it said in a voice like an avalanche. 'A monument to My greatness, built from the ashes of Asgard. Built from the timbers of Yggdrasil, it will endure. *I* will endure. And the gods – their stories, even their names – will be erased from history. You've seen it. You know it will happen.' The Oracle looked down expectantly, focusing its eyes on me. 'And now, Trickster. Where is the General?'

'Ah. Well. He got left behind,' I said, glancing quickly at Jonathan Gift.

The Oracle's giant voice took on a dangerously trollish tone. 'Really?' it said. 'I wonder how? And why have you brought my host into Dream? Were you hoping to use him against me? To make Me prophesy, perhaps? To force Me to give you the new runes?' The Oracle laughed again, and its voice filled the cathedral with thunder. 'The new runes are not for *you*,' it said, 'but for the next generation of gods. The children of the Fire; the ones who will build the Worlds anew.'

At this, Heidi's face lit up. 'And I, Father? What about me?'

The Oracle's laughter redoubled. 'The new runes are not for you,' it said. 'Of course, I admire your ambition, but there is no place for you in My plan.'

Heidi's eyes went wide at that, and her Aspect dwindled even more, reducing her to an angry child, denied some anticipated treat.

'My daughter,' went on the Oracle. 'I hope you know me well enough to understand that I mean you no personal ill. But we are too much alike, you and I. We share a common hunger. We also share a *reluctance* to share; an admirable self-interest. Just as it was inevitable that Odin's brothers would one day fall to his growing ambition, I've always known that one day, too, both of us would come to this.'

Heidi frowned. 'I don't understand. I sought you out. I *found* you.'

'But I didn't ask you to come,' said the Oracle. 'My orders were to bring Odin.'

Heidi shot me a glance. 'I thought—'

'*You* thought I might prophesy,' it said. 'You were afraid that Odin might learn something to his advantage. And so you defied Me – your father – and now you expect a reward?' The voice, already steely, grew sharp. 'And as for you, Trickster, what do you think *you* deserve for this escapade?'

I did not reply. My experience is that my idea of what I deserve doesn't always coincide with the majority opinion.

The Oracle made a dismissive sound. 'In any case, that's over now. It might have been amusing to make Odin suffer as I did, but his time is over. Mine begins. With the new runes, and the General's Horse, which you have thoughtfully provided for Me, as well as a corporeal host, I can travel wherever I please. But as for letting *you* leave this place – I'm afraid that's out of the question. All I need is Jonathan. The rest of you are expendable.'

'*Expendable?*' said Heidi. Her Aspect shifted uneasily; one moment small and petulant, the next a looming monstrosity. 'You're telling me that I spent the last few hundred years searching for you through Death, Dream and Damnation, and now I'm just expendable? That this – this *human* – inherits the Runes?'

And assuming her primary Aspect – clothed from head to toe in flame; merciless and terrible (I'm not going to lie. I *was* aroused) – she took a step towards Jonathan Gift, and flung a single runebolt—

Hagall, the Destroyer, crossed with *Sól*, the sun-rune in its most deadly, primitive form: a powerful combination. Flung with all the strength and guile of Gullveig-Heid, the Golden One, the missile whickered across the hall—

'*Stop her!*' I cried to Thor, and quickly flung up the runeshape Ýr as a shield to protect the architect. Meanwhile Thor – never much of a thinker, but faster than you might imagine when it came to taking action – had finally realized who it was that he *really* wanted to hit. He closed on Heidi, moving fast; but

Heidi's rune was powerful, and, punching through the rune-shield, it struck Jonathan Gift full in the face.

Jonathan cried out in pain, clapping his hand to his left eye. But the runeshield had done at least something to halt the speed of the Temptress's runebolt. The damage was superficial, although the wound looked like a nasty one. Jonathan Gift was still standing, blood dripping through his fingers. But now the Oracle's presence swelled invisibly all around, filling the air with incense and the sound of breaking glass.

On all sides of the great hall, stained-glass windows were shattering. They went one by one, from east to west, as if every door in the Nine Worlds were slamming shut almost at once. The fall of Odin. The last stand of Thor. My fall from the sky with Heimdall, pulverized into shining dust.

'YOU DARE TO ATTACK ME?' it said, in that giant, inhuman voice. 'AND HERE, OF ALL PLACES? USING *MY* RUNES?'

I winced as shards of stained glass scattered around us like shrapnel. This, I thought, was where my plan might be starting to get just a little out of control. The Oracle was already enraged. Every strong emotion meant a risk of it waking up. And a wakened Oracle would mean the end of this dream, with great risk to the rest of us. So far, the dream had been strong enough to survive our retrieval of the Head and its transportation to another World. But the presence of Jonathan Gift made for a volatile chemistry. The colours of the dream had become ominously lurid, boiling with captive energy. I was only too aware that the bubble shielding us from the raw and deadly stuff of Dream might burst at any moment.

I started to move towards Sleipnir, my only avenue of escape. The Oracle loomed over me like a curse. One more surprise might awaken it—

And then, from behind me came a voice, both familiar and new. I turned and saw Jumps, standing calmly in the eye of the storm, looking up at the Oracle. 'But they're not *your* runes. Are they?' she said. 'The runes were meant for someone else.'

4

I'D ALMOST FORGOTTEN JUMPS IN the drama of the scene. This was not her world, but mine; a world of uncertainty, and tricks, and colossal powers in conflict. She was trapped inside the mind of a god – or something very like one – and to be honest, the fact that she wasn't climbing the walls and gibbering came as a bit of a surprise. I mean, a life of fluffy toys and penguin slippers and having kind of a crush on the guy who plays Thor in the movies, and wanting to be skinny, and worrying about what the other kids might say if they knew you liked kissing girls – it's not much of a preparation for something on a grander scale.

And yet she seemed calm enough to me. Certainly calmer than she'd been the day she flipped out in the English exam. I struggled to understand how a test on twentieth-century novelists could be more important than being trapped between Worlds with an entity that could swallow you up as easily as the World Serpent inhaling fish, and found that I really couldn't.

She thinks she's asleep. She still thinks she's going to wake up if it gets too freaky.

I gave her a warning nudge. 'Shh. For gods' sakes, let him forget you're here. You're in the flesh now. You can be hurt.'

But her words had had immediate effect. The light from the dome began to darken ominously. Suddenly, shadows appeared at the base of the great marble pillars; long shadows that crept like snakes across the colourful mosaic floor.

Heidi and Thor had paused in their circling of each other, glam trembling at their fingertips.

'EXCUSE ME?' said the giant voice of the Oracle.

Jumps gave a little shrug. She seemed a little older than the last time I'd looked in the mirror: as if over the course of a single dream, she had left adolescence behind.

'Just saying,' she said. 'They're not your runes. Isn't that what your prophecy said? *New runes for Odin's heirs*?'

Hot damn. She'd been paying attention.

The temperature in the great hall dropped a sudden thirty degrees. The pillars that looked so like *Isa*, with their swags of ornamentation, now gleamed with baleful blue light. The Oracle's voice swelled, the rage in it trembling.

'WHAT?'

'You said that Odin had heirs,' said Jumps. 'That means the runes belong to *them*. Not to Gullveig-Heid, not to *you*—' I tried to make her be quiet, but Jumps was never what you'd call open to suggestions.

'ODIN'S HEIRS ARE NOT YET BORN,' said the Oracle's booming voice.

'Doesn't matter, does it?' said Jumps. 'You said the runes would come to them. You should know. You're supposed to be an Oracle.'

'YOU QUESTION ME?' said the voice from every corner of that World. All of us – corporeal or not – put our hands over our ears, but the volume did not abate.

'Just saying,' said Jumps. 'Odin's heirs. You ought to know who they are. Who they'll *be*. I mean, if you know the future.'

'OF COURSE I KNOW,' said the Oracle.

'OK,' said Jumps. 'Whatever.'

The temperature had dropped still more. Snow began to fall

from the dome. The ice on the pillars began to bloom like massive clusters of white moss.

'DID YOU JUST SAY "WHATEVER" TO ME?'

Jumps made an odd little gesture, half shrug, half head-waggle. I'd noticed it before, when we were discussing food choices. I'd found it infuriating then, and it seemed to have much the same effect on Mimir.

'Well, to be fair,' said Jumps, 'I haven't actually heard you ever *make* a prophecy. So far it's just been a whole load of intimidation and threats.'

'I SPEAK OF TWO YOUNG SHOOTS THAT GROW,' said the Oracle, in a grating voice. 'ONE THE OAK, AND ONE THE ASH. ONE THE HORSE, AND ONE THE BONE. ONE FROM EARTH, AND ONE FROM STONE.'

I saw Jonathan Gift look up. One hand was still clapped to his eye, but I could tell he was paying attention. Heidi, too, was listening. Even Thor seemed aware that he'd heard something of importance.

Jumps alone was unimpressed. 'Bit vague. Just saying, that could mean anything.'

'I SPEAK AS I MUST,' said the Oracle. 'I SPEAK AS I MUST, AND WILL NOT BE SILENT.'

'No, you never shut up, do you?' said Jumps.

I told you she was annoying. But at that moment I could have kissed her, if that wouldn't have been a bit creepy, even for me. And yet, as I was cheering her, I could also feel one of those human sensations that I didn't quite understand: a fear that was not on my own behalf.

'Don't,' I said. 'You've said enough.'

She grinned. 'Was that a prophecy?'

I nodded.

'So, it's what you wanted, right? This is what you came here for?'

I nodded again. 'But it's dangerous. Remember, in this world, he's a god.'

'He's not a god. He's a bully,' said Jumps. 'You taught me to stand up to bullies.'

'Er, not the same thing,' I said. 'Bullies are people who call you *names*, not immortal megalomaniacs with the power to crush your soul.'

Jumps grinned. 'Let's see, shall we? Let's make it prophesy again.' And she turned back to the Oracle, its head high up in the icy vault, waved her arms and shouted:

'Hey! Hey you up there!'

Once more, I tried to silence her. But I could see it was too late. The dream was beginning to collapse. Ice fell from the ceiling; darkness descended from the sky. Against the dome, the river Dream roiled and crashed and tumbled. I knew what that meant. I'd expected it – although, to be fair, I'd rather planned on being over the hills and far away by the time the proverbial excrement hit the proverbial ventilation unit. Destabilized by recent events; its power challenged, its vanity hurt; tricked into revelation: at last, the Oracle was waking up.

5

It STARTED WITH THE CEILING: that gorgeous dome of crystal glass, now cracked down the middle and swinging chandeliers of bundled ice. Swags of ice hung from the vaulting, tumbled down the pillars. The Oracle was still declaiming, its giant voice filling the Worlds:

'I SPEAK OF SEVEN SLEEPERS, BOUND WITH RUNES UNDER A MOUNTAIN. AND ONE WHO, IN A NET OF FIRE, STILL LIVES IN WISDOM'S FOUNTAIN.'

'Another verse of prophecy, right?' cried Jumps above the roar of Dream. 'Do you need to know any more?'

I shook my head. *Seven sleepers.* The Vanir, perhaps? *Wisdom's Fountain.* Mimir? Mimir's Well? A clue, perhaps, to where the Vanir slept?

'Forget the prophecy!' I said. 'We have to go!'

'Hang on,' said Jumps.

I saw that her Aspect had changed again. In dreams, that often happens, though I'd never seen it happen to a human in corporeal form. Now she was a young woman; strong, not unbeautiful, but a far cry from those girls at school and in those magazines she read. And although she must have been frightened – gods, even *I* was – she seemed to glow with her own inner light, a light that almost rivalled that of the Oracle's fantasy.

That's the thing about the Folk. They burn: they burn so brightly in their little span of time that even the gods cannot compete. And Jumps, so small, so weak, so scared – too scared to eat a pizza, too scared to be seen going out with a girl – Jumps was somehow suddenly, inexplicably marvellous.

Addressing the Oracle, she cried: 'Is that really all you've got?'

'I'M SORRY?' said the Oracle.

'Is that all you've got?' repeated Jumps. 'A few lines of verse – and *bad* verse, at that. Is that the extent of your power? I mean, who do you think you are? Telling people what to do? Thinking you're better than everyone else, making them do whatever you want? Did you never think to yourself that Jonathan might have dreams of his own? Dreams that don't involve being the pawn of a great big headless wonder?'

Beside me, I heard a hiss of what might have been laughter from Jonathan Gift. Heidi and Thor had briefly interrupted their fight and were looking at her incredulously. I tried in vain to quiet Jumps, but she was past being quieted. I'd seen her like this twice before: the night she'd threatened to cut her throat, and the night she'd confronted Heidi – and I knew she meant every word she said – after all, I'd been in her.

'A WHAT?' said the voice of the Oracle.

A silence fell on the great hall. But it wasn't a comforting silence. It was the silence that precedes an earthquake or an avalanche, the silence of sleep paralysis. All around us, the dream had begun to shimmer, and shift, and soften. Great rents in the fabric of that World had opened, showing the many horrors without.

And then the Oracle spoke again, in a surprisingly level voice: 'I SPEAK AS I MUST, AND WILL NOT BE SILENT. I SPEAK AS I MUST, AND YOU WILL HEAR. I SPEAK OF WORLDS BOTH OLD AND NEW; OF GODS BOTH NEW AND BROKEN. I SPEAK OF WAR ACROSS THE WORLD, AND WAR ACROSS THE OCEAN. I SPEAK OF

A ONE-EYED WANDERER, ALLFATHER, ARCHITECT OF DREAMS. I SPEAK OF A SLEEPER AWAKENED—'

The giant voice suddenly stopped.

Oh-oh, I thought. *Mimir got wise.*

I looked at Thor. Once more I wondered if I should try to explain the goat, the wolf and the cabbage. But he wouldn't understand – and besides, the dream was coming apart. I could see it losing cohesion at last, as the walls and vaulting started to stretch like bubblegum.

'Get ready,' I told him. 'Something's going to happen. And when it does, I hope you'll know what it is you have to do.'

'What do you mean?' said Thor.

I took a breath. 'What I mean is,' I told him, 'you're going to have to stay here.'

Thor gave me the look of a thunder god goaded beyond endurance. 'Why should I?' he said.

'Because *someone* has to, Thor,' I said. 'Because you're loyal. Because you're brave. And because (although to be honest, I'm not a great authority on bravery or sacrifice), you're actually pretty noble.' There came a sound from above our heads; the sound of the last of our time running out. 'I'm going to say something now, Thor, that you might not have heard very often. I mean, it's not as if we were *friends*, but of all the Aesir, you were perhaps the one who hated me the least. And Jumps always liked you, of course. She knew that if it ever came to someone making a sacrifice, of giving up their life to save the future of the gods, it would be you.'

Thor frowned. Above him, a sound like metal girders at breaking-point.

'*I'm sorry*,' I said, but I couldn't be sure whether Thor had heard me, because at that moment, with a single blast, the dome shattered into space dust, revealing the turbulence of Dream in all its dreadful glory. We were out of time at last. I flung myself on Sleipnir's back, dragging Jumps and Jonathan Gift along with me through the flying debris.

267

I looked back at Jumps. 'Remember the riddle I told you about the wolf, the goat and the cabbage?'

She nodded. 'What about them?'

I gestured at Jonathan. 'Meet the wolf.'

Jumps' eyes grew wide. 'You mean—'

Jonathan grinned – a *familiar* grin – and winked at me from his one good eye. 'Pleased to meet you, Jumps,' he said. 'Captain, I'm ready. Let's ride.'

6

THE STORY SO FAR: A FERRYMAN must carry, one at a time, a goat, a wolf and a cabbage, whilst ensuring no cargo happens to snack on another. It looks impossible at first. Whichever order he takes them in, at some point either the goat will be left alone to eat the cabbage, or the wolf will be left with the goat, with predictably gruesome results.

And yet there *is* a solution – straightforward enough, as long as you're able to deploy some mental flexibility.

First the ferryman takes the goat, leaving the wolf with the cabbage. He drops off the goat at the far side of the river, then comes back for the cabbage, leaving the wolf on the near side. But (and this is the important bit) as he drops off the cabbage, *he picks the goat back up again*, bringing it to the near side with him. Then he ferries the wolf to the far side, leaving the goat in its original spot, and drops off the wolf with the cabbage. Finally, he goes back to collect the goat. *Voilà*. Problem solved.

But in the fracas that ensued, I had no leisure to explain to Jumps the details of my sleight-of-hand. Nor did I have the time to point out to Odin how much better *my* riddle was than his cat-in-the-box scenario. Dream was engulfing the bubble-world like Skól and Haiti devouring the Sun and Moon. I was holding my runeshield with all the strength I could muster; Thor was wrestling Gullveig-Heid, who had suddenly realized that her ride was about to set off without her. And Odin, in the body of Gift, was grinning at me like a scythe.

'BETRAYAL!' roared the Oracle, having seen the deception at last. 'YOU TOOK ME OUT OF MY WORLD BY STEALTH! YOU STOLE MY SERVANT AWAY FROM ME!'

I could have pointed out that Jonathan Gift had been more than happy to give up corporeal Aspect in exchange for that of a fluffy white dog, but there was little time to go into details. The Oracle's dream was breaking apart, allowing glimpses of Jumps' World through the fragmented cathedral. I could see Castle Hill in the distance; the light reflecting from Evan's chair. I could see figures: Stella, Meg, and Evan, his face half turned towards me in the moonlight. And there was an object in his hands, an object the size of a cabbage, perhaps: an object that I recognized.

I mouthed a desperate, blasphemous prayer. I'd hoped that my plan wouldn't come to this. I'd hoped for an easier form of escape. Failing that, I'd hoped that in case of emergency, Evan would know what to do. That memory of Jumps, and the eye, like a marble in her palm: that should have told him something. But whether or not he had understood the importance of the symbolism – the link between the eye and the Head – the message I had tried to convey to him through that distant memory—

Frankly, I had no idea whether or not the boy would know how much my life and the life of his friend depended on his actions. In the same way, I'd had no idea whether his role-playing skills would be good enough to convince Gullveig-Heid that Odin was still inside him. And now I had no way of knowing if what I had asked him to do would work, or whether it would be *Game Over*. I wasn't happy about these things, but I can't see what else I could have done, given what limited material I had to work with.

Please. Just do it. Just do it, I thought, clinging to Sleipnir's mane as we fled towards the far edge of the dream. The bubble-world was breaking up even faster than before, pieces of the cathedral circling us like planets. Any one of those pieces might obliterate Jumps or the General, or knock our steed right out of the sky. At any second, the Oracle might awaken completely, leaving us to be torn apart in the vacuum of nonexistence.

Worse still, Heidi had finally understood the extent of my treachery, and had cast a web of binding-runes after Sleipnir as we fled. *Naudr*, the Binder, held us back, keeping us from leaving that World as it broke apart around us. But for Thor, whose courage was sadly not equalled by his intelligence, the penny either hadn't quite dropped, or was somehow still dropping.

'*Odin?*' I heard his rumbling voice like thunder through the bubble-world. '*Odin* is the architect?'

'Oh, get with the programme,' said Heidi. 'This was a ruse from the very start. Don't you see, you great oaf? This dream was a trap that is closing in. And, bodiless, without the General's Horse, both of us will remain here—'

But Thor, at last, had understood. His loyalty to the General meant that he was ready to do whatever he could to buy us the time we needed. Heidi had lifted a hand to cast another rune at Sleipnir, but Thor's bulk was blocking her. For a moment, Temptress and Thunderer stood almost close enough to embrace, and then his arms were around her, and hers around him, and locking tight—

This had better be worth it, he growled, his words reaching me from across the impossible delta of Dream.

'I swear I won't let you down,' I said. 'We'll meet again, some day, somewhere.'

Now why did I say that? I thought. It wasn't like me to make such a promise; still less like me to mean it. Close contact with Jumps must have made me soft – she'd always had a soft spot for Thor – but I knew that my plan had always been to use him as a sacrifice.

The Oracle was wakeful now: soon it would be back in the

Head that it had occupied for so many centuries. In a second the dream-World would be gone, the bubble dissolved into nothingness. And during that time, I had to make good my own escape, while ensuring that Jumps returned to her World, and Odin ended up as far away from the Head of the Oracle as I could manage to take him. Forget the goat and the cabbage; this was a juggling trick of colossal proportions.

But Heidi had one more trick up her sleeve. Assuming her full Aspect, she flung off the Thunderer's embrace and raised her hand to summon a rune. I flung up a shield – the runeshape *Ýr* – knowing it wasn't nearly enough to stop Heidi's attack, and braced myself for the impact of *Hagall*, the Destroyer, and my subsequent fall from the sky and back into Pandaemonium —

But what the Thunderer lacked in speed, he made up for in perseverance. Hurling *Thuris* at Heidi's rune he intercepted it in mid-air, causing a violent release of glam and a sound like two armies colliding. A flash like the forges of Chaos, and both of the combatants were gone, blown into Dream by the impact, extinguished as completely as a candle-flame in a window. And then, as that dissolving World finally popped into nothingness, revealing the scene on Castle Hill, I shouted:

'Evan, throw it, now!' and the boy threw the Head like a rugby ball, using all of his human strength, into the maelstrom of Dream.

For a moment it hung there, shining like a bauble on a Christmas tree. Odin reached for it, but too late; summoning what was left of my glam, I caught it in a net of runes and flung it like a stone from a sling – flung it right *through* the skin of that World and into the honeycomb cell beyond – which, if Odin's theory stood, should contain some *other* version of Castle Hill, maybe even some other version of Meg, or of Jumps, or Stella, or Evan.

For a moment, Jumps' World was all around us, safe and real. The stars shone down on Castle Hill; Evan stared up at the sky. Stella was there too, watching him, her face alight with something that might almost have been admiration. But I barely noticed her. Meg was running towards us, her golden eyes like pinwheels of fire. For a second I thought her smile was for me, until I remembered Jumps at my side, and, summoning what strength I had left, I gave her an almighty *push*, sending her tumbling from the Horse onto the grassy crest of the Hill.

'Sorry.' I said. 'Things to do. Worlds to see.' And then we were off again into the air, faster than the speed of Dream.

'*No!*' cried Jumps, as we passed overhead.

I gave her a little wave.

But will you be OK? she said.

'Of course I will. I'm Loki.'

Then Odin and I were shooting through Dream, with Sleipnir's colours around us like a giant array of Northlights. For a second I thought I saw Jumps from very, very far away, her arms around Meg, both of them surrounded by something as bright as runelight. I'm not an expert on these things, but I thought at the time that it might have been one of those human emotions, viewed through the lens of my truesight. On the other hand, it might easily have been a fragment of Dream, or a mirage, or a ripple running through that distant reality. As for Thor and Gullveig-Heid, there was no sign of either.

Odin looked at me and smiled. The eye that Heidi's runebolt had struck was a mess: the socket empty, a bloody slash across the cheekbone that looked almost like the rune *Raedo*, reversed. As a consequence, the smile was hardly warm, and yet I took it as promising.

'Well played,' he said. 'I'm assuming you had all this planned from the start?'

I grinned. 'I had a few ideas. Not least, getting Heidi out of the way.'

'And getting rid of the Oracle?'

'I thought that might be safest, yes.'

'Why?'

'Because you don't want it in your life,' I said. 'It's nothing

273

but trouble. It's never told you anything it didn't plan for you to know; it didn't give you anything that you could use to help yourself, or save us from the End of the Worlds.'

'And what about my son?' Odin said.

I shrugged. 'My options were limited. Thor was our best chance of escape. He gave his life to save you.'

'And the Vanir?'

'Let sleeping dogs lie,' I said. 'Why wake what's best left sleeping?'

Odin made a derisive noise. 'I know you too well, Trickster,' he said. 'You've got that innocent look on your face, but I can read your colours. This isn't the first time you've heard the Oracle prophesy. It told you something, didn't it? When you and it were together alone?'

For a moment I wondered whether to lie. But no: I had an advantage now. And I meant to play it for all it was worth.

'So shoot me. Yes. It prophesied. But I'm not going to tell you what it said. Not for the moment, anyway.'

'Really? And why's that?'

'Because each of us has something,' I said, 'that the other party wants. I have the missing segment of the Oracle's prophecy. Which I will deliver to you just as soon as you give me what *I* want.'

'Which is?' said Odin.

I told him. 'Now swear on your name you'll do it,' I said. 'And give me your word you'll let me go free.'

Odin gave a wry smile. 'You've got this all covered, haven't you?'

I made Jumps' favourite noise. 'Meh. I believe in being prepared.'

He sighed. 'Very well. We have a deal. Now, what did the Oracle tell you?'

7

I<small>T'S ALWAYS A RISK, WHEN YOU'RE</small> working with things
that can tell the future. Oracles, though unable to lie, are seldom
ever trustworthy. But Odin had never been able to let go of his
erstwhile counsellor, and now that I was the only one who
could give him Mimir's prediction, I knew that I could count on
him to get me what I needed. To whit: a corporeal Aspect, with
a working runemark – which happened to be *precisely* what
Mimir had asked of Jonathan Gift, and which he, in spite of his
scruples, had been so close to providing.

In his World, Gift had told me as we travelled together
through Dream, runemarks (or *ruinmarks*, as he called them)
were considered to be an evil sign: a throwback to Tribulation;
and those unfortunate enough to be born with one were often
shunned, or sometimes worse. A girl with a visible ruinmark
was unlikely ever to marry; elder sons with the mark were
passed over in favour of their siblings. And yet these sporadic
fragments of glam were all that was left of the Aesir: all that
was left in this World of our power to shape and recast Reality.

Jumps' World, though marvellous in so many ways, with
its screens and its magical gateways, had no such connection
with the primal Fire. The World of *Asgard!*™ had such a connection, but it was a flawed reality, which mirrored ours in so

many ways, but which could not be trusted to separate Reality from Dream. The World of Jonathan Gift was riddled with our leavings. Runes, the tales of Asgard of old; even the cinders that fell from the sky when Bif-rost collapsed onto the plain – everything was still in place, waiting to be exploited. All Mimir would have needed was the right physical presence in which to be reborn, and in this World he could have regained his Aspect, his powers – even his godhood.

'So Gift had already located a host?' said Odin, his one eye revealing his eagerness. 'A host with a workable runemark?'

'Absolutely,' I told him. 'But Jonathan was plagued with doubts. He knew the Oracle, you see; he knew of its ambitions. And he knew that in the right kind of host, its power would be dangerous.'

'Whereas *you*, of course,' said Odin, 'would present no risk at all.' I was glad to see he agreed with me, even though he was smiling. 'So – where is this host of yours, and how do you mean to command it? Waking humans have minds of their own, and unless you intend to enter through Dream, you may find it has other ideas.'

'Don't worry. I've got a plan,' I said.

He sighed. 'That's what I'm afraid of.'

8

ALWAYS HAVE A PLAN, I SAY. Always have a backup plan. Always have *another* plan for when the backup plan fails. And always plan an exit route for when you abandon the plan and flee. I may sound over-cautious, but it's a strategy that has always worked for me so far, and I've been to some pretty dark places.

Even so, when we landed in darkness, I wondered if we'd mistaken the place. Jonathan had been very precise in giving his instructions, but as Sleipnir came to rest in the corporeal World, I could see that we were not above ground, but in some kind of a large cellar, with an earthen floor and rocky walls and a smell of dust and spices.

Odin climbed from the back of the Horse, which had assumed the Aspect of a small, short-legged pony of the type the Tunnel Folk use in mines. It was an appropriate form to take: the tunnel was low, though not narrow, and seemed to lead to a larger storage space. In my discorporate Aspect I could not quite see, but could certainly *sense* the topography of that space, and I knew that this was only a part of a sprawling series of tunnels and vaults that ran beneath the University of World's End.

'What are we doing here?' said Odin, striking a light – oh, not with glam, but with a humble tinder-box that he must have found in Jonathan's pocket. The little flame flared, and we saw rats running away into the walls.

Have patience, I said – voicelessly, although he could still hear me. *I'm going to need you to say a word. Or rather, I need you to speak a* name.

I fed it directly into his mind, syllable by syllable.

'And this will do what, exactly?' he said, by then beginning (quite rightly) to feel that some kind of trickery was afoot.

'Jonathan had helpers,' I said. 'Just as we did in *Asgard!*™. That World was closer to ours, in some ways, than the one into which we were born. And the Oracle had been planning for years its transition into the flesh. But a willing host is not easy to find. A man with no runemark, a weakling, may sometimes be commanded. But the stronger mind resists. And the Oracle *wanted* a stronger mind: a mind that could control the runes – and fight with them, if need be.'

Odin frowned. The blood on his face looked stone-black in the light of the flame. 'But you said he *had* secured a host.'

'Oh, yes.' If I'd had a body, I would have been grinning from ear to ear. The Oracle had indeed found a host – the perfect host for its purpose, and mine. Young, strong, but malleable – and yet with the gilding of glamour that came with knowledge of the runes.

'And after you deliver it, then I can give you the prophecy.'

Odin frowned again. I knew that he was deeply suspicious; and yet, he had read my colours, and knew that my oath was binding.

'All right,' he said at last, and spoke the name: '*Smá-rákki.*'

9

A NAMED THING IS A TAMED THING, as they say in World Below. And tamed things are nicely obedient. As Odin spoke the word, there came a rumbling sound in the underground, a scatter of rats across our path, and when the dust had settled, there was a short and hairy individual standing in the passageway. Not one of the Folk, I surmised: more likely one of the creatures of World Below that had survived Ragnarók by mostly being somewhere else at the time. I was reminded of *Asgard!*™, and its goblin minions, although this creature seemed less generic, its golden eyes shining, its long tail twitching like a squirrel's.

'I come like you said,' said the creature, addressing the Aspect of Jonathan Gift. 'Now mebbe we could discuss payment before I hands over the package.'

'The package?' said Odin.

The creature tutted. It looked aggressive in spite of its size, bristling with mismatched armour. An overlarge helmet covered its head; a breastplate shielded the generous paunch above its bowed and stumpy little legs. I'd had the odd dealing with goblins before: they were often erratic creatures, but their self-interest was reliable.

'A hundred barrels of ale, you said,' went on the creature. 'That was the deal. A hundred barrels, and then we'll talk.'

'We'll talk now,' said Odin. He didn't know the details of Jonathan Gift's arrangement, but he did have plenty of experience in giving orders. 'Or do you doubt my intentions?'

'No need to be *nasty*,' said the goblin sulkily. 'We had a deal. I done my bit.'

Meanwhile, with my ephemeral senses, I was searching for the host. I thought a runemark ought to have some kind of a tangible presence. Even here, the colours should be bright and unmistakable. But in the dark of the passageway all I could see was the butterfly-blue of Odin's shadow against the wall, and the goblin's golden signature, jumping like a cracker.

'An 'undred barrels of ale, you said,' repeated the goblin stubbornly.

'You shall have them,' said Odin, clearly forgetting that in this World he was Jonathan Gift, not Allfather. 'You have my word.'

The goblin sniggered. 'You'll 'ave to do better than that,' he said. 'Words don't do nuthin when you've gotta thirst on.'

Odin was looking frustrated. 'Give me the prophecy,' he said, apparently addressing me (although strictly speaking, I wasn't there).

When I'm in the flesh, I said, *I swear that the first words I speak will be the words of the Oracle.* Which was totally true, of course, though not quite as Odin expected it. And now I reached out to the creature, standing with its arms crossed, looking up at Odin with an air of belligerence.

Pay no attention to Jonathan Gift. This is where the money is. Stick with me, Smá-rákki, and I promise you a lot more than a few dozen barrels of ale.

The goblin narrowed its golden eyes at the figure of Sleipnir. Goblins don't have runemarks, but they do have glam, of a lesser kind. Glam enough to move through walls, and to see things hidden to the Folk. I knew it could see me, ephemeral as I was, and the Horse, behind its disguise. The goblin's colours flared suspiciously.

'Like what?' it said at last.

You'll see. Now, when I give the word, do as I say.

The goblin gave a whole-body shrug. 'I don't much care for—'

Not aloud, Smá-rákki. A named thing is a tamed thing. Thus are you named, and bound to my will. Now, when I give the word—

'Yes, sir,' it said.

It's all about the timing, of course. The trick, the tease, the sleight-of-hand. Odin should have known that, but he was distracted – perhaps by his wounded face, perhaps by the promise of prophecy. I'd been counting on his being slow to respond, slow to react, slow to understand the fact that he was being double-crossed again. And yet, even given his weakened state, his mind still unused to Jonathan's, I was wary. His instincts were good. He might, even now, obstruct me.

Now, I whispered silently.

The goblin beckoned. 'Over here!'

Odin stepped away from the Horse. For a moment I saw him peering one-eyed into the darkness. And then the goblin took Sleipnir's mane – rather gingerly, I thought – and hauled himself into position beside me.

'I'm not so sure about this—' he began.

Odin turned, and his one eye gleamed as he saw Sleipnir shifting Aspect from the mundane to the ephemeral. He started forward, anger and fear flaring through his colours, but it was already too late – we had begun the shift from the corporeal plane into Dream. I heard him call my name, and sent him the tiniest of waves.

'No hard feelings, brother,' I said. 'See you on the other side.'

Then I urged the Horse out of the World, passing through the thick stone walls and galleries of the underground, then rising above the towers of the University of World's End, and into the clouds, riding fast over valleys and rivers and peaks towards the place where my new host lay, fast asleep in his cradle.

281

10

IN THIS WORLD, JONATHAN GIFT HAD SAID, babies with
runemarks were often seen as changelings, left by the goblins
in the place of a normal child. In rural parts, such babies were
sometimes even abandoned at birth – a practice frowned on
by the Church, but commonly ignored by it, too. Jonathan Gift
had been under orders from Mimir's Head to seek such a child,
a child with a mark of power, which could serve as its human
host.

On Sleipnir, our journey lasted only a matter of moments.
My co-conspirator's wail of alarm had barely ceased to resonate
by the time the Horse touched down, somewhere in the North-
lands. Goblins don't like sunlight, and as soon as Sleipnir's
hooves hit the ground, it scuttled under a fallen rock, leaving
me to take in a scene of almost perfect tranquillity.

We had landed on the crest of a hill, overlooking a valley. In
my current form I could not breathe the sweetness of the air, or
feel the warmth of the dying sun; but I took a moment to take
in the view, the gentle grassy slope of the hill, softened by tufts
of rabbit-tail grass. Crows scattered across the purple sky; from
the valley below came the sounds of sheep and cattle grazing.
A valley of woods and meadows and fields, enclosed by a chain
of mountains and containing several villages of no great size

or importance, surrounded by farmlands and wetlands and woods. A good place to grow up, I thought, as Sleipnir, in mundane Aspect again, started to crop the grass of the hill. A good place to lay down some roots.

> *On what was once the battlefield*
> *A New Age dawns. Its children*
> *Find the golden gaming-boards*
> *Of bright Asgard, the fallen.*

I hadn't realized I'd spoken the words of the Oracle aloud. The goblin, emerging from under its rock to find that the hill was in shadow, blinked at me, golden-eyed, and said with some suspicion:

'What's that?'

'Oh, just something I heard once,' I said, still looking out at the valley. I knew I'd never been there before, and yet I couldn't help thinking that the place seemed vaguely familiar. Something about the shape of that hill and the ring of distant mountains behind, with the sunset turning the peaks to brass all around the skyline. I thought there was something familiar, too, about the shape of that valley: the soft steep incline down from the hill, and Sleipnir's signature in the sky making a kind of runeshape—

In my mind came Jumps' voice: *It's not a rune, it's a vapour-trail.* I could hear her perfectly, even though she was Worlds away. And somehow I felt those feelings again – very, very far from home.

Every World has its counterpart. That's what Odin taught me. Every action, every choice, every mistake, every move we make is re-enacted somewhere else, with different players, different results. And the Worlds we know are honeycomb, cells crammed together side by side, awaiting their chance to begin again. Even Death is but one of the Worlds through which the river Dream runs its course, collecting its stories like flotsam, building its reefs and its islands, making them into new cells, other Worlds for the taking. The thought of it almost moved me – another of those little gifts from Jumps' World, not memory, but *nostalgia*, and unexpectedly scented with cherry-coconut cake and smoke—

Goodbye, Jumps. I'll miss you.

The goblin was looking shifty, and I guessed it was thinking about escape. *Go on. Try that again,* I said. *I'll suck your tiny mind like an egg.*

The goblin gave a hiss of protest. 'I never!' it said. 'I'm as good as me word. See? I told you. There it is.' And it waved its arm to indicate a figure on the path to the hill: a girl of seventeen or so, carrying a basket, and leading a small white goat.

Is she the mother?

'Laws, no. That's Nancy, the wicker-man's daughter.' The goblin waved a stubby arm. 'She found the baby Tuesday last, on a market-trip into the Ridings. They must have left it out to die, ruined as it was, poor thing. But Nan meant to care for it herself, whatever her folk or the Parson said. She's a stubborn one, that Nan. The villagers call her crazy.'

Bring her to me. I need to be close.

'Yes, sir. Right away, sir.'

I waited with impatience in my ephemeral Aspect. The girl approached, still leading the goat, with the basket tucked under her arm. From the swaddled thing inside, there came a wail of protest.

'*Shhh.*' The girl's voice came to me over the misty brow of the hill. 'No one's going to hurt you, little one. I promise you. Everything will be all right.'

I wondered how she could say that with such a careless conviction. In my experience, nothing is ever all right, and everyone's out to get you. But babies must be easier to fool than normal people, because this one simply hiccupped a bit, then stopped wailing, and went to sleep.

I could see its colours now: they flared with a violet signature not unlike my own. And now, with my ephemeral vision, I saw that the rune on the baby's arm was *Kaen*, the rune of Wildfire – *my* rune – although it was reversed. That was a disappointment. I'd hoped for something more workable. But even reversed or broken runes can channel power, and besides, I wasn't in any position to be picky on details. The child was healthy, accessible and open to my influence; what came later was yet to be seen.

Finally, the girl and her little goat reached the summit of the hill, where Sleipnir was still cropping grass. The girl approached my steed, smiled and, tethering the goat to a rock, she brought out a piece of carrot from one of the pockets of her apron and offered it to the General's Horse. That made me smile: if only she'd known what a rare and terrible beast was hidden beneath that humble disguise, she might not have been so eager to feed him scraps. But Sleipnir accepted the carrot greedily, nuzzling her shoulder. Then she turned to the goblin, still holding the basket under her arm.

'Take the goat for her milk,' she said. 'And use the blanket when it gets cold.'

'Well, that's very kind, miss,' said the goblin, reaching for the basket with a gleam in its golden eyes.

'I meant for the *baby*,' said Nancy sternly.

The goblin assumed an air of exaggerated innocence.

Nancy gave him a long, hard stare. 'You drink that milk – *or eat the goat* – and there'll be no more beer for you. The baby needs it. Understand?'

The goblin wilted under her gaze. The girl was tougher than I'd thought. That was good. I would need her strength. For a moment I thought she could see me, so earnest was her scrutiny. But she made no comment, and simply placed the basket gently onto the Horse's back, and looked at the baby from keen eyes, which, now she was closer, I thought looked quite a lot like Jumps' eyes; as did the hair, the stubborn chin, and that stiffness in the spine, as if in anticipation of someone saying something mean.

'I don't want to leave you,' she said to the child, although her eyes were levelled at me. 'But you'll be safer under the Hill, in the care of the Good Folk. There's food there, and shelter. They say if you go down deep enough, you'll find the Land of Roast Beef, where children play in the golden fields, and no one ever goes hungry.'

That sounded like pure fantasy to me, but still I let her have her way. She wiped her eyes, which had started to leak, and said at last to the goblin: 'You promise he'll be cared for? Swear it on your true name?'

'Aye, miss,' said the goblin, with a sideways glance at me. 'Cared for like a princeling, don't you worry yer head about *that*.'

The girl who looked like Jumps gave a sigh. 'Then take him,' she said. 'Look after him well. And don't forget. I'm always here. If ever he needs—' Her voice broke. And then she bent over the basket and kissed the bundle on the cheek, and I spoke the word to Sleipnir – *Stay!* – and slipped back sweetly into flesh.

Game Over

1

I'VE DONE THIS SO MANY TIMES BEFORE. And yet being newly corporeal never ceases to surprise: the rush of it; the dizziness; the avalanche of sensations. Time has no meaning in Dream. I felt as if my last incarnation had been over a hundred years ago. And flesh, so deceptively similar from the vantage point of Dream, is so profoundly different when experienced in person.

Being in Jumps was like being in a cavernous vault, filled with memories, teeming with sensations and thoughts, coloured with her personality. Being in her vacated skin was like being in an empty house, furnished by a stranger. Being in Jonathan Gift had been like being inside a library. But this *new* location was narrow, small: a warm and lightless cave, in which the only hint of a presence was a small sense of discomfort; some curiosity; no sense of self, just a memory of darkness and warmth and the strong sound of a maternal heartbeat.

So now I'm a baby, I thought to myself. Not the most practical outcome in some ways, but necessary, if I were to fulfil my oath to the General whilst keeping the Prophecy to myself. A neat solution to what had seemed like an insoluble paradox.

I reached out for my host's glam. I found a thread of violet light, dim compared to what I'd had, but still far better than nothing. Perhaps it would grow as I did, I thought. Perhaps I could work with it later. How long would that take? Two years? Three? In any case, not very long, in the general scheme of things. For the present I tried to move, and found myself alarmingly weak and strangely uncoordinated. I opened my mouth, and a sound came out – a sound both young and very old, a sound both new and broken. A fear like nothing I'd ever felt wrung me like a piece of rag – a nameless fear, like a bad dream, or the sudden crash of mortality. *What's happening?* I wailed soundlessly. *What in the Worlds is this torment?*

'He's hungry,' said the girl, and though I understood her words, they were *huge,* swimming in the air like fish, and her face, like the giant face of the Moon, moved into my line of vision. The unformed presence of my host recognized the giant face and made a kind of bleating sound. Then I was rising dizzily into the arms of the giant girl, and I thought that yes, I *was* hungry, and summoned my glam to command them to my bidding:

Bring me cake, and ice cream; and wine to soothe my frazzled nerves, and maybe some pizza, if pizza exists in this version of my World; and bring it to me quickly, for I find myself in need of sustenance —

What the Hel is that?

It was a bottle, made from some kind of animal skin, smelling most definitely of goat. The liquid inside was a little sour, and none too appetizing. But my host latched on to the teat, and drank, and seemed to be enjoying it, and I went along without protest. The urge to feed was too strong to resist. Besides, my host was hungry, and I was beginning to realize that in my current circumstances I was not likely to be giving orders to my minions any time soon.

Still, that was a small price to pay for a new start, in a new World, in a new skin, far from those who would do me harm. Safe from my enemies, safe from my friends, I had a lifetime to plan my next move; to explore the limits of my glam; to taste every pleasure this World could give. And it felt good to be in the flesh; to breathe; to feel; to taste; to touch. And guilty as I undoubtedly was of crimes too numerous to list, there was a kind of hope in rebirth, even a kind of innocence. Who knew? Maybe there would be the chance to revisit the Prophecy: to inherit some of those rewards of which the Oracle had spoken.

> *I see Asgard built anew*
> *Gleaming over Ida's plain.*
> *I have spoken. Now I sleep*
> *Until the world's tides turn again.*

And maybe things will be different this time. Maybe this time I can be—

Oh, please. Don't let's get ahead of ourselves. Wildfire I was, and that I remain. Don't ever doubt my nature. But maybe this time I can be in this World without ending it, or ending myself. Maybe I can leave that behind. *There's* a dream worth pursuing.

And so I closed my eyes and fed, and finally I fell asleep, and as I slept, I dreamed: and saw Asgard as it used to be, and Odin, to whom I owed a debt, and Thor, to whom I had sworn an oath that even I didn't understand. And in my dream I was Loki again, with my runemark unreversed on my arm, and all the Worlds once more at my feet, and Bif-rost hanging overhead.

And then I dreamed of Jumps, and Meg, and Evan, safe in their own World, sitting around Evan's computer, watching him play *Asgard!*™. And in the game, I tried to say some part of what was in my mind, but all I could do was run and fight, and finally fall to my enemies, and look into the cold blue sky and see the words: *Game Over!*. And Jumps' face was as big as the Moon, swimming over the console, but she was smiling, and she said: *See, it's not the End of the Worlds. We all get a chance to start again.*

'Jumps,' I said.

She smiled again.

'You were OK. For a human.'

You were OK, too. For a dick.

And in my dream she laughed, and the sound was like a thousand birds flying free, and in my dream I must have been a lot more sentimental than I'd ever been when I was awake, because I felt something strange and new, something that was almost grief—

And then there was Evan, and he said: *See you on the other side*—

And then there was Meg, and she didn't say anything, but smiled and smiled, and her face was like the rising Sun, and her eyes were shining. And then in my dream I saw Gullveig-Heid, searching through the flotsam of a vanished World; Gullveig-Heid, awake, alert and filled with relentless patience. And lastly, I dreamed of Mimir's Head, caught fast in its net of runes and spinning through Dream like a spindle, gathering with it the threads of our lives, twisting them together.

Asgard was falling. The plain below was cratered with fires and laddered with smoke. Ragnarók, the End of the Worlds, lay upon us like a pall. Odin had fallen; and Thor; and Týr. Gullveig-Heid, the Sorceress, stood at the helm of the Fleet of the Dead. Surt, on dragon's wings, approached from out of fiery Chaos, and where his shadow fell, the dark was absolute, and terrible. Bif-rost was broken, and as I fell, clutching at the last of my glam, I saw the great bridge come apart at last in a fractal of brightness, spilling its millions of cantrips and runes into the wild and shattered air, so that, for a moment, everything was rainbow . . .

And then I awoke on the hillside, and the girl had already gone, and the goat was cropping grass, and the goblin was holding the basket with a look of mournful endurance.

Dusk had come. The sky was striped in purple and lemon-yellow. The vapour-trail above us had gone, and there was no sign of Sleipnir. Except for the outline of a Horse against the flank of the grassy hill – apparently cut into the turf, and very slightly luminous.

I don't know why I was surprised. After all, I had told it to stay. Just as it had beneath Castle Hill, now it slumbered under the soil, its spidery limbs sunk into the ground. I wondered if perhaps I should have sent it away into Dream instead, rather than risk its presence alerting unwanted attention, but I guess it's too late now for me to change the programme.

Instead I will allow myself to be taken far beneath the Hill, into the tunnels and passageways that only such creatures as goblins would know. It will be warm and safe down there; there will be food and security. My little cousins under the Hill will care for me until I am grown. There I will explore my domain, discover my powers; flex my glam. Odin, trapped in his mortal skin, will never know where to find me, or how to redeem the bargain we struck – my life for the Oracle's prophecy.

But that thrice-damned bauble never spoke a word that wasn't twisted beyond recognition. Let it rot in its webwork of runes: let it tumble for ever in Dream. Even if I knew where it was, I wouldn't lift a finger to find it, or to bring it home.

And yet, my oath to *him* will be kept. Although he will never hear them, my first words, whispered in the dark, will be the words of the Oracle. Put together it almost makes sense. It almost makes a picture. A picture of new gods, lost loves and new Worlds for the taking. A picture of a World at war. Who will fight? Who will stand? Even now, and in this form, I can't help being a little aroused at the possibilities. So shoot me; it's my nature. I never could resist a war. But right now it's all too much. I'm barely a week old, after all. Let others deal with the Prophecy, or ignore it, as they choose. I have my whole life ahead of me – well, technically, someone else's. The safest thing to do would be to stay down here, under the Hill, and enjoy the pleasures of the flesh – at least, such pleasures available to a being in my tender state.

And yet I can't help wondering. Much like the cat in Odin's tale, my nature is to be curious. Perhaps that's what will kill me. Or I may live for ever. Who knows? Like the cat in the box, maybe I shall manage both at once.

But for the present, let there be simple pleasures: milk, and sleep, and the warmth of a lambswool blanket. Let there be dreams of jam tarts, and penguin pyjamas, and coconut cake. Let there be light, and open skies, and the scent of growing grass. And let there be – as always – the occasional dream of Asgard.

PROPHECY OF THE ORACLE

I speak of One who is Nameless.
And yet his name is Legion.
He will bring Order to the Worlds,
And bring about a Cleansing.

From the Cradle to the grave,
He lives in rage and malice.
And his parting gift to you
Will be a poisoned chalice.

I speak of two young shoots that grow.
One the Oak, and one the Ash.
One the Horse, and one the bone.
One from Earth, and one from stone.

I speak of seven Sleepers, bound
With runes under a mountain.
And One who, in a net of fire
Still lives, in Wisdom's fountain.

I speak of Worlds, both old and new,
Of gods, both new and broken.
I speak of war across the Worlds
And war across the ocean.